DEP

The Lost Khaki Girls

G000058555

The Lost Khaki Girls

Ronke Odewumi

Ronke Odewumi

www.ronkewrites.com[1]

Cover design: Sunkanmi Akinboye/ linebug.carbon-made.com/

Cover photograph: Adetoun Adekambi

ISBN: 978-1-9999662-1-8

EBOOK ISBN: 978-1-9999662-0-1

First Printing: February 2018

---

1. http://www.ronkewrites.com

Captivating and full of suspense and witty humour. I was hooked from the beginning to the end. A must read!
Detola Amure (Bestselling author – Super Working Mum)

The Lost Khaki Girls is a gripping story of love and murder. A chick-lit and thriller all in one. A dark and lovely read. I enjoyed it.
Bunmi Layode (Author – Leaving to Live)

To Olufemi, Oluwatofarati & Oluwarominiye
For all the joy and sunshine you bring.

Acknowledgement

I wish to acknowledge a few of the people who have in one way or the other contributed to the publishing of this book and to whom I will remain forever grateful.

Toluwalope, Kolawole, Olasunkanmi & Titilayomi Akinboye (for your creative comments, title choice, cover design, logistics & support – best siblings ever).

Bankole Olayebi, Bunmi Layode, Oyesumbo Thomas, Detola Amure & the Super Working Mums group (support, advice & everything else in between)

Gabrielle Ede and Mojiroluwa Adebosin (editing); Adetoun Adekambi (cover photography) and Mrs Elizabeth Ogundiya (aunt & first editor).

My parents - Akintayo and Adebola Akinboye (dream nurturers, world's best parents).

Olufemi Odewumi (husband, best friend and hype man).

These people are partly why you will suffer through or enjoy this book, they made me do it and I love them for it.

If I have forgotten to mention you or your contribution to this little project, please forgive me. I appreciate you and thank you from the bottom of my heart.

Be kind, everyone you meet is fighting a hard battle – attributed to Plato and various others

Pre Day 1 – NYSC Camp

BECKY

I started my journey to the NYSC Orientation camp on a Sunday, in a bus that pulled out of the Yaba Lagos motor park at 6.30am. I expected the journey to last about 13 hours, but nothing is ever as expected in my world, so the journey lasted 20 hours instead.

First, we had a flat tyre on the Benin-Auchi road around noon and we all had to sit on the road side while the driver changed the tyre; still it was a relief that he had a spare, but our luck was about to run out.

Another three hours into the journey and we had another flat tyre on the Okene-Lokoja road and this time the driver didn't have another spare so we had to wait in the bus while he went in search of a roadside mechanic to repair the tyre.

He returned an hour later with a dark squat man in tattered shorts and a torn singlet and together they rolled the tyre away to shouts and curses from the passengers.

"Let thieves not even come and catch us here ehn" one of the passengers, a fat woman with her headscarf at a rakish angle, complained.

"God forbid. If we see anybody strange coming, we will run into the bush" another woman answered.

We were all sitting by the roadside under the shade of a large mango tree, in a place from where we could safely watch the bus and our luggage in it.

"And you think if thieves want to catch you in the bush they won't? It is better they don't come at all" the fat woman replied.

"We will keep praying; God will keep us"

I stopped listening to the conversation at this point, it was about to descend into a holy supplication for help from helpless humans to a benevolent but unpredictable deity. My worry was less about here and now and more about getting into camp and being at the fore of the registration before everyone else. Camp opens on Monday with a 48-hour registration window and I was hoping to get registered on the first day before the panic and bedlam I knew would happen on the second day.

Six pm and the flat tyre was repaired and sitting proudly on the back wheel of the bus, ready to take us the rest of the journey. The driver cranked the engine and we got underway but the bus was quiet, we were all tired and worried about safety and being on the highway at midnight.

We finally arrived at the Jos motor park in the early hours of the morning; tired, filthy but relieved; some passengers, mostly men got off the bus and hurried off in various directions, but the rest of us were a bit hesitant. The driver, seeing our hesitation advised us to remain in the bus till the safer hours of the morning.

I rested my head on the hard back of the seats in front of me and tried to sleep. The bus driver woke us at 5.30am with shouts of, "Mama! Aunty! Morning don come!" He showed me where to get a bus to the NYSC camp at Bukuru and I walked off on rubbery legs, my travelling bag slung on my shoulder and the cold morning wind slapping and whipping up my thick cotton skirt.

Day 1 NYSC Camp
ADUNNI

The city woke up slowly, like a giant trying to beat the effect of the drunken bout of the night before. The morning air was clean and sharp; still devoid of the smell people create every day. A few people trekked along the road briskly while bus conductors on the early shift sat on the edge of their seats and called stubbornly for passengers, like they were trying to get them out of bed; soon these same conductors would be hanging precariously from the rusting edge of the bus screaming the names of their various stops while tempting death.

Swiftly the electric poles, neon signs, empty kiosks and bright yellow telephone booths rushed by and the nearer we got to the motor park, the more neon signs were broken and without their fluorescent tubes. It seemed this hoodlum-ruled part of town rebelled against something as civilised as lit neon signs. The signs glowered back defiantly, their loose wires and empty slots giving them the appearance of toothless old men laughing at a private joke.

At the motor park, I boarded a bus going to Jos, careful to choose a window seat; not the window seat directly behind the bus driver but the one in the next row. The window seat directly behind the driver is for the novice traveller who will find out in the course of the journey that this is where the engine sits; which means little leg room and a lot of hot air from the engine. The driver also hangs his "attempt at health and safety awareness" fire extinguisher and ratty looking dustbin in the face of whoever sits in that window seat. I was not a novice traveller.

It was going to be a long journey, one that could have been better done by air on a Virgin or Arik airline but I was saving all my money for drugs so flights were now a luxury I could not afford. I was of the opinion that since I got myself into this situation, I must also deal with the consequences alone. I already sold my car as I believed I wouldn't be needing it for the next year.

I tried to gain some level of comfort from the poorly padded seat and shifted around till I was fairly comfortable; at N6000 it was not terrible.

My mum and my siblings - Tunji and Abeke - waited till the bus filled up and left the park. I had hoped to come to the motor park alone in a cab, but shaking off my family proved to be a trying task; one I didn't have the strength for, so I gave up and let them tag along.

I was going away for one year of National Youth Service Corps generally referred to as NYSC; three weeks in a boot camp and the rest of the year doing whatever volunteer job I was asked to do while pretending to serve my country. My family was immensely proud and couldn't keep it off their faces. They were at the motor park to see me off to Plateau State where I was to live for a year. I hoped to visit home as infrequently as possible and perhaps not at all.

In a country where people love to show off the evidence of good living without any grace, the NYSC programme is ample evidence that I have actually graduated from University; that I was not a ghost student (one of those who hang around lecture halls and live in University hostels but were not actually registered students of the University) and have a degree; that I have now joined the throng of University graduates who are fighting over a few jobs. For the next one year, I and thousands of other recent University graduates like me are "Youth Corpers" and would be addressed by the locals at our location as "corpers" or "ajuwayas" bastardisations of our temporary title.

I did not have high expectations of the Youth service programme, and this was largely due to the many tales I had heard; but strangely I was glad to be going. The three weeks in camp would be respite from my family and the love in their eyes and the hurt they will feel in the future about me. It was escaping Abeke who was growing suspicious and had questions in her eyes that were pushing her to ask repeatedly if I was fine. I was going off with mixed feelings, I didn't want to be with the family I know I have let down. NYSC camp wasn't my idea of the perfect escape or hiding place; but it would have to do.

I waved frantically as the bus pulled out of the park. My excitement was temporary, a short lull from the misery, fear and deep sadness of the last few weeks. I wondered how fast the three weeks would fly and if I might wake up one day to find everything was a dream and the pain in my chest imaginary.

I gazed out of the window at the tarmac as it rushed under the wheels of the bus and the trees flashed past us in backward motion. I soon got tired of watching the trees and greenery and dozed off, to a myriad coloured dreamland of breeze and flying kites, of green rolling hills and faint strains of relaxing music; my first peaceful dream in weeks.

I woke up to find my travel neighbour staring at me, I stared back at him in confusion and some irritation; he smiled unabashedly "sorry I didn't mean to stare" he said without taking his eyes off me.

I nodded silently knowing that he wanted to be caught staring. In another world I would be amused, I would be wondering what he was thinking and I would be stealing small sideways glances at him with coy half smiles; I would be wondering if this was the start of another beautiful, delightful romance, the remit of every young girl; but this time I was not.

"So how was dreamland?"

I ignored him, turning away ever so slightly.

"You actually slept with a smile on your face; you must be one happy person"

I couldn't imagine myself smiling in my sleep; but I must admit it was flattery I couldn't fault... I couldn't exactly say I surely wasn't smiling in my sleep. How would I know? But I knew; I knew the good looking man beside me whose interest I would normally have encouraged was lying. Despite the placid dream of rolling hill I had woken up from, I knew I was too sad consciously or unconsciously to be smiling in my sleep. How could a person as bereft as I was, as lost, confused and alone as I was, be smiling while sleeping? I thought.

"Thank you" I answered.

My response took him aback; it was an unexpected one. He thought he had a perfect conversation starter, one that would yield positive or negative results but not indifference. He refreshed his faltering smile and proceeded doggedly to make himself glibly agreeable.

"Going on a holiday?"

"No" I replied wearily. This one is not going away, he is staying. I was too smart now to blame my looks for this attention. It is nothing to do with looks, even if they sometimes facilitate things. It is the way things are. He is a hunter who has spotted a suitable prey.

"Oh really? First time in Jos?"

"Yes" I willed him to notice my monosyllabic responses and stop talking to me, he did not.

"Fantastic place I tell you. Ignore anything you might have heard about unrests and violence, it's a fantastic place" he said. I glanced at him and he continued in a rush, as if he was afraid I might put a pause to his spiel "you should make sure you visit the National museum, the Wildlife Safari Park, and Assop falls, now that is one waterfall you want to see. You should let me show you around, I've been in Jos for a while, and by the way I'm Seye"

I smiled sadly, I didn't volunteer my name. I wished I could say yes show me the city, take me out, tell me all the tall tales you can think of that will make me like you, but to what point? The futility hit me hard, in the centre of my head and I decided to put a stop to all this talking now. I had too many hours to spend in this bus and the earlier we both realised we would not be friends, the better.

"I don't feel like having a conversation, or making a new friend, I want to sleep if you don't mind"

"Oh okay; I won't bother you anymore" he replied politely. There was slight embarrassment in his eyes but I was not bothered, I have learnt that men, the kind of men I have met and I was always meeting were not easily hurt... they had rhinoceros hides sitting firmly over their emotions.

Still I was conscious of his features out of the side of my eye. Slim dark features, a light moustache, tan polo shirt on black chinos pants, soft black suede loafers. He was well dressed, an aspiring young man... probably worked in a bank or one of the telecoms companies... even consulting. We fell into a silence, initially uncomfortable but gradually fading into the silence between strangers, where we ceased to be aware of each other.

Six hours and forty-five minutes later, most of which I spent with my head against the window, eyes closed, mind in the same tumult that has become the norm, the bus turned into a busy motor park in Jos City. Still unwilling to give up completely, they never seem to; he took out a neat business card, turned to me and put the card in my hand.

"I'm Seye Odunlami, I hope you will call me to say hello if you get bored around here. You could also send me a text or WhatsApp message" he continued tentatively a smidgen of hope in his voice.

I continue to look ahead silently.

The card was engraved in blue with 'GT Bank Plc', and down in the left-hand corner, Seye Odunlami; of course I was right... he was a banker.

"Good-bye"

"Good-bye" I answered walking away clutching the card. My life seemed full of goodbyes, like a person destined to constantly say good byes; to people, to places, to love, good-bye even to living. I felt tired of living, what is the purpose anyway? To wake up, to eat, to struggle for material things, to chase love, to find what you want and then lose it in as painful a way as possible, then to do it all over again... pointless activities.

I dragged my legs one ahead of the other in search of further transport to take me from the motor park to another park where I would get a bus to the Youth Service camp in Bukuru. I found it in the form of a motorbike famously called Okada and it's filthy, dust covered driver.

Okada drivers pick passengers on the single seat behind them and rush you to your destination, hurrying back with another passenger. As dangerous as they were, a lot of people rode them to avoid the traffic that has cars crawling bumper to bumper and sometimes like I was about to do, you ride them because they are the only available means of transport, having beat the rickety buses and taxis out of the market in the particular geography involved.

Unfortunately, the Okada driver I chose was suicidal and destined straight to hell. His dirty scarf flapped in the wind, and his grime coated cap sat rakish on his head as he raced and wove his way between cars, trucks and along the edge of sidewalks, his tyres barely missing a plunge into the slime filled roadside gutters. I quickly realised I was only an unfortunate luggage on his suicide journey and quickly started praying to a God I rarely talked to. He drove at a mind spinning speed, and turned corners at a dangerous spin, bearing down on the road as if he bore it a grudge for stretching on ahead of him.

"Take it easy please" I begged him.

"Don't worry auntie, don't worry at all" he was amused at my concern.

"Idiot" I mumbled while trying to keep my grip on him and at the same time keep my mind on all the terrible things that could happen as he weaved in between cars and raced alongside trucks.

JAY

"Have a safe journey my love" he whispered.

"Thank you" I whispered back moving gently out of his embrace.

"Call me the moment you land in Jos"

"You know I will." I turned and waved again before turning the corner into the corridor leading to the departure lounge and another wave of security personnel.

I was relieved to be out of sight and going away for a few days. I needed space and time to clear my head and get my thoughts in line and with happy, thoughtful Yomi around, constantly checking on how I was feeling it was near impossible articulating a single thought.

"Your bag please" I was snatched out of my reverie by the polite voice of an airport customs officer, a lady in a grey uniform.

"Please open your bag madam I need to take a look in it" she repeated gesturing at my hand bag with her right hand, she was wearing a latex rubber glove.

"Yes, sorry" I quickly removed my handbag from my shoulder and passed it to her.

"And your hand luggage"

I pushed my carry-on along the metal table to her, she did a quick riffle through my handbag, looked up and smiled at me.

"This is a pretty bag aunty" she caressed the leather, "I want to carry a Mulberry bag too oh"

"Thank you" I smiled, collecting the bag she was returning to me while she patted and rubbed the corners and bottom of my small luggage.

"Have a lovely day ma'am" she finished zipping up my luggage.

"You too" I headed into the departure lounge and the rows of joined chair where I sat along with the already seated crowd waiting to be called to board our flight from Lagos to Jos.

I was on my way to Jos for three weeks of NYSC and despite the horror and surprise expressed by almost everyone I knew including my boyfriend Yomi, I was looking forward to Orientation camp. It was time away from them all - Yomi, Rolake and Anne my two closest friends and my brother Fola. Time for me to think about my next steps.

My NYSC posting should have been to the Lagos Orientation camp, daddy spoke to Uncle Kay about it and Uncle Kay promised to sort it out, but instead I was posted to Jos.

Initially on receiving the call up letter and reading 'Bukuru, Jos' I was petrified and stood rooted to the spot, staring at the piece of paper in my hand.

Rolake and Anne peered over my shoulder to read my posting details.

"Bukuru, Jos." Anne read out loud, "that can't be right" she exclaimed, alarm in her voice "Rolake and I have been posted to the Lagos camp.... You can't go to Jossssssssssss" Anne wailed.

"Somebody definitely messed this one up somewhere." Rolake sighed, "you are not going to Jos" she continued, her voice taking on more authoritative tones, "you will need to wait till the next posting and hopefully the idiot who messed this up can correct it" she finished sighing again more theatrically. She is most dramatic and says everything with a theatrical sigh and a roll of her eyes. I am convinced her eye balls get more exercise than the rest of her.

"But why not?" I asked, irritated by the assumption that I wouldn't want to go to Jos or couldn't cope in Jos.

"What do you mean why not?" Rolake countered, predictably rolling her eyes.

"You want to go to Jos ni?" Anne asked.

"Maybe" I replied shrugging.

"Come on Jay, this is not the time to be rebellious"

"I think I will like Jos" I replied folding the piece of paper and tucking it into the pocket of my tan trousers.

"I don't think so, let me tell mummy, she will speak to General Akeem and he will get your posting corrected back to Lagos" Rolake said opening her car doors and sitting on the edge of the driver seat gingerly before swinging her legs in "I thought you had this sorted, you said your dad was sorting it out"

"Yes my dad said he was sorting it out, and no you will not speak to General Akeem about my posting" I replied.

"Yes I will, stop all this nonsense. Your face looks all funny by the way, I think you need to change the foundation you are wearing" Rolake continued all in one breathe.

"I'm wearing the Estee Lauder Foundation we all like"

"Well Estee Lauder isn't working for you right now, you look ashen, I think you should try the Kat Von Range, I'm so into that now"

"I'm wearing the foundation by BMPro and it's not bad at all, I told you about it when I got it, remember?" Anne said helpfully peering at me from beside Rolake where she always rides shotgun.

"Let's go over to Banke Meshida's studio this weekend and get a makeover, you can always trust Banke to find you the perfect foundation and everything else in between" Rolake said shutting her car door.

"See you tomorrow babes"

"See you" I turned and trudged to my car, my feet heavy under me; that was when I decided to go to Jos for my NYSC programme.

I got home and told daddy my NYSC deployment is to Jos; he was so surprised he sat down hard on the sofa behind him; "don't worry princess, you are not going to Jos, Kay is a silly boy for not sorting this out" he said, getting up from the sofa purposefully.

"I don't mind going to Jos daddy, actually I want to go"

"No you don't, you will enjoy it for the three weeks in the camp and after that you will hate that place, and so you are not going" he said firmly

"Since I'm the one that's going to hate it, why does it matter?"

"It matters because daddy will worry and Jos is not safe with all these Islamic insurgents that won't go away, why are we even having this conversation? We already agreed you will do your Youth service in Lagos or not at all" my dad finished impatiently.

"Okay, how about if I go for the three weeks of Orientation camp and do the rest of it in Lagos here? I would like to see Jos and like you said I will enjoy the first three weeks, so why not?"

He was silent, thinking about it.

"It will be an adventure and if after the first week I don't enjoy it or it is unsafe, I'll come home" I learnt from a young age that cajoling works with my father, outright rebellion rarely ever.

"Okay, let me call that Kay of a boy. I don't know how he could have messed this up"

Daddy got on the phone with Uncle Kay and I could hear Uncle Kay explaining and apologising for the mess up. He promised to correct it so that my posting to Jos would be rerouted back to Lagos in time for me to continue my Youth service in Lagos after the three weeks in the Jos Orientation camp; so all of that settled, I gladly set out for Jos via Arik Airline, business class of course.

Yomi took the news of my deployment to Jos the worst, he was upset and kept saying "You don't have to do Youth Service at all. You don't need Youth Service, not right now anyway, not in the light of all what is happening now, it can be dangerous. There is always next year. You can do all of this next year. Trust me honey, trust me. Leave this NYSC business for now, let's sort out the business on our plate"

I wanted to shout, "the business is on my plate, on my plate Yomi and I'm going to Jos because I need space, because I need to think and because contrary to what everybody seems to be thinking, if thousands of other Nigerian graduates can survive three weeks of Orientation camp in far flung locations, I can too, I'm not made of glass. This is my chance to have three weeks to myself, far away from you, Fola, everyone and your constant suggestions, ideas, and advice. I want these three weeks and I am not letting you or your 'shoulder of support' stop me" but I did not say this, I merely smiled and said, "I will be alright, don't worry love, and you can visit".

Fola, I didn't even tell at all, he was away in Kuala Lumpur and was not expected to return for another two weeks. I was glad for the respite these three weeks offered but I was also afraid of the decision I would have to make by the end of the three weeks. My mind was in a whirl and all that kept running through my mind was – how could I have been so stupid, so indulgent? How could I have lived my life as cavalierly without thought or plan? Now what do I do? What am I going to do?

ADUNNI

Somehow I arrived at the NYSC Orientation Camp in one piece and watched with fascination through the gates into the camp; like a street urchin barred by the unfortunate circumstance of birth from the children's party holding in the rich man's house up the street.

I was a bit surprised to see soldiers inside the gates of the camp, rummaging in the luggage of would-be Youth Corpers who were on a queue in front of them. Of course, it's a sort of military camp yet somehow I never imagined that soldiers would be in charge. I expected a host of old university types herding us like flock and forcing us to attend numerous boring lectures on a wide variety of topics. I was wrong. The camp was run by soldiers who were at the camp gates with forbidding faces and a long list of "prohibited items". I watched as they delved into bags and boxes impatiently, seeking out items that fell into their contraband category and throwing these unceremoniously into a big heap while declaring "you can collect them in three weeks' time"

It didn't take long to figure out what was contraband and how of many of these I had in my brown box, an electric iron and an electric coil for boiling water. I had no intention of handing over my electric iron and coil, they cost good money and wouldn't survive for three weeks in the metallic mountain the soldiers were creating; so I stepped away from the queue, opened my luggage and reconstructed the tidy arrangement to a more suitable one, one that had worked since my boarding school days of sneaking things into school.

I got back in the queue and watched the soldiers confiscate black shirts and trousers from the baffled fellow in front of me. I dragged my luggage up to be searched, hoping the soldiers would prove as human as every house mistress and master I had in boarding school.

"Open your box" a female soldier barked at me.

A male version of her stood behind her pretending nonchalance, his curiosity a scarcely hidden concern.

I threw open my brown box and sitting grandly atop my clothes were lace and silk panties in varying shades of powder blue, hot pink, zebras, fresh violet and satin yellow; a pack of sanitary towels vied for attention and brassieres grinned back at the ogling pair.

"Anything in your box?" she asked irritably.

Her partner gasped and swallowed and some boys on the queue behind me craned their necks to see the cause of his hyperventilation.

I started to reel off a list of the harmless items in my luggage, "My clothes, my shoes, my..."

"I didn't ask you to list them. Anything else there?"

"No" I shook my head.

"You can go"

I snapped my box shut and joined the next stage of the registration in front of an old man sitting behind a scarred worn out table.

"Write you name here... here..." he tapped at the exact spot he wanted the baffled candidate to write his name. A prototype of the old men who took charge of faculty registration every session throughout my undergraduate studies and who I have come to believe were there for the sole purpose of teaching students patience, endurance and native intelligence.

I peered over the shoulder of the individual who didn't know exactly where to sign his name and read what he had written under the direction of the old man's pointing finger; 'Effiong T. Attah, MBBS Medicine, University of Ibadan. I gawked at him inanely as he shuffled on dragging his box; I was sure we had travelled in the same bus from Lagos; he was the novice traveller who sat directly behind the driver.

"Write your name here" a loud impatient voice snapped me out of my musings.

"Do quick oh, people dey wait" he said to me in broken English; the next target of his irritation and self-importance.

I hurriedly scribbled in the brown notebook he was pushing at me and set off into the camp dragging my luggage whose tires were refusing to roll in the sand I was forcing them through.

The camp was a large state school 'Zanc Commercial School' which was most likely a school with boarding facilities during term time. It was fenced with brick and cement walls in peeling white paint and a dust road with white painted stones arranged in a line along both sides of it, led from the black gates up to a white building about 50 yards on. The white building was long and one end of it stretched almost to the brick wall fencing the camp. Its five or six wooden doors were interspaced with rows of windows; like classrooms; many of the wooden windows had lost a hinge or two and hung loose while others were flung wide open. The roof was a rusty dusty brown and wore different shades of brown squares where leaks had been patched down. The building, its doors, the windows, everything was covered with the same film of dust snuggling in my sandals and settling on my brown suitcase and knapsack.

I later found out that the white long building that was partitioned into makeshift rooms with plywood was called the administrative building and housed camp officials at one end and the clinic at the other. The three flag posts in front of the administrative building were bare except for one flying a straggly national flag in green and white. Its tips were torn and it fluttered feebly in the wind as tired as everything else I could see so far.

The white building stood facing a large football field with two goal posts that had no net for catching the ball.

One goal post stood unevenly, its hold in the soil enabled only by rocks arranged artfully around its ailing leg. I suspected a lot of our time would be spent on the grass field that was artfully being called 'the Parade ground' because of all the marching we were going to be doing.

To the left of the administrative building were two storey buildings that later served the multipurpose jobs of dining rooms, meeting rooms and registration rooms; although much bigger and painted brown, both buildings were in the same derelict state as the administrative building.

A large number of luggage dragging graduates mostly young like me with a few looking suspiciously too old to be here were all heading down the narrow pathway beside the brown storey buildings, so I followed them. I found there was more registration to be done.

I was suddenly faced with a longer and rowdier queue and no notebook carrying old men in sight. People were queued up in groups and at some point the queue appeared to have two lines, at other points, six. I quickly scanned the crowd for a familiar face to identify with; someone to tell me exactly what was going on here. I discovered a long time ago that I have no luck on long queues; I went through my undergraduate days hating the first few weeks of registration; the odds were seldom ever in my favour. Registration either ended a few minutes before my turn, or I would find out I did not meet a vital requirement three hours after joining the queue; if not that, then a fight would erupt on the queue and I would end up losing my turn. If it can go wrong, it will; so I have learnt to be fast and wily on queues. Jumping queues is an art I have been forced to master. In this country, queues are not the orderly things you see in other countries. Here, queues are time wasters; they reward bullies, queue jumpers and early comers who are able to present an aggressive attitude. On graduating I had naively again assumed that my days of endless queues and registrations were over and everything from hence forth would be orderly and dignified, but here again I was wrong.

"Hi, Hello, 'scuse me" someone tapped me; I turned around and it was Jadesola Savage. It felt strange to see a familiar face in this motley crowd even though a few minutes earlier I had been scanning for one.

Jadesola who everyone calls Jay, and I matriculated and graduated the same year from the same University and during my third year she visited my roommate Marilyn who was also her friend and classmate, very frequently. I believe she even spent the night a few times; but she was not a campus resident. She was one of those who schooled from home. It was usually the rich kids who did this at my University. Home for them was not a place to run away from or escape; home meant maids, drivers, zero chores and sometimes even a swimming pool. Hostels were the unbearable places. I know this because I have dated them.

Jay was bubbly and constantly smiling. She was one of those "happy, life-is-a-dream, friend-of-the-world" kind of people. She had a chirpy hello and a small happy wave for everyone. I preferred to ignore her most times, irritating as she was, always like a puppy with a bowl of milk; although I figured I would have a lot to be happy about if I drove to school in a shiny new model Honda Accord and didn't have to live in the horribly dirty and poor serviced hostels the University charged us through the nose for.

"Hello! What a surprise" she said, in her posh lilting voice.

"Yeah" I replied "and this queue is crazy" I added; for want of something to say.

"I knowwwwwwww" she rolled her eyes and fluttering her designer strapped hand at the queue.

About five feet three inches, she is dark and slim with small breasts that gave her a pretty prepubescent look, she looked like a fourteen-year-old on the cusp of maturity. She was dressed in a way that accentuated her boyish figure, giving her curves in places you didn't know they existed. Her appearance, dressing, manners and speech all screamed cultured, moneyed and sheltered; I could almost see the silver spoon dangling from her mouth. I assessed Jay again while also trying to have a conversation with her and wondered what she was doing in a backwater like Bukuru.

"How long have you been on this queue?" I asked.

"About ten minutes and it's no use" she shrugged.

"Really?"

"You need to see how long this queue is" she said "between here and the first person, there must be three hundred people shoving and pushing each other"

I watched the crowd and it truly appeared to be dancing in unison to some slow music, weaving and swaying, the noise deafening.

"And I haven't even done my photocopies" she continued.

"What photocopies" I asked, groping in the recesses of my brain for any information that pertained to photocopies and coming up blank, trying not to panic I dived back into the murky waters of my memories, and came up blank again and gasping for air.

"Your documents, all of them, you are supposed to make six copies of each one," Jay explained "and if you haven't, which from your face I think you haven't, then we need to go and do them right now"

"Where" I asked, a bit put out, I looked around me and I saw nothing as orderly as a business centre or a photocopier machine, only some local children who had somehow found their way into the Orientation camp and were staring at us like birds of prey who knew we were food and were only waiting for us to realise it and oblige them.

"Outside, I think we need to find out; let me make sure we have a slot on the queue to return to"

"Yeah sure"

She tapped Effiong Attah who was now on the heaving mammoth queue and talked to him briefly and he nodded in reply. I surmised he had agreed to save a space on the queue for us till we returned from our photocopy adventures.

"Do you want to exchange phone numbers; in case we lose each other in this crowd? Then we can WhatsApp" Jay asked me fishing out her phone.

"What's that?" I asked feigning ignorance.

"You don't know what WhatsApp is? That's wild" Jay said smiling and shaking her head.

I shrug.

"Okay no problem, it's an app and its literarily free to call and message on it; so if you download the app, we can chat on WhatsApp" Jay replied cheerily.

"Okay" I nodded. I had no intention of downloading any privacy invading application. I like the silence in my world and planned to keep it that way "Let's exchange phone numbers for now, if we lose each other, we call okay?"

"Yes sure" she replied, looking slightly perplexed as we exchanged phone numbers.

At the camp gate, we discovered a load of people trying to get out and the soldiers manning the gate, refusing them exit, their faces like masks spelling out their will; negative and immovable.

"I guess there goes our going-out idea" Jay mumbled shuffling the grass with her right foot and looking very mournful. "I have some money, maybe if we offer them some money, they'll let us through"

"Not with a hundred people all trying to get out"

I sighed inwardly and headed determinedly towards the soldiers, straight at the one with eyes that roved like he was looking for something.

"*Oga* well done" I cocked my head to one side and flashed him a warm smile.

"Hmm" he grunted, staring at me like he was now taking a proper look at the person addressing him.

"*Oga abeg I wan commot quickly I go soon return, now now I go return, make I go small come back*" I continued in broken English.

"*Henhen, I no suppose gree you commot*" he replied in the same vein.

"Please oga, I no go tey"

"Henhen, you go bring something for me?" He was weakening.

"I go try. Abeg" I moved slightly closer to the gates. He paused as if he was thinking, while greedily roaming my face with his eyes, drinking me in.

"No too tey oh you hear? I no wan stress fine girls like you, na why I dey allow you be that" he answered as he opened the gate enough to let Jay and I out amidst complaints from the others who also wanted to get out.

We returned an hour later to find the queue extinct and replaced by an even larger crowd pushing and shoving viciously.

Jay and I watched the milling crowd for a while; surprised and confused, we quickly realised that we would not be getting any more of the required registration done that day.

"This is no use" she moaned.

"Let's go" I urged and we went off in search of cold drinks and a tour of the Orientation camp.

There were more of the brown storey buildings, and they were split into class rooms, with long wooden chairs and tables and a ceiling that looked suspiciously leaky. The Mammy market was slightly more impressive; an array of raffia roofed sheds selling food, drinks, toiletries, books and fruits. A lady was setting up a hair dressing stall, and a snooker table was already up and surrounded by young boys. We bought buckets and food flasks from a woman who was arranging and displaying her stall of brightly coloured plastic wares.

Two banks had set up stands offering immediate account opening services and their staff smiled at us invitingly. One of them followed us, trying to cajole us to open accounts with their bank. When we refused, he stared at us thoughtfully and said, "Your money will be stolen and you will say I told you so"

"Blah blah blah" Jay muttered and giggled.

I glanced at her for a second, a little irritated, I hoped she is not also a giggler because that would just make her more difficult to live with. I can't run away from my happy crowd to come here and play best friends with another happy duck. Can everybody just be sad for a second? I am sad, you should all be sad... I don't care how amazing your life is, if I'm sad I want you to be sad... like why is the sun shining?

Still lost in thoughts, I found myself and Jay in the administrative building. It housed a clinic where six beds were already laid out and the press room where we met an officious looking Youth Corper who was already in the standard youth corper uniform. He looked like he had been there all year long. He stood at the door of the Press room and importantly informed us that the Press department and room would be manned only by the most intelligent Corpers including his esteemed self. We both burst out laughing and left him wondering what the joke was.

Then we headed to the hostels; there were four of them, long white buildings similar to the administrative building. Two of the buildings had rusting metal boards hanging from the room beam declaring the buildings named after incumbent Governor Jonah David Lang.

"Jesus Christ of Nazareth!" Jay gasped, there were rows and rows of bunk beds, all packed together tightly in the long rectangular room.

"You didn't go to boarding house?" I asked her.

"No" she shook her head, "did you know it would be this bad?" she continued.

"No, but I guess it is what it is. Don't worry it's not so bad and it's merely three weeks" I shrugged.

Although my attitude to the decrepit state of the hostels was nonchalant, I was undeniably shocked at the state of the rooms we were going to be living in for three weeks. Sometimes I think I am the most selfish person in the world and I can be very mean and here is my mean streak showing itself again. The hostel looked worse than any I ever encountered during my days of boarding school and I was more freaked out than I was letting on. Still a perverse side of me, instead of allaying her fears by showing some of mine, chose to act blasé and unmoved.

A lot of the bunks had no mattresses yet were spotting various signs of ownership – luggage, buckets and shoes.

"Let's go and get our things and lay claim to two bunks before they are all gone" I offered now feeling contrite.

"Okay" she nodded humbly, still short of words and probably wondering how to survive in this place for three weeks.

We got our bags and boxes and returned to the hostel; some of the girls had been busy at work and now had the bunks joined together in twos with a small space enough for standing and turning carefully, in between every two bunks.

"Let's take the upper bunks of two joined bunks so that we can be side by side" she suggested.

"Alright" I replied a little surprised, I wouldn't have imagined Jay and I hitting it off well enough to be bedding down side by side for three weeks.

It later occurred to me that she had chosen me merely because I was a familiar face in an alien environment and there was no else. I brushed the thought aside; it didn't matter anyway, so why dwell on it. I continued to scrutinise the two rickety bunk beds we had chosen to be sure they were sturdy enough to carry our weight for three weeks, I shook them vigorously.

I looked up from our bunk inspection, to see a girl dragging in a mattress.

"Excuse me, where did you get the mattress from?"

"There's a store room, near the Mammy market, before you get to the Press room, where mattresses are been given out but you will have to drop your call-up letter to get one of these"

"Oh thanks" I turned to Jay "what do you think?"

"If we drop our call-up letters, how do we register tomorrow? I think the call-up letters are needed to get registered and if we make an early start tomorrow, we stand a better chance of getting things done" Jay reasoned.

"But we need something to sleep on tonight" I countered.

"So what do we do?"

"I'll drop mine" I offered and we'll both sleep on one mattress, so while I'm returning the mattress, you could get on the registration queue and I'll join you when I get my call up letter back"

"Okay, that's a good idea"

The queue was short and moved fast, "the others don't know about this yet" Jay whispered conspiratorially.

A few minutes later, I realised that the coordination between the man collecting the call-up letter and the man handing out the mattress was poor. The call-up letter guy was working very quickly, oblivious of the dilemma of the other guy who had to drag out the beds from the huge pile in a dark smelly room. A small crowd of those who had dropped their letters was forming in front of him and he worked frantically to reduce the crowd. He wasn't looking at the faces, merely handing out the mattresses, his face sweat-streaked. An idea formed in my head as I joined the waiting crowd after dropping my letter. I collected the mattress that was handed to me and passed it on to Jay who started to walk off with it assuming that I was following her. I stayed put and without batting an eyelid collected another mattress that was handed out. When Jay looked back and saw me with another mattress, a triumphant grin on my face her jaw practically dropped "how did you do it?" she asked as I caught up with her.

"Observation and calculation my dear Watson" I replied smugly.

We emptied half a can of insecticide on both mattresses for fear of bed bugs before we set about laying the bed, and then returned to the Mammy market in search of dinner. We later found out that the camp provided horrible prison style meals three times a day. We never ate the food provided by the camp.

We returned to the hostel after a heavy dinner of steamed rice and fish stew. We sat on our side by side bunk beds and talked for about an hour, learning about each other's life before our meeting again in Jos. I was cautious in telling Jay my story; I talked about my mum, a teacher in a state school and my siblings; my dad I mentioned briefly, what's the point of talking about how much you loved someone who is dead? It only picks at the scabs of a wound that never heals. My father died of cancer when I was fifteen and every time I say that out loud or in my head the phrase that always comes to my mind in a mocking voice is 'Physician heal thy self'.

I was right about the silver spoon dangling prettily from Jay's mouth; her father is a retired diplomat now running a fish farm in Epe, a few hundred miles outside the Lagos metropolis. She is the last of four kids and has lived all over the world as her dad went from one diplomatic post to another. We were clearly from different sides of the fence, with glaringly different experiences of life.

Feeling I had now given my food enough time to begin the process of digestion, I slid down on my bed in exhaustion. I was so tired I was sure I could sleep for two days; a rough road journey, a hectic day and the powerful drugs had all worked together to sap me of all energy. I felt like sleeping and never waking up although the thing is I didn't want to die in this crappy place. My last thought as I drifted off to sleep was this: I don't want to die but I find living exhausting.

BECKY

I arrived at the camp gate around seven am on Monday, the first day of camp and there was a straggly queue of other tired looking men and women. The soldiers were looking through everyone's luggage but one look at my cornrowed hair and the big bible sitting on top of my clothes and the soldier waved me through. I cannot fully explain how well this "Christian sister" stereotype works for me, one look at me and I am basically assumed to be naïve, clueless, guileless, pious and at most annoying.

The next stage of registration was putting my name in some attendance register manned by an old man in a faded Ankara shirt with matching trousers.

"Rebecca Oni" he mouthed after me, "where are you from?"

"Lagos" I replied, trying to smile.

"Hehehehe, I mean originally, everybody likes to say Lagos, Lagos, Lagos, where is your original hometown?" the old man said, laughing and slapping his thigh.

I could hear some people giggling behind me; I stared at the old man memorising his face "Ife, my parents are from Ife"

"Good, good, that is better, my wife is from Ife too, particularly troublesome people. Sign here and here, move on, move on. Next"

I joined the next stage of the registration and the next; it all progressed quickly after that and by 12 noon I was a fully registered Youth Corper in the dusty city of Jos, Plateau state ready to serve state and country.

When my white and green khakis were handed to me by a smiling official, I felt flush with pride, which surprised me. I was not sure why I was suddenly so happy and proud, but I suspect it is the reminder that I was indeed a university graduate and my country and its systems recognise this singular fact; added to this was the awareness that I had finally completed the notorious anxiety inducing registration without so much as a hitch. It went as smoothly as Vaseline on a baby's bottom.

After khakis were issued to me, I was directed to visit the camp stores to collect my mattress and head to any female hostel of my choice. Off I went to the camp stores where I was handed a measly looking, bug infested mattress, definitely the thinnest and saddest looking mattress I had ever seen; holding it made my skin crawl.

"Can I have another one?" I politely asked the camp staff handing out the mattresses, he paused and glared at me and I could see his face change from indifference to dislike.

"No, you can't have another one; that is the one I am issuing to you; please leave the queue, you are disturbing"

I looked behind me, there was no queue, just a straggly group of smirking boys.

"Help the S.U. sister bros, you don't want her to smell more than she is already smelling" one of them said. The others laughed.

I waited a little, staring at his face, willing him to change his mind but he went back to hauling mattresses out of the store and on to the pavement in front of the store in readiness for mattress requests.

I watched him, memorising his face. I hate this, I don't want to do this, I don't want to learn people's faces for later, but here we are again; life is a vicious cycle.

I must confess that this mattress incidence was the first negative in a day filled with bright orderly positives excluding the silly old man at the registration desk.

In the first female hostel I came across, I chose the lower bunk, I'm too heavy to spend the next three weeks climbing up and down these metal frames. I focused on spraying the mattress with insecticide before covering it with the bright yellow bed sheet I brought from Lagos. I refused to think about all the other bodies that might have slept on this mattress before me.

Shortly after, a slim tall girl with a head of spiral curls trudged into the hostel, a mattress under one arm, dragging and trailing on the floor and her head bent to one side talking into a phone insistently. I watched as she dropped the mattress nonchalantly on a bunk and walked out again, still talking on her phone. I waited till her voice faded before picking up the mattress she so nonchalantly dropped; it was a much thicker mattress than mine. I sprayed it with insecticide and laid it beneath the sad ugly thing that had been issued to me earlier; then I covered them both with the bright yellow bed sheet. It looked a little better; it's a survival of the fittest in this world.

***

I first saw him as he walked through the gates, slim, dark and wiry. He turned to smile at someone and I was transfixed, in addition to his hooded broody hawk eyes, he had the most startlingly beautiful smile ever. He was oblivious of me, but I could feel him in every cell in me, every hair on my body stood on end and I watched him as he hurried to the registration table where the same old man was still sitting, barking at people and pointing at the next line in his big book.

He wrote his name and moved on, I wanted to run to the old man, snatch the book and read his name. I watched him as he headed wrongly to the Press room. I wanted to run to him and say "not there my love, here; right here" He was beautiful, tall enough, slim enough, everything enough. I continued to watch his every move.

He later joined the queue for the next stage of registration and without thinking or remembering that I was already registered, I queued up behind him; like a thief I inhaled his smell, sweat and a musky man smell. I greedily drank it all in and hoped the queue would last forever.

I watched the hair at the back of his head as it curled into tight little rolls, like little roses waiting to burst out. I imagined my hands in the curls brushing them out, his hair was cut low but I could still see a few sprinkles of grey. He couldn't have been more than 26 years old yet looked so distinguished. He shifted his weight from one leg to another and I felt my insides turn to liquid. I wanted to touch him so desperately and luckily the heaving moving queue made it happen; I was pushed into him.

"Sorry" I mumbled, "People keep pushing"

"It's alright" he replied without even turning round to look at me.

I wanted to say hello and introduce myself but I was tongue tied, I could not find the words; I forgot my name and anything else I could have said in the circumstance. The unsayable thought on my mind was "Hello soulmate, I have waited for you forever, I love you already, you beautiful chocolate work of art"

I gaped at the back of his head in fascination, letting my eyes travel down his back to his waist where his checked shirt went into his brown trousers, held up by a brown belt. I was jealous of his belt, of his trouser, of his shirt, they were all so close to his body, his smell clinging to them. I was filled with sudden sadness and despair at the knowledge that I was not his when a small wispy girl came to speak to him.

"Hi, I'm Jay" she said to him.

"Hi, Effiong" he replied, his voice is strong and deep and travelled down my spine in waves.

"My friend and I need to dash out quickly and we don't want to lose our space on the queue, so please remember we are in front of you here" she finished pointing.

"That's okay" he turned slightly and smiled at the two girls.

Rage coursed through me, I felt betrayed. He bestowed his shining earth-shattering smile on two idiots who did not deserve it while I was standing here, waiting and loving him.

I watched the two of them as they sauntered off, their pert bottoms in some designer jeans. I wanted to run after them and tear their eyes out, to stab them again and again and again until their blood ran richly into the mud earth and they became lifeless.

I shook with rage and left the queue quickly before I did something unseemly; returning to the hostel and my bed where I laid down in deep sadness. I came back out at 7pm when the bugle went off for a horrible cold supper and returned to the familiarity of my bed.

The girl whose mattress I stole, came into the hostel screaming and cursing whoever stole her mattress. I managed to ignore her and suppressed the urge inside me to go over to her and slap her screaming face and knock the teeth out of her.

This was my chance to change my life, to change over a new leaf and I was not going to let some flimsy negative people and their negative aura make me do any less.

Day 2 NYSC Camp

JAY

It was 4.30am and the sun was still in bed but I could hear the urgent noises of my new roommates, their chattering, laughing and walking around, the girls on the joined bunk on my left were whispering loudly.

I could see some girls running out of the hostels carrying their mattresses, clearly returning them to the collection room. They looked like rats abandoning a sinking ship. I got up quickly and woke Adunni and together we piled our luggage on one bed, dragged the bedding off the other and joined the girls running out of the hostel; past two girls on the bunk by the south exit door who were fighting bitterly. The tall dark skinny one pointed her finger and screamed her disgust and anger at the other girl, she looked ready to foam at the mouth and the veins on her neck bulged; her opponent leaned on her bunk and rained curses and obscenities back. I watched in fascination for a moment before hurrying after Adunni.

An hour later, we were all heralded unceremoniously onto the grassy field and those in the hostels were chased out to join us.

"Don't we get to shower first?" I asked Adunni unable to keep the surprise out of my voice.

"Doesn't look like it" Adunni replied, stamping her feet in the early morning cold.

"Good morning young men and women, I am the RSM" someone bellowed. We later found out that an RSM is basically an Army Warrant Officer and the head honcho in the camp.

"Registration will continue today. Tomorrow, you will be split into Platoons and from then on you are required to participate in camp activities with your Platoon members. Discipline is essential and the Camp Commandant will be here tomorrow to make you aware of the rules of this camp. Today is the day of grace"

"Sadist" someone grumbled.

"Torture master" another said.

"I wan go sleep oh" someone else said in broken English from the edge of the gathering, everybody laughed.

The RSM then asked for two volunteers, one Christian and one Muslim to lead a prayer session. "What about us? Alternative religion over here?" someone screamed from within the crowd. Everyone laughed and tittered. The RSM ignored the question, a pained expression on his face. The prayer session lasted about fifteen minutes. My legs shook with the effort of standing and I bent down twice to rest on my hunches.

After the prayer session, the soldiers briskly divided us into groups and for an hour we stretched, jumped and bent over. We jogged round the parade ground twice, one straggly group after the other then returned to more jumping and stretching. When we started to groan the RSM called off the soldiers and we were made to assemble again. He then laboriously reminded us of the advantages of discipline and good behaviour and the need to complete the registration process today as full camp activities would be starting tomorrow.

"Discipline and good behaviour, two words with new meaning to me. If I had been disciplined and of good behaviour say in the last five years or maybe if I had said 'No' that once, I would be happy and carefree now, looking forward to what life had to offer; but I wasn't any of those things so here I was, miserable as a drunk goat; sick to my stomach.

The RSM called up an old wrinkled soldier carrying a bugle and asked us to listen conscientiously to the different sounds that would signify drills, call to dinner, wake up call, light-out and a salute to the flag. The crowd listened and clapped vigorously after each blow on the bugle like ardent aficionados at the opera. I was slightly irritated by this united ability to derive fun from an ostensibly unappealing activity. I let my mind wander to more pressing matters such as how I was feeling, the dryness in my mouth, the tiredness I felt all over and the slight headache that was coming on. I honestly had no idea how I was going to survive the next three weeks.

"You can now get back to your registration and settling in" the RSM shouted dismissing us.

On the way back to the hostel, I noticed some people at the registration area already scrambling for space and shoving each other. They have either taken their baths at some ungodly hour or care nothing for personal hygiene and have chosen registration over it. I thought. Adunni and I continued the journey to the hostel and the bathroom. I could feel the sweat trickling down my back, the sand from the parade ground in my shoes, on my skin, nestling in the cracks of my elbow, fingers and neck; I walked faster.

The hostel was in an uproar, another two girls were already beating each other up, another two were trying to separate them; about twenty others were lying or kneeling on their bunks shouting encouragements and insults at the irate girls; while the rest of the hostel expounded their opinion of the matter loudly. The din was deafening, Adunni glanced at me, horror in her eyes and without any other form of conversation we both understood that we needed to clean up and get out of the hostel as fast as we could.

A plate of Jollof rice and a maggi cube sized piece of meat was breakfast, I willed my stomach to keep it down; this was not the time for theatrics, gratefully it complied.

The sight of the registration queue we had to join almost put my heart in my belly and I was convinced I would be the last corper registered in this camp.

"I think I should walk up the queue and maybe I will discover a gentleman who will allow me to jump the queue" Adunni said, dragging me out of my negative thoughts.

Adunni is incredibly pretty, from her dark perfectly arched eyebrows, to her straight nose, bow shaped lips and jet black hair packed in a sleek pony tail, long limbs, slim delicate fingers, graceful hips and legs that go on and on; she was devastatingly beautiful. Yesterday when she smiled, I noticed her teeth – perfect rows of pearly white, equally and evenly distributed in her mouth. Adunni's beauty is the kind you notice, who or what you are is irrelevant, you see her and it hits you between the eyes – this is a beautiful woman with a face to remember and a perfect body.

Like many beautiful people, Adunni knows she is beautiful but she is sardonic about it. It is almost as if she finds it annoying, yet she is willing to use it, to make it work for her. I always had her pegged as a party girl, in and out of flashy cars in front of Moremi hall; seldom smiling but looking immaculate as usual. Unlike me I don't think she has to try. I don't think she noticed me even when I lived next door to her in the same hostel in our third year except for those few times on the hostel corridors.

"I know a lot about jumping queues, trust me on this, I have perfected the art of jumping queues and I feel no remorse about it" Adunni said. "When you want to jump a queue, you should never appeal to the good sense of another female, they have no such thing on queues, go for the men; charm the men" Adunni continued, pulling me along as she walked up the queue.

I don't think girls would find it difficult to hate Adunni. You take one look at that face and think oh God! She has it all; but I know she doesn't, nobody does. A lot of people have taken a look at me, at my life and thought exactly the same thing, I have seen it in their eyes; and yet I know how wrong they are.

Scrutinising faces as we went up the queue, I noticed a few baleful glares from some girls; they knew what we were up to.

"There are some guys who will not give you the time of day" Adunni wagged her finger "these are usually the I-stand-on-a-morally-higher-ground-than-you ones, don't even bother with those, they are worse than the females, they will not only refuse you, they will lecture you on the virtue of patience 'go-to-the-back-of-the-queue' or discipline 'you-should-have-gotten-here-early-like-we-did'"

We were right at the front of the queue now; I was too scared to look behind us.

"Hello"

I turned and it was the guy from the day before, I think his name is Effiong, he saved us a spot on the queue yesterday; I smiled at him in recognition.

"Hi" Adunni smiled warmly at him too. I was not surprised she was smiling at him so warmly. I bet she's nicer to men than women.

"I'm surprised you are still on this queue. I guess you didn't register after all" she said.

He grinned happily, he was delighted at her warm response "No, I did not and I'm Effiong Attah"

"I'm Adunni Momora, and I'm sure you will register soon" she shrugged, "you are almost there now"

"Yes, are you on the queue too?" he asked.

"Yeah, we are way at the back" she replied, stretching her hand like we were queued up at the moon.

"Ahw" he grunted, screwing up his bushy brows in a thoughtful frown.

"Could I possibly join the queue here?" she smiled fully now, it was like bringing out full military artillery for a street scuffle. The smile crinkled up her eyes and spread to her perfect cupid shaped mouth slowly. I felt pity for Effiong, he didn't stand a chance.

"Of course" he said moving back and smiling happily like it was he who had received a favour.

"Thank you" Adunni slipped into the queue and pulled me in. I felt like running down the length of the queue apologising to everyone for what Adunni and I had done but I think I was more frightened of Adunni and the idea of returning to the tail end of the queue than I was of the angry glares on the queue, so I stayed.

Soon it was past noon and hunger started to bite, I was tired of being elbowed and manhandled and of the unnecessary contact so many bodies were making with mine while the length of the queue remained unchanged. When Adunni suggested lunch, I agreed eagerly, feeling faint at the thought of food.

Adunni watched intently, frowning slightly as I got off the ledge, I read her eyes, "fragile, over pampered child" and I wished I could say 'Adunni, you are wrong like everybody else, I am not fragile nor pampered, I am tired and I have good reason' but as usual I said nothing, and together we went to the Mammy market.

At the Mammy market which appeared to be famous with all the corpers, we had a hard time making up our minds. We walked up and down the dust road in the middle of the market in search of the perfect meal amidst cat calls and whistling from mischievous boys. At last we opted for one of the many bukateria, its floors looked freshly swept and clean. The fragrant smell of fried tomatoes and fresh chillies wafted out from the bukateria where rows of people were sitting on wooden benches bent over steaming bowls. Adunni and I hurried inside.

"Aunty, good afternoon, what would you like? A chubby light skinned woman asked us as we entered.

"Rice and plantain" Adunni replied choosing a table near the door.

"Meat?"

"Yes, two pieces" she held up two fingers.

"How about drinks?"

"I'll have a Sprite"

"Aunty and you?" she asked turning to me.

"Same thing for me but I'll have a Coke instead"

"Okay Ma, please sit down"

"You prefer Sprite to Coke?" I asked Adunni.

"Always a Sprite, never a Coke, I like Sprite more"

"It's sweeter I think"

"Maybe" she shrugged.

While waiting for our lunch to arrive, I looked around the buka, plastic chairs were arranged around three plastic tables and the rest of the space available was taken up by long benches arranged in twos; the lower one serving as the chair and the higher one as the table. A big white freezer hummed and vibrated in a corner. Three guys in the heat of a loud argument sat at the table opposite the freezer.

"I am telling you, one guy entered camp three days after camp opened, all this yamayama registration rush was over" the guy in a red shirt with his back to us said slapping the table surface.

"Na lie" another one shot back in broken English, shaking his head and stamping his foot simultaneously; he was dressed in a brown sleeveless vest and had bushy hair.

Our food arrived and while I ate I continued listening to their conversation.

"You shouldn't say it is not possible, the question is - how did this guy do it?" the third guy stated, his clean shaven head glistering slightly with perspiration; he then turned to red shirt "young man, you can't be telling us someone did it, how did he do it? That is what you should tell us".

"Why are you asking him?" the bushy hair sneered, "I can bet my next meal that he doesn't know, he's making up the story"

"What next meal are you betting? Will there be one for you? Mad man. It is not a story, I know the person, and it was two batches ago" red shirt insisted.

"After registration had closed?" clean shaven asked.

"I am telling you it was three days into camp opening, the registration rush was over, they simply registered him in a small back room" red shirt replied shifting in his seat.

"They registered him in one back room? It's a lie. If you had said it was a girl now I would have believed you, but you have messed up your story by saying it was a guy, they won't register a guy like that, never ever" bushy hair replied.

"They did, I'm telling you, the guy had the right excuse and the dough to share, plenty of it, and register him they did" red shirt shifted some more.

"And we all know there is almost nothing money cannot buy" clean shaven head pointed out.

"Thank you David, girls, cars, houses, fun, name it" red shirt said nodding.

"Those are material things" bushy hair pointed out.

"What's wrong with this guy? What do you want to hear? Hope, love, joy, peace? Get a life man" red shirt shouted turning slightly in our direction. I looked away quickly not wanting to be caught enjoying a conversation I was not a part of.

"Adunni" he gasped, slightly hesitant as he got up.

Since meeting Adunni at the camp, I was starting to re-alise that these three weeks was likely to be filled with men gasping Adunni's name.

"Toni" Adunni replied with a wry smile, "Long time no see"

"Yeah"

"How are you?" she asked.

"Fine, fine, so good to see you" he replied in a gruff voice, admiration and delight shining from his eyes.

"Toni, Jay, Jay Toni" Adunni said, suddenly pointing at me and back at him in introduction. I quickly swallowed the last morsel in my mouth and nodded hurriedly at him.

Not surprisingly, he invited us to join him and his friends at their table.

I quickly pushed my now empty plate into the hand of the serving girl and requested for another plate of rice. Adunni glanced at me in surprise and I shrugged my defiance, mind your business lady.

Bushy hair is called Bolaji and clean shaven head is David and for about an hour we discussed every topic that came to mind; then we remembered registration.

We checked on Effiong Attah and our space in the dancing queue and found both intact, although the queue was rowdier and some frustrated registrants were now arguing with the camp officials who didn't look happy either.

"This queue is not getting anywhere" he mourned.

"You are kidding me" I said for lack of something better to say, I could see he was still on the same spot where we had left him.

"I kid you not"

"That's just terrible" I sympathised as sincerely as I could.

Adunni and I went off again with Toni, David and Bolaji to sit under a shed, a small distance from the registration area where we peeled and ate the oranges that David had paid an exorbitant price for. Toni and Bolaji regaled us with life in the male hostel. In a day the whole hostel was chummy and like one big family, Bolaji bragged.

"Well we can't say the same at our end, there have been a few nasty fights" I said.

"Is that so?"

"Girls beating each other even"

"Did they tear each other's clothes off?" Bolaji asked.

"Why would they do that?" I asked.

"You said they have been fighting, that's part of fighting isn't it?" Bolaji reasoned.

"He is imagining things already" Adunni smiled.

"The guy is a juvenile, don't mind him" Toni said.

"Abeg, leave this guy to imagine, it can't kill him" David said jabbing Bolaji playfully with his elbow.

"I'm not pretending, unlike the ratchet girls in your hostel who will come out later looking and talking all posh"

"Acting like the sun shines out of their bums" David added.

"These girls sef" Bolaji said shaking his head "No offence to you lovely ladies here" he added.

"Wow, you guys are bitter; all this anger; all single; no girlfriends I'm going to assume" I jibed back to show I wasn't offended.

"Doesn't matter, we are honest, single men" Bolaji answered.

"So you attended the same Uni. with Adunni" Toni said turning to me.

"Yes I did, and studied Mechanical Engineering"

"Cool, although I would have pegged you for someone in the Arts – Economics, Philosophy..."

"Why?"

"You have that their look" he said, smiling.

"Are you calling me a party girl?"

"Of course not, you simply don't have that serious nerdy look that Engineering girls have; you seem rather trendy for an Engineering student, sorry graduate"

"That's strange, always fancied myself as looking a bit nerdish"

"Hardly and that's a compliment" Toni smiled. I didn't agree but I kept quiet.

Bolaji who appeared to be full of fascinating, and I suspected well embellished stories launched into the tale of the best soup ever made which of course he ate in the room of one of his many girlfriends or like he said 'obliging friends'. Shortly into this very outlandish story of a soup that couldn't possibly exist, the weather changed; storm clouds raced along the sky and huge cold droplets of rain started to fall rapidly, we ran for our respective hostels as the sky released a cold deluge.

At the hostel door, I stuck my hand in my pockets to check my phone and papers and that was when I realised my wallet was missing. It had my passport photographs, ID card and call up letter. I continued to run for the hostel, bewildered and confused, wondering when exactly I could have lost my wallet. This is Karma for jumping that useless queue, I thought.

"I shouldn't have jumped the queue" I wailed silently "This is what happens to people who jump queues, life screws them"

The rain stopped around 9.15pm and Adunni and I went out in search of my wallet, some stubborn people were forming queues again but the NYSC officials ignored them, preferring to engage in their own discussions.

Effiong came along and joined us in searching for my wallet. It was dark and even with two torch lights, there were so many papers and debris lying around ...all wet...it was a useless search. We walked around till a few minutes past 10pm when we gave up. I got into bed imagining my wallet somewhere dark and wet, all trampled over and its contents unusable and I felt extremely sad; there goes my 'I will be fine for three weeks'; everything is already going pear shaped.

BECKY

The hostel is a long rectangular room with doors at both ends; metal bunk beds were arranged in long rows along both sides of the long room with one row of bunks running down the middle of the room.

My bed is the first bed in the middle row; putting me close to the door and far from the rowdiness and disorder that increased gradually from both doors and peaked in the middle of the room. The number of bunks in the hostel has also turned an otherwise big room into a small claustrophobia inducing space. Fortunately for me, the space in front of the open door which goes the whole length of the room created a lot of free space beside my bed and reduced my feeling of being squashed in with a lot of stupid vapid people in a small space. I also liked the leg traffic coming through the door and I would lie on my bed and watch everybody coming in and going out. I liked to make up stories about their lives and the kind of secrets they were likely to have, because everybody has secrets. You may be shaking your head and saying oh no I don't have secrets but trust me you do, there is that one thing or two you don't want anyone knowing, yes that one, that's your secret right there.

On the downside I got a bit of draft from the door at night, but considering it was fresh air which was much needed in a hostel that was growing more fetid by the hour, I wasn't complaining. I couldn't say the same for the idiot in the bed above mine; she complained non-stop and our conversations tended to go like this:

Her: "It's cold here"

Me: "Wear a cardigan"

Her: "There is so much leg traffic though"

Me: Silence

Her: "This is the hardest mattress in the world and there are definitely bedbugs in this bed"

Me: Buy insecticide at the Mammy market and spray your mattress again"

Her: "Why do we have to wake up so early? I can't do this for three weeks"

Me: "You can and you will"

Her: "Mammy market food is crap"

Me: "Camp food is worse"

Her: "I hate camp"

Me: "Silence

In two days she already had a long list of everything that was wrong with camp and was insistent on directing her whinging at me. I hate people who whinge, they are weak, cowardly, vacillating people as far as I'm concerned. If you have a problem you either resolve it or learn to live with it, you don't need to tell the whole world and their mother about it.

I also believe strongly that for order to exist, there should be hierarchy in all situations and I could already see order breaking down in this room of vacuous undisciplined women; so to establish my leadership position I decided on the second day of camp to lead an hour of impromptu prayer meeting in the big space in front of my bed and to continue to do so regularly till the end of camp. In as much as I despise it, there is nothing like a bit of religion to hold people in thrall, I have seen it work too many times not to believe it.

My garrulous bunk mate Adesuwa came in handy with rounding up attendees. I only asked her if she was interested in having a ten minute prayer meeting in our corner with our room-mates and without a word she jumped off her bunk and went round the room shouting "Prayer meeting in 10 minutes by the first bunk South. Ladies come and pray and thank God for bringing you here safely" she went round the room twice and 10 minutes later I had six girls waiting by my bunk.

"Good afternoon ladies, thank you for coming here" I started in my most solemn voice, holding my bible open and leaning against my bunk "This is a short prayer meeting, it is a time for us to gather and thank God for bringing us here safely, for giving us the opportunity to be here, to be University graduates. It is not by our power or might, it is by the grace of God. We are not better or holier than those who didn't make it this far, we are here only because God counted us worthy"

"Hmmm, hmmm" my congregation murmured.

"Do you think you are here by your own power?" I asked.

"Noooo" they chorused.

"Or is it by your grace that you are alive?"

Answers of "How" "Noooo" "It is all God" came back to me.

"Good. So we need to praise the God that brought us here and invite Him to be with us. To guard us and guide us; even as we are here, there are evil spirits and workers of iniquity in this hostel, in this camp, amongst us. Here to wreak havoc and to remove the grace and glory of God from us"

There is nothing to get people praying and hollering like the mention of evil spirits and workers of iniquity. I talked for a few more minutes, whipping the girls up into a decent frenzy, 'Brethren of God Assembly' ministers would be proud of me.

When I saw they were ready I said, "So we will praise and worship and pray them into bondage" I paused while they clapped and stamped their feet "Let a blessed sister who is led of the spirit lead us in praise worship"

Immediately a short dark lady with her hair cornrowed into a basket design broke out in high song like she had been waiting for my cue. We sang boisterously for ten minutes, then I flipped my bible to a suitable passage in the book of Isaiah, before leading them in prayer.

"Let us meet here again tomorrow at 12noon, before lunch, God bless you all"

A few more days of these and I should have a steady fol-lowership and my own team of devotees with Adesuwa as my personal rabble rouser, perfect.

***

They kept managing to be around him; the two girls from the previous day before, I learnt their names - Jay and Adun-ni. At the registration ground I saw them get in front of him again on the queue. He smiled at them and touched Adunni on her elbow when she joined the queue. I don't get it. Some women are born witches; even when a man is not interested or willing, they will hang around him and bewitch him into doing things he doesn't want to do.

It was obvious Effiong, my Effiong did not have any in-terest in being friends or getting to know these girls. I knew he was going to need my help to avoid these girls and beat their bewitching skills especially that one called Adunni.

Jay bothered me a little less than Adunni; childlike with a small pixie-like face, small hands and tiny wrists, she re-minded me of our Rachel in many ways; Effiong also did not stare at her the same way he stared at Adunni; following her around with his hooded dark eyes; eyes that should be look-ing at me, loving me.

Adunni is a Jezebel, once you see her, you know; like a waif she is tall and slim with long limbs and long fingers that end in perfect nails. Her ant-hill coloured skin is clear and dewy like an advertisement for expensive body cream. She is a siren, a seductress with kohl rimmed eyes and a beguiling smile. I hated her so much, I still do; even if Effiong wasn't looking at her so fascinatedly, I would still hate her with her long lean sinuous body. She has probably never had to refuse food for fear of gaining weight, probably has no idea what teenage pimples are or hair breakage or fat handles or any of the things that plague normal women like me.

She acted indifferent, like she did not care that she was beautiful but I was not fooled, her indifference hid arrogance and disdain for others. She was so confident of all the attention she was receiving that she could afford to ignore it all. I planned to keep my eyes on her for the three weeks of camp. Meanwhile I took to following Effiong at a distance and I watched him go into the Medical building again; it was the fourth time since I started following him, I felt nauseous at the thought that he was ill.

"Hello" I smiled at another Youth Corper in front of Medical building, a fat girl sitting on the pavement reading a tatty looking book.

"Hello" she replied frowning slightly.

"The guy that went in now, is that the head of the NCCF fellowship? They said he is here"

"Who? That guy?" she said pointing at Effiong's retreating back.

"Yes him"

"Noooo, that's Doctor Effiong, he is here to resume his shift, I don't think he is the NCCF leader or anything like that" she shrugged.

Ah! ah! He is not ill, he is a doctor, a healer of the sick; what could be more perfect.

"Oh thank you" I turned to leave.

"Go inside" she said waving, "the person you are looking for might be inside now, you can't be sure unless you check, do you have a name though?"

"Paul, I replied hurriedly, "Pastor Paul"

"Go inside" she repeated returning to her book.

"Thank you" I headed into the Medical building where I surprisingly roamed free. I was not stopped by anyone and in ten minutes I had walked round the building twice and brushed against Effiong in a passage way; so I decided to leave.

Somebody had put up a shelf of books outside the long corridor in front of the Administrative block and stuck a piece of paper on the bookshelf saying "free novels, pick, read and return" written on it. As registration was still going on, those of us who were already registered didn't have much to do, so I picked one of the free books and sat on a pavement near the Medical Building from where I could watch everyone going into and out of the building. I was waiting for Effiong to finish his shift. I wanted to say hello to him, introduce myself to him and get to know him. This could very well be the beginning of our journey of destiny.

Day 3 NYSC Camp

BECKY

Three days into the NYSC experience and I could feel my initial positivity and relief ebbing away. Camp was starting to feel less like the escape I thought it would be when I left Brethren's Campsite three days earlier in exhilaration. In retrospect, I wondered why I had left so happily, after all it was very unlikely that anyone would find Brother Daniel and look to me for answers. As I got dressed slowly in the darkness of the still quiet room, I couldn't help thinking about Brother Daniel, Brethren Campsite and my days as a Kitchen Manager.

I volunteered at the Assembly headquarters generally known as "Brethren Campsite" every term break from my first year in University till my last. Initially, volunteering at the campsite was merely an excuse to be away from home because it was much better than home and was the only excuse my off-the-wall parents would accept. I made a point to ask them when Elder Jeremiah was paying them his weekly visit so they were forced to acquiesce with happy grins which was quickly replaced with a grudging sullen silence after Elder Jeremiah left. So using the church as an excuse, I stayed away from home.

The church ground is about 3 miles wide and 4.5 miles long, a rectangle fenced with red bricks arranged one on top of the other and cemented together; lovingly done by a team of bricklayers from within the church, their tithes, their giving and their penance. The church hardly ever had to pay for hard labour in its construction process as much of it was carried out by a mix of expert skills and enthusiastic volunteering and the sheer availability of ignorant man power. This resulted in an appealing architectural piece; wooden windows constructed with pretty little leaves painstakingly carved into them by a master carpenter sat in misguided rectangle pretending to be squares and walls standing a little bit off to the left but lovingly and meticulously plastered. The church buildings, walls, windows and doors in their incongruity were beautiful to me, there was exquisiteness mixed in with blunders and inexperience, the ugly and the good – I loved it all. Sometimes I walked round caressing walls, touching doors that gave me splinters and staring up at crooked beams of timber.

The Campsite was a far cry from home; at the campsite, there was no cleaning up vomit or washing mountains of clothes with cold brown rain water; no sitting in a dark damp room in between endless chores pretending to read my bible while keeping a look out for my father; instead I was assigned basic duties such as sweeping the large dining hall and washing the dishes after the meagre but filling dinners served daily and I took to my duties with vigour and asked for more. The other volunteers simply couldn't keep up with my strength and enthusiasm for work.

The duties I was assigned in camp were so much lighter than what I had to do at home, it was almost a laugh; yet in camp I was treated like a saint. Sister Becky's selfless nature and hard work was well talked about and pointed out as an example of how a Christian sister should be. The Senior Pastors made it a point to greet me warmly whenever our paths crossed around the camp, shaking my hand and saying my name clearly.

Sometimes I made it a point for our paths to cross to gauge how warmly they would greet me. It always filled me with a sense of justification; a reminder that I was the good one, proof that I am not useless, evil or wrong. These exalted people think I am good and hardworking; worthy of their acknowledgement and warm greetings.

I stayed at the campsite as much as I could, going home only because of Caleb who still lived at home with the parents; brilliant 16- year old Caleb who was itching to leave home forever, like the rest of us. Rachel ran away three years ago when she was his age and I know she is living with an older man somewhere in Surulere. She drives his car around, playing the wife. Abraham lives in Maroko with his girlfriend who is a prostitute by night, he is her pimp. You could describe him as a 23 year old college educated pimp to a 28 year old woman who has been selling her body since she was 14 and it would be a fair description by next year when he completes his university degree. The first time I saw her, I thought she was closer to 40 years old than her 28 years. Their life together disgusts me solely because I know that Abraham can do better, he is seeing himself through college on money he raises from working in a gas filling station and money he gets from her. As far as she is concerned my brother is going to marry her one day and she is merely investing in her future spouse by working all night; the idiot.

Over the four years of my undergraduate programme, I became very popular at the Brethren Campsite and gained more responsibility. As a volunteer dishwasher I developed the dish washing chain to make the washing of 800 odd plates and cutlery more efficient. It was such a simple idea that I still do know why no one thought of it, but they didn't, I did. All the dirty dishes went into a giant bowl of hot soapy water, where they stayed for 15 minutes and all the oil and scum fell off, then they were dumped in a second bowl of warm soapy water for a rinse and then into a third bowl of clean water for a final rinse, there was no individual sponging of plates or cutlery. I washed record amounts of plates in record time. Initially the kitchen manager complained about the amount of hot water I was using, she moaned about the electricity bill and the extravagance of the dish washing chain until she saw it in action, then she went quiet and let me be. I got all the dishes washed single-handedly, that was enough for her.

Then I became the kitchen assistant and accompanied the cooks to the market every week. The journey was made in a white van, two cooks and I in the back and the head cook in the front with the driver. We laughed and joked and sang praise songs that were heavily modified, sometimes we mimicked the praise worship leaders and the various ad-libs they liked to add to the praise songs. I would forget my troubles and all the things that hailed and worried me. The kitchen staff were the most jovial lot at the campsite although I also think they restricted their happy laughter to our market journeys.

In my fourth year of University and volunteering at the campsite, I became the Kitchen Manager with sole responsibility for the weekly shopping. The church agreed to pay me a stipend and gave me a room on the camp site; to them I was worth it. I returned to my room on the campsite from school every weekend. It was a small, cosy room with a single bed, a wooden table and a chair; a blue flowery curtain billowed at the wide window which kept the room cool at all hours. I had gradually become a permanent fixture at the Church campsite with its crooked walls and perfect plastering.

By the time I left for my year of NYSC, I had served at the Assembly for 4 years and 6 months and as the Kitchen Manager for a year and three months of this. I loved every moment of my volunteer job and the church seemed to love me too.

The week I was leaving for my NYSC posting, I was called out during the evening service on Sunday and Senior Pastor Solomon led the congregation in prayer for me. They swayed and hummed and the prayer was frequently interrupted with shouts of 'Hallelujah' and 'Praise the Lord.' The prayer went on for about fifteen minutes, every possible ill was considered and prayed against and every possible good thing I could need during my Youth service was requested from God. The church presented me with a new study bible and a box of toiletries and tinned food - towels, tinned sardine fish, powdered milk, sugar, cocoa powder, toilet tissue, tooth paste and body cream.

I found the box of toiletries and tinned food rather thoughtful of them and I wondered who had thought of it. I muttered my thanks between effusive tears and promised to visit the Church regularly during my one year of NYSC.

I was going to miss my life as Kitchen Manager and all the perks that came with it. In addition to having access to regular filling meals, I had access to the best portion, the food that was cooked and served to the Senior Pastors whose meals were of better quality than what was served to the rest of the camp.

A few months after becoming Kitchen Manager, I realised the benefits of receiving a stipend and all the wonderful things I could suddenly afford, many of which I had to squirrel away under my bed in my little room. I also realised if I had a little more money I could afford a few more things, like proper leather sandals instead of the rubbery rubbish I was wearing around; moisturising Dove soap which although doesn't come cheap I had developed a deep liking for and even chocolate bars, Mars bars, Twix bars and the so lovely KitKat; so I spent a lot of time thinking of ways to augment my stipend.

As the kitchen manager I was in charge of the funds allocated for buying groceries and dry foods for camp use weekly and I decided that if I could find a safe way of keeping some of it for myself, it would supplement my now so measly allowance. I wasn't going to do something as stupid as stealing the funds outright and not doing the shopping at all, but I thought that if I bought lower quality produce, I wouldn't have to spend all the money in the weekly shopping account.

I didn't feel any guilt, after all it was free food which nobody worked for beyond attending numerous services and meetings during the week at the campsite. I didn't see why I couldn't stretch the shopping allowance and have some left over for myself; after all he who dwells at the altar eats at the altar is what they say.

So I added water to the beans or the porridge after the Senior Pastors' portions had been served. I watered down

the milk we used for the teas, added the cheaper garden vegetable to the more expensive Kale and Pumpkin leaves that
we cooked on Thursdays and some cocoyam mixed in with
the yam went a long way. I made sure we bought two types of
garri, a good one and a poor one and I mixed them together. I
had to involve the senior cook in my ingenious plan; she was
never far from the kitchen and pantry and there was no way
I could have carried it off without her, outside of killing her;
the thought of killing her frequently got me giggling quietly.

At first she was reluctant, not because of any moral hold
back or conviction but merely because of the risk of been
caught. The senior cook was not a volunteer at the camp; she
was a paid employee and was concerned about her job; but
after I pointed out the fact that the only person who could
catch and report her was the Kitchen manager, namely me,
she quickly relaxed and even suggested a few more ways of
stretching the budget and subsequently the food.

We started adding water to the stew and buying rotten
baskets of tomatoes to mix in with the fresh ones we normally bought. It's amazing isn't it? Inside each of us is a little devious devil that needs the right encouragement to lead us down
unexpected paths. In about three months, Senior Cook and
I were running a seamless and effective little operation that
filled our pockets with ever growing funds; until that sniv-
elling Brother Daniel came along with his curiosity and the
dried saliva encrusted at the corner of his mouth.

Why some people can't walk away from situations is
completely beyond me; it leaves me baffled and amazed. I
see them in movies all the time, people who ask where the
body is buried; people who want to know things for knowing

sake and act completely surprised when they are made to take their knowledge to an immediate grave. What did you seriously think? I still shake my head in frustration at the thought of these stupid people.

Brother Daniel was the Head of Facilities at the Brethren camp and so would hang around buildings, locking doors, checking windows, and turning on and off the diesel-run generator whenever the electricity company cut the power supply. A dogsbody with a huge sense of importance he would strut around the camp with a thoughtful look on his face and a hand constantly rubbing his chin as if he was thinking of something more mundane than the blocked toilet in block E or the leaking taps in the Pastors' yard.

I sometimes wished I could scream at him "you are just a gofer with an elevated title, please clean the corners of your mouth while you are at it, you disgusting little fool." I didn't do that of course, although I now wish I had.

Anyway, Brother Daniel started dropping by at the kitchen, he was suddenly the voice of the populace and would come by to say things like 'the stew was rather watery today Sisters, hope tomorrow will be better', 'the eba stuck in our throats today and the watery soup didn't help matters', 'I know where you can get better garri than the one you have now, let me know when you have time and I'll take you there', 'today's tea tasted like coloured water' and so on. He largely said these things to the cooks and service group although it filtered back to me.

Senior Cook came to me in jitters one afternoon *"Sister Becky, I no dey do again oh, e be like say Bruoda Daniel don dey suspect us, you hear wetin he talk today?"* she asked.

"What did he say?" I asked coolly.

"Him ask me, he say, Mama Cook, where you buy these tomatoes so? Dem don spoil na. And these vegetables, na Ugu bin dey look like this? Somebody suppose look into the food wey we dey chop fore dinin' these days. E no good at all, how person wan do better work with food wey dey run belle?"

"What did you tell him?" I asked continuing to study the purchase list for the coming week.

"Wetin I wan say? I say make him leave me, make I do my job, make him go do him own, aproko no dey pay, na wetin church money cover we dey cook, if e wan better food, make him give better offering on Sunday na" she replied shrugging, *"I don dey cook before dem born this boy, he come dey talk to me anyhow"* she continued indignantly.

"Don't worry about it Mama Cook, I will deal with him. Just continue what you are doing, next time he bothers you, tell him to talk to the Kitchen manager" I smiled.

"Thank you. I know you no go take nonsense from him. Asking me queshion like say I be small pikin cook, idiot"

I watched Senior Cook as she walked away, her indignation still evident in her shoulder and the jerk of her rolling gait, I could still hear her muttering angrily, she seemed to have forgotten we were the ones cutting corners on the cooking.

I continued to study the grocery list, although my mind was no longer there, I was also fuming angrily at the infuriating behaviour of this Brother Daniel, the galling dirty faced monkey. Who asked his opinion? Bloody freeloader. The cheek of him. Your station is facilities, why can't you stay the hell there, you this useless son of a diseased camel? But he didn't, he came back to the kitchen again and again, getting Senior Cook worked up and the other kitchen staff fascinated. They all started commenting on the quality of the tomatoes and peppers they had to cook, the roughness of the garri they used in making eba, the quantity of water in the morning teas. I knew I had to do something about Brother Daniel, quickly before things got out of hand.

So the next week I told Senior Cook we would return to the old shopping list going forward and buy everything at the quality we used to buy them before.

She appeared relieved and said *"yes sister, make we do am like that, make Bruoda Daniel and all his wahala go away, his trouble dey too much for me"* I was further infuriated by the fact that this useless self-appointed spokesman and detective was about to put an end to my source of income even temporarily; but I smiled; Brother Daniel and all his wahala definitely needed to go away.

"Yes Senior Cook, let's go back to the old way until Brother Daniel leaves camp"

"He dey leave? She asked doubtfully, *"na who tell you so?"*

"Yes he is leaving and I have my sources. I hear he is not happy here and has been complaining about everything"

"No wonder" she nodded as if everything was suddenly clear to her *"I too don notice am, he be like say he dey vex all the time, na him make he dey come to the kitchen to dey complain so?, make he leave if he wan leave na, make e no dey find wahala wey no dey"* she finished.

"Leave it to me" I replied and walked off, stage one completed.

The next day I invited Brother Daniel for a chat late in the evening to discuss his complaints. He arrived in the small back room I had turned into an office and started off with "I knew you didn't know about all these things Sister Becky, I am sure it is that unchristian Senior Cook that has been creaming things off the top. You can never trust these people who are employed and not volunteers; they are not committed to the church like we are. I just don't trust them at all"

I ignored his diatribe, "walk with me brother" I said as I headed to our mini abattoir. We recently received a machine for cutting up the beef and pork we bought weekly. A shiny new angel of death which unfortunately was getting less use than it deserved solely because the cooks were a bit afraid of its efficiency; the fear of losing a finger in a moment of carelessness kept the machine idler than it merited. In my less busy hours, I used the machine to cut up the meat in storage and I quickly became very adept in its use. I found its mechanical whirring very mollifying.

At the abattoir, he continued to tell me in detail of all his observations – he had noticed more than half of the ways in which we were cutting corners, brother Daniel definitely had to go.

"Thank you brother Daniel, I am shocked at these things you are telling me, and I am also disappointed, to think the people we entrust with our dietary care are failing us in such an appalling manner" I moved closer to him, "I myself have been on a 40 day fast so I have not been eating the food from the kitchen, this must be why I have not noticed these things"

He nodded "thank you Sister Becky, people are complaining oh, yesterday a lot of people didn't eat their dinner and the beans was just left in the dining hall to waste"

"I will definitely look into it and I assure you that it will never happen again, next week is going to be the beginning of new things, meal wise by God's grace"

"Thank you sister, God bless you Sister Becky"

"And you too brother" I moved closer to him to hug him, he was momentarily surprised that I wished to hug him and he hesitated. I stretched out my left hand and with a smile he moved into my embrace; he didn't notice my right hand until the cutting knife I held was buried in his stomach, slicing in through the soft flesh. He gasped and tried to move away but I held him close and pushed the knife up and twisted it, leaning my full 200 pound weight into the knife, "it's alright brother, it's over now" I whispered to him. He relaxed, leaned into me and emptied his bowels as he breathed his last.

I dragged his body up on the table beside the shiny electric meat cleaver and went off to lock the door; then I sat down and waited for the evening service to begin at 6pm.

Predictably at 6.02pm I heard Sister Elizabeth's strident voice as she said the opening prayer, this was followed by loud singing. Sister Hannah's voice struggled to stay above the din of the drums, electric guitars and keyboards. I had about 30 minutes before the singing would end so I got down to business and switched on the electric meat cleaver; it's whirring expectedly drowned by the loud singing coming from the praise hall. I hummed to myself as I destroyed all evidence of Bro Daniel's existence.

I told myself that by the time they noticed his absence, I would be far away on NYSC posting and Senior Cook will be there to tell them, she heard he wanted to leave. As I have shown no animosity towards him at any time, nobody would think I or anyone else had anything to do with his decision to leave; perfect.

Without a body, there would be no assumption of foul play; of course there is a lot more meat in storage for the whole lot of them to feast on. I hope they enjoy it, I hope it poisons them actually. There were days when I wished I could just poison the whole lot of them, throw some arsenic into the huge bubbling pot of stew and watch the cooks serve up the good-bye meal, but I knew I couldn't do that; the fingers would quickly point at me especially if as the Kitchen manager I was the only survivor.

Despite attending the Assembly with my parents since I was 10 years old, serving at the headquarters for four years and six months and enjoying the generosity of the pastors, I loathed them for their kindness and servitude, their blind devotion to their faith and their bible. I abhorred with passion their repetitive songs, fervent prayers, and supplications to a god they were not even sure existed, yet so convinced were they, so faithful and consistent in their worship. I hated them for not noticing that my parents are abusive crazies who have broken every one of their children; for turning a blind eye to the behaviour of the drunken lout that is my father and accepting him in "love", for not noticing the pain in our eyes or the bruises on our young bodies. I despised them with every cell in my body; but not as much as I despise my parents.

Two people who should never have married nor had children. Yet they not only got married, they went on to have four of us and to share with us all their pain and antipathy, all the rage they feel against the world and themselves, both imagined and real. For four year and six months, I hid my loathing, and hid it well; in my opinion, Brother Daniel's death was a fitting expression of my hatred of Brethren Assembly and their hypocrisy.

ADUNNI

I was walking down the aisle at Shoprite; pushing a trolley of chocolates, cakes, a big pie and a big glass bottle of something red. I picked it up to peer at it and its content moved. There was a child inside the bottle swimming in what I could now see was blood and it was trying to get out. It turned to look at me and I realise it is my child, the one that will never be born and it knows it's all my fault, my entire careless fault. I wanted to drop the bottle, but it was suddenly incredibly heavy and I couldn't drop it. I threw up all over the bottle violently. Five or six menacing looking store attendants started to run towards me while I kept trying to put the bottle down gently on the floor without success; as soon as one of the attendants laid a filthy rotting hand on me I woke up.

I swung my legs off the bunk and jumped down racing for the door at the same time, I could feel the nausea rising. I barely made it outside before throwing up and like in the dream it was violent. I retched till the bugle sounded the wakeup call. I sensed someone beside me as Jay pushed a bowl of water into my hands; I grabbed the bowl weakly and washed my face and mouth. Almost like another surreal dream, Jay started throwing up too but then I figured seeing me throw up must have disgusted her very much; well I didn't ask her out here, I shrugged carelessly.

I left her outside and went back inside the hostel. The drugs give me bad dreams, sometimes they make me nauseous and I throw up and sometimes they leave me unimaginably exhausted. I am a laid back person on most days, I take my time to get things done. I just have never been one of those people with boundless energy running around with to-do lists, joining groups, making friends, participating in everything, it's just not me. Growing up I would come home from school every year with my report cards saying things like "Adunni needs to participate more" "Adunni is frequently disinterested in class activities" "Although making good grades, Adunni seems lazy" and so on, my mum would scream and shout and warn that I wouldn't get far if I kept on like this. Oh well, here we are; the one time I decided to participate, to be interested and live life with vigour, it just went and slapped me back like – oh shut up and sit down! Not now, not you... stupid irony.

I struggled into my clothes, my eyes half open and slogged off to the parade ground with Jay who had also returned into the hostel and looked as bad as I felt. "Suck it up Missy, surely I can't be the first person you have seen vomiting. If you were half as sick as I am you wouldn't be here at all, I thought with a little anger.

My wristwatch read 4.30am; it was dark and windy outside yet the dusty main road leading from the parade ground to all the hostels was already filled with sleepy people in ghostly white vests and shorts walking to the parade ground. I have always hated getting out of bed early, my mum had to drag me out of bed every day throughout primary school; going to boarding school didn't help either, it merely reinforced my dislike for early mornings. In my final year in secondary school, I made use of my senior year privilege to the max and slept for as long as I could get away with. I can count the number of 8am classes I attended in University; I would rather wake up at noon and go to bed at 2am which was very good for my clubbing and partying activities.

On the parade ground we were split into registered and unregistered groups, a few were registered now although most of us were not. I managed to do the jumps, jogging and stretching as much as my tired body would allow, the soldiers were barking in the face of the stragglers. Soon I was as warm and flush as everybody else appeared to be and I felt much better than when I first woke up.

Still flush, we were further split into smaller groups and a soldier assigned to each group. The soldier in charge of my group glowered at us and shouted his name loudly, although I still didn't catch it.

"You will learn how to march" he screamed, "Now, listen well and learn it quick" he paused.

"Attention by number, score one" he bellowed, lifted up his right leg, hung it in the air for a few seconds and screamed again before dropping his leg to the ground firmly.

Laughter rippled through the group while some people gallantly clapped and cheered him. We all then followed suite, lifting up our legs in unison while our Commandant screamed repeatedly. We kept up this superficially silly activity until we were totally worn-out.

Around 9am we were released to go for breakfast and despite my dog tiredness, I ate heartily.

The camp provided a breakfast of stale bread and tea; Jay and I took one look at the grey tea and rocky bread and we fled for the Mammy market.

Everything at the Mammy market had us heaving, nausea threatening to break through... the bean cakes, the frying eggs, and the fish simmering in hot oil in wooden stalls haphazardly built and scattered across the Mammy market. We hurriedly bought fresh loaves of bread in the first stall where we found some and sat in a corner far away from the market smells to eat our plain bread; it was all our rebellious stomachs would take.

"We will eat Akara next time" Jay said.

"Yes, sure" I nodded.

"So what is wrong with you?" she asked, watching my face intently.

"What is wrong with YOU?" I answered back coolly, although my inside had turned to water at her blunt question.

She giggled "nice comeback Adunni, well played, okay let's hurry, I need to take new passport photographs to replace the missing ones, not like I look fantastic right now. I'm also going to look around for my missing documents, I might still find them" she finished.

"Yeah sure" I nodded again although not actually believing we would find her missing papers in the sea of dirty papers scattered all over the camp.

After our miserable breakfast, which I don't think I tasted, we walked over to the photographers' shed where Jay snapped a new passport photograph – eight copies at triple the normal price. She looked worried in the pictures, worried, tired and slightly confused. There was more to Jay than my "well-off diplomat's child" first impression of her. When I took a few minutes away from my worries and thinking about my drugs and how well they were working or not working, I would notice her deep in thought, gnawing on her lower lip.

So, we set off for the registration area again in search of Jay's documents in the piles of rubbish around the camp. We asked those whose faces had become familiar in the last two days and peered at every piece of paper and envelope in the dirt, turning them over with our feet to get a better look.

"Hello, girls" Effiong said striding up.

I was starting to wonder if our repeated stumbling into him was a coincidence or if Effiong was making it happen.

"Hi" Jay said. I mumbled a hello under my breath busily turning over a piece of paper in the dirt and willing it to be the missing documents so that we could stop this futile search. I was realising that pessimism concerning the missing documents did not bode well for me, Jay had no plans of quitting the search for a while. I was now willing these documents to reappear right away.

"I've been looking for you guys, I looked out for you on the parade ground this morning; I couldn't find you guys though. I asked members of your Platoon where you guys were; in case of next time can I have your phone numbers?"

Nice try brother, I thought. Why are you looking for us anyway? It's not like we know you now, is it? I was getting irritated with Effiong's distracting and inane attempt at conversation.

Jay exchanged phone numbers with him, I ignored them and continued to flip pieces of paper in the wet sand with the toe of my right foot.

"One of the camp officials has found your document and he has been looking for you" he continued.

I stared at him, "why didn't you say that all the while?" I snapped. Jay was grinning happily "Oh great, thanks Effiong" she said, reaching out to hold his hand briefly.

"But that is what I have been trying to say, I have been looking for you guys, because the guy refused to give them to me, he is insisting Jay has to come and collect them herself"

"That's okay, where is he?" Jay asked now holding Effiong's hand. She is like a child at times, friendly and warm, willing you to like her, she smiled at Effiong again. It is difficult not to like Jay.

"He is inside the registration building, he is one of the officials carrying out the registration, light skinned big guy" Effiong continued waving his hand vaguely, "Come lets go, I'll point the guy out to you" he said heading off still holding hands with Jay.

"I hope this is for real and they are my documents, not those of some lucky girl whose search for missing documents will soon end" Jay quipped.

"No, no, they are definitely yours, I took a look at the passport photographs" Effiong assured her.

At one of the faded white crowded buildings, Effiong pointed at a tall albino man wearing an oversized white shirt with a frayed collar; and wandered off leaving us to talk to the man whose large feet were tucked into brown leather sandals that have also seen better days.

"Good afternoon sir" we chorused.

"Good afternoon ladies, how are you?" he replied at the top of his voice.

Why is he shouting? I wondered

"We are fine; I was told you found my missing documents and passport photographs" Jay replied.

"Ah, ah, you are the young lady. Yes, yes you are right, the picture... it is you" he said smiling and wagging his finger at Jay who was nodding helpfully.

"Okay, so why were you so careless? I found the documents yesterday and I have been on the lookout for you" he was talking to Jay but staring at me. I was irritated and turned away. Taking a small step back, I saw Toni from the corner of my eyes and waved to him. He saw me and turned to head in my direction, smiling boyishly. Toni and I grew up on the same street; our houses right next to each other. We rode bicycles, chased cats and bought sugary candy from the corner store together as kids. Then we moved thirty minutes' drive away when I was twelve and I had only seen Toni twice since then, till our chance meeting in camp.

"How are you babe?"

"I'm fine, you?"

"Great, doing great"

"Good" I smiled.

"Babe, I like your friend" he said abruptly.

"We are not friends per se" I shrugged. My response surprised him.

"Weren't you friends from Uni?" he asked.

"No, we more like struck it up here, so I'm not the best person to tell this thing"

"But you are, you are" he insisted, "you are friends here and I like her, she's totally cool"

"Yeah that she is" I agreed, "but liking her might not be a good idea"

"Oh come on Adunni, don't block me now; be nice to me. I'm your friend too, you know" he replied tapping his chest and smiling.

"I'm not trying to block you, I think Jay might not be what you want exactly, loads of girls in camp here you know" I replied quietly, keeping a firm hold on my thoughts; there's no point getting irritated, what's obvious to me is not necessarily obvious to everyone else.

"I need you to put in a good word for me with her, can you do that?" he asked.

"You will have to say your words first before I could put in a good one" I replied; now abandoning any attempt to discourage his inopportune professions about Jay. He will find out soon enough, I thought.

"Fair enough" he agreed. We both turned round to check on Jay and her continuing conversation with her benefactor. He was still talking to her; she was smiling and nodding, not saying a word, he had found a willing audience and was not letting go easily.

"I found your documents somewhere there, trampled and dirty" he pointed towards the end of the registration queue where we had been standing yesterday "I was going to the Mammy market when I saw your pictures face up, so I picked them up, one of the passport photographs was torn but the others were in good shape, very good shape, definitely usable, no need to take new pictures. You would have been unable to register without those documents, it's good I found them"

"Thank you so much" Jay said cutting in.

"So what is your name?"

"Jadesola Savage"

"Which Savage is this? Are you related to that musician Tiwa Savage?" he asked frowning thoughtfully.

"No I don't think so" Jay replied.

"Ah, very interesting, very interesting" he nodded.

"What school did you finish from?" He continued now relaxing into the wooden chair he was sitting on.

"Unilag"

"And your friend?" he asked turning to smile at me, I stared daggers at him silently.

"She finished from Unilag too" Jay responded patiently.

"Unilag girls hey?"

What about Unilag girls?

"So what course did you study?"

"Engineering, please let me look at the document, I need to know if you've found the important ones" Jay said, a trifle impatiently.

He ignored her request.

"Ok, ok and your friend?" he continued, turning to me slightly, I continued to ignore him.

"Her name is Adunni and she studied English"

"The Queen's own language" he enthused. There was no appropriate response to this, so we kept quiet and both stared at him; "good, good....beautiful girls... you are both very beautiful" he finished lapsing into an awkward silence. We stood there saying nothing, waiting for him to give us the documents.

He got up laboriously, as if it cost him so much effort to abandon his conversation with us "Let me get your things" He dug around in some files he had on an adjacent table and fished out the worn out looking documents.

"Thank you Sir"

"You are welcome, Mr Julius at your service"

I smiled at Jay as we walked off, Toni in tow, "Happy lady Jay"

"Yes, I am happy. I almost screamed when he started that ridiculous conversation, I almost hit him" she said giggling.

"You hid that well, I'm not sure I did though, I think he realised I wanted to murder him at some point. I'm glad we will no longer be digging in the dirt like peasants"

We both broke into relieved giggles.

"Did you get your documents?" Effiong said materialising again from nowhere and shaking Toni's hand while peering at the documents Jay was holding.

"Yes I did" Jay replied grinning at him.

"Ah, so now you can smile, you should have seen your face a few minutes ago, I'm glad I helped to make you happy though"

"Me too, thanks, let me buy you a cold drink, you have all been fantastic" We all trooped to the Mammy market again.

We spent the rest of the day trying to get registered, shoving and getting shoved. I jumped the queue with impunity, Jay refused and stayed on the same spot for three hours; she was repeatedly shoved and pushed for her perseverance; the look of dismay on her face was priceless.

Those who were registered were already spotting their white t-shirts, shorts, white socks with green stripes and white canvas shoes. They walked jauntily to the parade ground where they marched from noon till sundown looking like tin soldiers; soon the jauntiness was replaced with misery and we watched their unhappy faces as they sweated and groaned.

At about 4pm, the officials handed out numbered cardboards to those who were still on the queue, from then on the queue progressed very swiftly and efficiently and we all finally got registered; Jay and I into Platoon 5. I could only wonder why the camp officials didn't hand out these numbers on day one.

The khakis I got were two sizes too big while Jay's khakis were about four sizes too big; same with our canvas shoes. We went around camp trying to barter for our shoe sizes and to the tailors who were sitting under the mango trees and making good money from reducing oversized khakis.

All doctors were placed on rotational clinic duty for the three weeks of camp so right after completing his registration, Effiong went on his first duty at the clinic. Jay and I hung out with Toni and his friends in the same stall where we had lunch the day before for the two hours before the bugle went off and we were all required to turn in for the night.

Day 4 NYSC Camp

JAY

Our Platoon commandant Ahmed was a sergeant in the 83rd Command Unit, in his mid-30s he was tall and muscly with a single tribal mark from the upper ridge of his nose down to his cheek. Standing in the wet grass after the morning drills he informed us that all Platoon members will be required to participate and compete with the other nine Platoons in football, volleyball, cultural dancing, drama, cooking competition and a few other events. I had no idea how I was going to survive these much activities in three weeks; three days in and I was tired already.

"If you no bring all the trophies to this Platoon I swear I go quench all of you" Ahmed warned us in a heavy Northern accent before taking us out of the camp grounds and down the dusty red road linking the highway. We jogged for about two miles; everybody jogged, I walked because within the first few minutes I knew I couldn't do it. My stomach turned and rebelled, my arms and legs ached; I tried to keep up but it was a staggering feat, one I was failing miserably at.

"Jog my friend, Jog" Sergeant Ahmed screamed in my ear, spraying me with spittle and his cold sweat.

"I am tryingggggg" I responded, all my misery and tiredness in my voice. I watched as the others jogged on, feet thumping in unison, looking splendid in their whites and getting further away from Adunni and me.

"What is wrong with your legs? Can't you move them? Move those legs, lady" Sergeant Ahmed bellowed; he looked like he was about to have a fit.

"She is trying" Adunni snapped at him.

"Corper, don't answer me back" he yelled in her face "one more word from you and you will spend the rest of the week in detention! Detention my friend!" he finished in a scream. I don't dare look but I knew Adunni was rolling her eyes. Isn't she afraid of anyone? I wondered.

"Move girls! Don't be lazy; move!" he screamed once more before jogging on, abandoning Adunni and me to our apparent laziness.

I watched the receding backs of the others who were quickly becoming smaller in my sight, white, green-banded socks rising and falling in unison, young, vibrant and without a single care in their lives; I envied every one of them. I listened to the thud-thud of feet on the burnt orange mud road and tried to catch up a little, suddenly it didn't feel so bad to be here in badly cut clothes waking up at crazy hours to jog and stretch in wet grass.

"Is this the best you can do?" Adunni asked me, I could hear the smile in her voice, she was teasing me.

"Yes it is" I shrugged.

"Your jogging is shit" she replied.

"Look who's talking"

"I'm here to keep you company. I could shoot off into the horizon like all those ones" she replied pointing with her chin, the smile still in her voice, "but what kind of friend would that make me?"

"Whatever"

"So are you merely terrible at running or something else is wrong?" she asked.

"Like what?" my running had turned to walking again and even though I could see Sergeant Ahmed running back towards the two of us, fury in his eyes, I couldn't move any faster, the fatigue was firmly in my limbs and spreading.

"Just answer the question, are you merely shit at running or is there something else?" Adunni persisted.

"I'm shit at running" I replied "and for someone who threw up five times yesterday, you are one to talk"

"It wasn't five times lady, it was three"

"Hmm" I huffed as Sergeant Ahmed returned screaming "you are both spending the rest of today in detention; you lazy girls"

I had to stifle my laughter; his face was terribly comical as he tried to look angry and shocked at us.

"We are sorry" I replied meekly.

"You are not. You are lazy that is what. Lazy girls" the tribal mark on his face bulged at us angrily as he paused for a moment before running back to his more obedient troops.

Adunni and I made it back to camp, a long time after the others and we joined them in singing the ribald songs they were belting out while stretching and exercising; soon I was sitting down on the dewy grass and Adunni promptly joined me.

Sergeant Ahmed spotted Adunni and me again and made a beeline for us his comical frown back on his face; he was obviously intent on issuing us an appropriately severe punishment for our continued sluggishness. I could only wonder how this soldier would control troops with a face that makes you want to laugh.

"Both of you, come with me" he bellowed.

I got up from the grassy field and everything whirled; Sergeant Ahmed's face doubled and swam, Adunni's face doubled, one above the other, I couldn't hear what they were both saying.

ADUNNI

Jay fainted during morning exercises and came around in the clinic thirty minutes later feebly insisting "I'm fine, I'm fine". Effiong was on duty when we carried a limp Jay to the clinic and for once I was glad to see him. I gratefully left her in his care to return to compulsory camp activities.

I returned after the day's marching and thumping around was done and barely saw Effiong leaving the clinic and going around the back of the building; I called him and hurried to catch up with him.

He turned and the thoughtful look on his face changed to a glad smile, "Hi Adunni, how are you?"

"I'm very well thank you" I smiled, "Jay..." I started.

"Jay is fine, she is awake already and trying to have dinner I think" he cut in waving at the wooden clinic door.

I said, "I need to talk to you about Jay"

"Okay, is everything okay?"

"Actually no; I think Jay is pregnant. I'm not sure if she has told you or wants anybody to know, but we have to do something for her if she is pregnant, to keep her from jogging and running everyday" I said "Obviously, she doesn't want to be kicked out of camp and have to come back next year so we can't tell anyone she is pregnant. They send pregnant girls back home right? And they have to come back a year later to do this all over again? We can't let anyone know she is pregnant but she can't keep doing all these strenuous exercise, she can't" I finished with emphasis.

Effiong was silent for a moment and smiled, "it's alright Adunni, Jay told me about her pregnancy" he paused, "I'm the only one who knows though and I'm not going to tell anyone, but I have requested that the Camp Commandant exempt her from all strenuous activities as she is unable to fully participate due to poor health"

"And they won't send her home and make her come back next year?" I asked.

"No, not at all, as long as she stays in the camp for the duration of the three weeks she'll be fine"

"Oh great. Thanks a lot, you are brilliant" I said happily. "One more thing though"

"Okay?"

"She doesn't know I know about the pregnancy so can we not mention that we talked about it?"

"She doesn't know you know but you came to me to help her out?"

"Well I don't want her escaping this drudgery we are all in now do I?" I shrugged "Thanks again Doc" I headed into the clinic. I don't know why I am being nice to Jay or why I'm trying to watch out for her, but I am here doing it and I don't want to think too hard about it. It is what it is.

"Adunni wait" Effiong made a grab for my hand; his fingers were long and slim with neatly oval finger nails.

"Could we hang out tomorrow? You know? Dinner?" he smiled hesitantly.

"Maybe" I smiled slightly.

"Okay then, see you tomorrow" he smiled widely, his eyes crinkling at the edges.

"Yeah sure" I continued into the open female ward in the rather noisy camp clinic.

"Hey babes" I smiled at Jay who just pushed aside her dinner of yam swimming in stew. I wrinkled my nose in disgust at the meal.

"It is disgusting food and I couldn't eat it. I don't know how anyone is expected to eat that" She replied indignantly "the food here is truly horrible"

"I know and I brought you something" I said holding up the bottle in my right hand. Her eyes lit up at the giant bottle of Lucozade drink peeking from inside the carrier bag; "and some biscuits and chocolates, this is a nicer dinner no?"

"Fit for kings" she replied gamely, "come on, get on the bed" she patted the side of her bed, "I shouldn't still be here though, cos I'm perfectly fine now but Dr Effiong said I could have the bed till tomorrow morning if I wanted it, unless the clinic fills up and they have to kick me out which I hope they won't. It's nicer here anyway. Maybe I should faint every day" She finished winking.

Now he is Dr Effiong hey? More like co-conspirator Effiong.

"Maybe you should, then you will get sent home and I will kill you for leaving me alone in this horrid place" I got on the bed with Jay and broke open the pack of jam biscuits and Twix chocolates.

"So Jay, how is life in this grand old place?"

"It's kinda exciting to watch the doctors at work, there has been four cases of asthma attacks since I came in this morning and someone fell off a wall and came in here with a huge gash on his head. They stemmed the blood flow but I think he's been taken into the city for stitches. All in all, good fun; I also got to sleep, I think I was sleep deprived and needed a proper rest"

"Hmm" I sniffed, "but you are better now? Perfect?"

"Yes, I'm feeling perfectly fine now. Dr Effiong has been kind you know, he's spoken to the camp commandant and got me an exemption from strenuous exercise"

"And why would he do that? I thought you were just sleep deprived and have now gotten enough sleep"

"Well yes, but he doesn't want me fainting again and he thinks I might if I do anymore jogging and running"

"I see; you are a real pack of lazy bones aren't you?" I smiled at her continued duplicity.

She gripped my hand and squeezed them, I squeezed back and we tore into the biscuits and chocolates while I told her all about my day outside the clinic leaving out my conversation with Effiong a few minutes earlier.

BECKY

The things you hear when people think no one is listening. Effiong and that Jezebel called Adunni were discussing outside the Clinic, I was sitting right there on the ledge in front of the Clinic reading another free ditzy novel and as usual they didn't see me. I'm very good at being invisible when I want to be and I heard him say clearly, "Jay told me about her pregnancy". The dirty little trollop was pregnant; baby faced slut.

Adunni started off by telling Effiong about Jay's pregnancy like he didn't already know. He's a doctor, you fool. Of course, he knows. I wondered if she was just using it as an excuse to have a conversation with my Effiong, the useless immoral dirty tramp.

I wanted to get up and slap her hard and tear out all that shiny black hair that's probably half of her problem; stupid, stupid, whore.

She finally pushed him into asking her on a date or something, the whore. He was grovelling too, "Could we hang out?" he sounded so hopeful, I felt ashamed of him.

"Stop asking her to hang out with you" I screamed in my head, "She doesn't deserve you. I am here, I love you, and I will hang out with you as much as you want, for as long as you want"

They finished their silly little conversation and she went into the Clinic, still acting all indifferent, her responses to him vague and nonchalant.

Oh Effiong, my Effiong, why are you so silly? Why would a god like you grovel before a mere Jezebel like that? Is it her slim body or her long lashes that bewitch you? Her breasts are a tenth of mine and her thighs are the size of my arms, yet you bow and scrape for a hang out. A hang out? You disappoint me Effiong and my heart breaks at your treachery.

I struggled to control my fury and grief and instead focused on the secret I'd just heard. Jay is a pregnant woman in NYSC Orientation camp. One of the rules of participating in the NYSC Orientation camp is that pregnant women are not allowed in camp and when they are discovered are usually sent packing to return the next year with the job market largely closed to them till they had completed the NYSC one year programme; pregnancy was definitely a no-no if you wanted to complete your NYSC programme.

Who would have thought, that behind that sweetly innocent smile and wide eyes lives a complete slut? I was not too surprised though, birds of a feather flock together and she was best of friends with Delilah herself after all. The way they stalked my Effiong was unbelievable; always finding a way to talk to him, smiling and flirting; and that Jezebel practicing her art of pretend indifference that had him falling all over his own feet, his tongue hanging out in abject adoration. The whole thing filled me with disgust and rage, red hot rage.

I started following him on the first day of registration when I first noticed the unnecessary attention the two whores were giving him. Once he gave me a fright when he turned round and walked towards me, I was so sure he was coming to ask me why I had been following him around, but he just walked right past me like I didn't exist... like I didn't exist.

I wanted to tap him on the shoulder and say "tut tut Effiong, you are so naughty, pretending so well that I am not here, that you don't see me" at the same time I wanted to hit him over the head with a stick and keep hitting him till the big lump sitting angrily in my chest dissolved into a puff of pink cloud.

Nevertheless, it was rather gratifying to be proved right, I have always believed that you can spot a bad egg if you know what you are looking for, someone needs to be told about this dirty pregnancy; we can't have one bad apple spoiling the rest now can we? And camp rules do say pregnant women are not allowed here.

Still, I decided to hold on to the juicy information until the right time when I could tell the right person or people for maximum impact.

In the meantime, my bedside prayer meeting now lovingly named "Sisters in Faith Fellowship (SIFF)" was growing steadily. SIFF held meetings every day at noon and in four days grew from a small group of six girls meeting for ten minutes to a steady group of twenty, meeting joyously for thirty minutes. We had to procure plastic chairs from the administrative building and arranged these along the wall opposite my bed, all the way to the door and round back to my bed.

Adesuwa my bunkmate and ready assistant found us a praise and worship leader, Aina's sonorous voice sounded like a chapel bell and she happily belted out chorus after chorus till we were duly transported into a state of spiritual appropriateness and readiness to discuss cogent issues with our saviour as true warriors of heaven.

We did not collect any offerings and when I pointed out to Adesuwa the need for a SIFF fund she said it might frighten the girls away. "It's been almost two weeks you fool, it all ends in a week and then they will all be gone, we need the offering now not next week when they are all broke and ready to leave" I thought; but I agreed with her and shelved the idea of offering for the time being.

Some of the girls in the hostel started complaining about SIFF and how we were disturbing their 'before lunch nap', how they didn't see the purpose of SIFF when there was already an established general Christian fellowship in the camp; the Nigerian Corpers Christian Fellowship (NCCF).

This one is for the ladies in this hostel, I tried to tell them as gently as I could, the heifers.

"We need something for ourselves, where we can pray for each other and support each other. You can't take delicate and personal matters to the general fellowship" Adesuwa informed two of the nit-pickers firmly.

But these whiners never give up easily, and Adesuwa and I ended up having an unfortunate conversation with one of them, Marilee.

She started with "Becky, please can you not block my bed with these chairs? I can't even get out of bed without banging into a chair"

"Sorry" I moved the chairs slightly, her bed is next to the door, there was no way I could avoid blocking her bed with the chairs; our fellowship held for thirty minutes so I didn't see why she was complaining, but she is a whiner, that is their way.

"It would be better if you don't have the chairs here at all, putting it bluntly, this your daily meeting is a problem to be honest" she flicked her hand in my face, her nose in the air.

"The prayer meeting is just for thirty minutes; you could rest in your bed at that time" I countered, ignoring her ugly little nose.

"Rest in my bed? And you are telling me what to do because? What is the purpose of this fellowship you do here every day anyway? Is the NCCF not enough for you people?"

"You can join us Marilee, you will be welcome" I answered her serenely.

"I don't think you are listening to me. I don't want to join you, what I want is for you to stop disturbing the rest of us with your singing. Did you people kill Jesus?" she was shouting now.

Marilee had a strident voice and it was starting to grate on my nerves. I stared at her coldly, although I was smiling at her; "there is no need for you to be rude and blasphemous" I answered from behind my smile which was by then, very wooden.

I could feel the lump rising in my chest, a loud noise like rushing waters filled my head, I desperately swallowed the lump now in my throat and pushed the noise away firmly.

"Please, please, please, don't tell me what I can say or cannot say. Who died and made you god? You are not even the hostel leader. Are you the hostel leader?" she shouted.

I bit the bottom of my lips to control my still rising rage.

"Catherine over there is the leader, not you, and as far as I can see, she is not making our lives miserable"

"Catherine doesn't mind that we pray" I cut in.

"Then she should, and I will take this up with her, if she can't play her role as hostel leader, she should allow someone else to do it"

"Later on, you will say your life is not working" Adesuwa interrupted rudely, joining the rapidly deteriorating conversation, "how is it your business what we do in our corner? Is it your mouth we are singing with? Hen? Answer me?"

"Adesuwa leave it, no need to shout" I said cutting into Adesuwa's response.

"No let me tell this idiot what she wants to hear. So we are disturbing you? Is this your personal room? Is this your father's house? Answer me aunty" Adesuwa screamed.

Adesuwa is naturally rude, she was garrulous and always willing to shout and argue, this situation was Adesuwa's home ground, she was ready to posture and dance around while slinging insults at her victim at the top of her voice, her skinny arms flailing about.

"Don't put your stupid chairs in my corner and don't bang your silly tambourines in my face is what I was saying, and if you call me an idiot one more time, I will deal with you mercilessly. Do you hear me?" Marilee replied.

"Come and deal with me" Adesuwa screamed.

Although I was tempted to leave her to Marilee just to see how much she could hold her own, I also knew that if there was a fight between Adesuwa and Marilee, Adesuwa would lose badly. I mean this is someone who could barely carry her small plastic bucket ten feet without panting; but I decided to reward her loyalty to me by helping her walk away from the fight, so I dragged her out of the hostel.

Marilee, I planned to deal with at a later date.

Day 5 NYSC Camp

ADUNNI

Our fifth day in camp was also the 'swearing in' day. Wakeup call had been pushed to 7am and morning drills cancelled. The camp officials did not want us all sweaty and tired before the day's event; still the whole hostel was awake and buzzing at 5am and I felt I was the only one interested in making good use of the extra sleep time we had been given. The girls were giggling and chattering in loud whispers, while I tossed and turned in my bed and tried to drown out their chatter.

As the dawn broke clear, Jay returned to the hostel looking spry and already dressed in her white vests and stubbornly baggy green trousers.

We had a leisurely breakfast at the Mammy market before heading to the parade grounds at 9am.

"The dignitaries will not show up for the next two hours at the least" Jay said glancing at her watch "so I'm not even sure why we have to go to the parade ground now"

"Don't push your luck, they already cancelled morning drills and gave us two extra hours of sleep, so when the dignitaries arrive to shake your hand for agreeing to serve your country for a whole year, you better be smiling gratefully and marching like a tin soldier otherwise these soldiers will make sure there is hell to pay"

Still we both arrived at the parade ground with a noticeable drag in our feet and joined our Platoon, where we spent the next twenty minutes attempting to form straight lines as best as we could. Sergeant Ahmed was somewhere else, chasing rebellious corpers so his job with us was being shabbily done by three guys and a girl who had differing opinions on how best lines should be formed.

For three hours we waited for the Governor and his entourage to arrive. My legs shook with tiredness and within the first thirty minutes of waiting, Jay was sitting in the grass at the back of the queue; I just wanted to cry. A few dignitaries trickled in, but no Governor and the soldiers refused to let us off the parade ground; soon our tiredness and disenchantment overcame our initial excitement and the noise of grumbling started to rise along our standing ranks.

A few people decided to risk the soldiers' wrath by running in different directions; the soldiers gave chase heatedly, caught up with them and pushed them roughly back into their lines.

Others, like Jay and me, sat on our hunches and the soldiers came running again "Get up, all of you... no sit down... no sit down ... Governor is coming... lazy girls" they screamed in broken English.

I am already exhausted from all of this activity, I wish I could scream my exhaustion or better still disappear into the cool earth and take a long nap.

We scrambled up and wearily went back into the now indiscernible line and like we were not miserable enough, it began to rain. We all ran towards the buildings for cover but the soldiers chased us. They insisted we stand in the rain and wait for the Governor. We were soaked to the skin, Jay and I shivered and shook and I was filled with righteous indignation. The camp commandant came out and in a loud and clear voice reminded us of our Youth Service anthem which they'd made us learn and sing repeatedly the day before.

The camp commandant went on to sing the cursed anthem and insisted we all sing along with him. At first, we mumbled it, but what the heck, in the heavy downpour; we accepted our cold fate and sang along with him:

"Youth obey the clarion call... Let us lift our nation high...Under the sun and in the rain... With dedication and selflessness...Our country's ours, our nation we serve"

The third line of the song, adequately chastised us all, and was also to haunt us for the rest of our camp stay, because the sun was relentless and the rain much more so, through most of camp.

The rain stopped and the wind blew and dried our clothes; yet the Governor was nowhere to be seen. Toni and Effiong came over from their Platoon to keep us company and make the waiting easier. I shivered and shook and my teeth chattered. I glanced at Jay worriedly a few times, she refused to go into the clinic and was sticking it out with the rest of us. Now I knew her situation, I admired her spunk. I wondered if her parents knew about the pregnancy; or if the wonderful boyfriend she loved so much had any idea his sweet girlfriend was pregnant.

Just when the tiredness was getting unbearable and the rebellion was threatening to become full blown, the Governor's representative zoomed in. The Governor had more important engagements and had sent a representative in his place; he probably couldn't care less what we did with ourselves and our poorly made uniforms, not that I could blame him particularly. I mean who would want to sit and watch a host of poor idiots stomping around in a wet field in wrinkled, badly made and now very dirty uniforms anyway.

An hour later, the ceremony came to an end and the RSM in a magnanimous voice informed us that we were a marvellous lot and therefore were getting the rest of the day off to do as we pleased. Guinness and The Brewery would be coming to the camp and would be throwing us a welcome party with free beer later in the night; lights out was also extended from 10pm to midnight. We cheered and ran off the parade ground in different directions, our noise joyous and relieved. I planned to drink myself into oblivion.

***

At the hostel, while we changed out of our filthy uniforms into our own clothes, Jay started telling me about Yomi and how she had met him at one of her father's high power parties. He had just joined the family business in a senior management capacity; a well-known bank with subsidiaries in manufacturing, pharmaceuticals and media. The Baloguns are a rich, powerful family with money going back many generations and his parents, uncles and aunties were in and out of the news and society pages; his mother always looked formidable and unsmiling.

At the time they met, he was fresh from the University of Cranfield UK, where he had gone to study for his MBA after a first degree in Economics from the London School of Economics and a few years working with the Credit Suisse. He came home, keen and full of innovative ideas to move the bank's business forward.

At the party, she had been bored and was starting to drink a little bit more than she should when Yomi came over to introduce himself with the words "are you as bored as you look or is that the face you wear at these kind of parties?" They had got talking and he had swept her off her feet.

She kept him away from her family for the first three months of their whirlwind romance; before introducing him to her brothers and that was when the misery started.

Being the last child and the only girl, her father and brothers doted on her; their mum had left them precipitously when she was four years old, and it had only made them even more possessive of her. They were ensconced in the belief that no boy was good enough for their princess.

Her older brothers, Dele and Richard were initially wary of her relationship with Yomi. Fola on the other hand hated Yomi from the word go and with a word here and a suggestion there, he convinced Dele and Richard that Yomi could not be trusted with their baby sister. Dele and Richard promptly developed strong feelings of animosity towards Yomi.

"Daddy is the only one who seems to like Yomi somewhat and I can only hope that continues, although if Fola has anything to do with it, daddy will soon start thinking of Yomi as the devil himself" Jay shrugged "Fola won't even stay in the same room with Yomi and is extremely insolent to him at every opportunity; his rudeness is childish and churlish" Jay said. "I know Fola can be ruthless but I didn't realise how ruthless till I started dating Yomi. He has been calculating in discrediting Yomi and making sure Dele and Richard distrust him, no matter what I say" she continued, a little mournful.

"But why? Has he ever told you why he dislikes Yomi so much?" I asked.

She smiled sadly, "He's jealous is why. We sort of grew up in pairs; Dele and Richard are just two years apart and are chummy while Fola who is eight years younger than Richard, and I are also two years apart and also close. Fola and I did everything together growing up and I think he's just jealous that I now have Yomi"

"Ahw, how sweet, that's understandable then, with time he will like Yomi I hope"

"I don't think so" she insisted.

"Men do have a way of sorting out these things don't they? Maybe you could have a word with Dele or Richard about it? Especially now that...." I trailed off.

"Now that what? Jay asked me smiling, "now that I'm pregnant you mean?"

"Ah! Finally, we talk about the elephant in the room" I exclaimed throwing up my hands "Sorry the baby in the room" I finished in a whisper.

Jay giggled. "Yes, I'm pregnant and I'm sorry I'm just saying something about it now, it's just not something I felt able to talk about with anyone"

"Yomi knows, right?"

"Yes he does, I told him shortly before I came to camp and he wasn't happy that I still came...he was angry actually, but I insisted. I'm doing this now and when I get back we can talk about it more. It's just three weeks anyway"

"He was happy then?"

"Yes he was delighted, but we haven't talked much about it" she shrugged, "we didn't have much time with camp and all"

"So will he be visiting sometime? I'm told we can have guests on weekends"

"Sure" she answered faintly.

I felt there were still gaps in the conversation but I was glad she was talking about the pregnancy. Now I don't have to pretend about watching out for her.

"You should slow down though, not do all the running, jogging and standing about, especially the standing about, now that you have your exemption you don't have to do any of it with the rest of us you know. It's dangerous"

"I know and I'm slowing down. It's just that slowing down means accepting that I'm pregnant, acknowledging it; just like talking about it, slowing down puts it in my face. I don't want to think there's another person; breathing and living inside me it's so surreal and frightening"

"Oh" I felt a bit sad for her, last time I had this kind of thoughts about a baby, it didn't survive my thoughts.

"Don't worry, you'll feel better about it as the days pass; how far gone are you now?" I asked brightly.

"Ten weeks" she smiled.

"Nice, congrats again. Weird question but tell me you are keeping the baby"

She was silent, "I don't know, I think so; sometimes I feel that I want it and sometimes I hate it; I hate it growing inside of me"

"So tell me Adunni, are you pregnant too?" she asked changing the topic quickly.

"Me? Hell, no. I don't even have a boyfriend; I'm definitely not pregnant" I replied jumping off the bunk so we could head back to the Mammy market and all the waiting beer.

She held my hand, keeping me in the little space between our bunks and the next "So why have you been throwing up so much?"

"The food here doesn't agree with me that much, but it's getting better now" I shrugged smiling drily, "Come lady, let's go have some fun out there and no drinking for you, you are going to be sightseeing" I said clapping.

She let it go, for the time being. I should have had a story ready, for her, for people who were insistent, who wanted to know what was wrong; a diversionary tale to keep them far off the real issue, the real pain; but I did not. I had been told the nausea and diarrhoea and vomiting would only be for a while then it would all go away once everything was under control so I had no answers to the questions and the puzzled looks. I shrugged and gave them my well-practiced inscrutable look; that one I learnt when my dad died and I needed to hide the pain of the heartbreak and the rage.

***

Everywhere was bubbly and colourful, the beer companies with their makeshift bars spewing foaming beers from taps attached to barrels were already set up at two different ends of the Mammy market. Girls surrounded two guys in promo t-shirts as they obligingly gave out branded bags and umbrellas to the girls based on their whim, ignoring most of the guys hanging around them.

"Hi girls"

"Hello"

"Don't you guys want to come closer to our stand? You can't catch any fun standing a mile off like that" he was wearing a promo t-shirt and his confident smile oozed like oil. His eyes showed he was accustomed to getting his way with girls; not particularly because of his good looks or charm but mostly because he knew how to spread his money around.

Jay frowned at him, I smiled and tugged at her and we moved closer. The oily guy smiled and ushered us into their blue branded tent; I ignored him pointedly as we entered the tent.

"Look at the pretty damsels I've got here" he said announcing us like someone who just got two little kittens.

"Wow, they are pretty", another one said coming out of the dark corners of the tent with a smile as oily as that of his colleague.

"I hope you will both be dancing tonight; we are going to have a dancing competition later and there are lots of prizes to be won by pretty girls like you" he chanted.

We smiled vaguely.

"Ita is my name" oily 2 said jabbing at himself.

I hate it when people introduce themselves like that.

"Adunni"

"Jadesola"

"Ahhhh, Adunni, Jadesola, pretty Yoruba girls, I have gifts for you beautiful ladies" he smiled handing out two bright blue branded knapsacks to Jay and I.

"Thank you" we replied and collected the bag, immediately turning and ducking out of his stall.

"Are you ladies leaving already?"

"Yes we need to get to the hostel" Jay said.

"What do we need these bags for now?" Jay asked turning to me and holding up the bag.

"Nothing, it doesn't matter" I shrugged.

"Okay, but I don't want to stay at the Mammy market anymore"

"Why?"

"It's a little too noisy for me" she said frowning, "the noise and the lights and all that screaming along with the music, seriously I can't deal with it"

"You are going to miss all the fun"

"I don't care; I think I'm tired now"

"But the party might pick up later, don't you want to dance? Dancing is good for pregnant girls you know" I teased, trying to lighten what was quickly looking like a bad mood.

"No, it isn't" she replied calming down a little, "You stay and have fun, there are loads of young men here who are dying to be gifted with your smile and to trail you like moon struck dogs"

"Bet they are all twats" I shrugged.

"Not Dr Effiong" she replied.

"Oh! oh! What makes him different then? Your knight in shining armour"

"I think he likes you, and I think he's a nice guy"

"I'm sure you think so, after all he got you that exemption" I replied wryly. I remembered his suggestion of a hang out and made a mental note to avoid Dr Effiong throughout the evening. "Are you fine to head back to the hostel alone? I asked Jay, "I'm going to stay and have a few drinks in this smoke-filled chaos"

"Yes sure, have fun and don't get too drunk"

"I'm going to get very drunk darling" I said to her tiny retreating figure and in my heart I began to hope that Yomi was nothing like Aidan and that he loved her as much as she loved him.

Despite her bubbly narration of a romance that could make Disney movies jealous, Jay was obviously unhappy about something, she had everything and yet a lot seemed missing and there was an unwanted baby in the mix.

I realised she was possibly exerting herself in camp in an attempt to induce a miscarriage; she maybe thinks a miscarriage would be easier to deal with that an abortion because a miscarriage wouldn't be her fault but an abortion would. Poor thing, I wished I could tell her the human mind doesn't work that way, that she would feel guilty whether it was an abortion or a miscarriage, she might even hate herself more for the deceit of an induced miscarriage but I could not say these things so I hoped that I was wrong and my gut instincts were way off.

***

I gazed into my lager glass and took a sip from the foaming top, it was ice cold and trickled down my throat into my stomach; most of the people standing around me were holding a glass of the free ice cold foaming beer which the beer companies were handing out generously. Even though the Camp Commandant declared the party a uniform- free affair; we were all in variations of the same get up. The uniform of our generation, straggly jeans, skin tight jeans, skimpy jeans and jeans that only occasionally saw a wash. The guys were wearing theirs hanging low, fashionably and disgustingly showing their underwear. Aidan would never dress like that. He was the epitome of the dashing gentleman.

I remember the first time I met Aidan; it was at the Eko Hotel. I had gone there to meet Dr. Sowande who I had been dating on and off for six months. Initially, dating Dr Sowande was exciting; he made me laugh and said the most intelligent things. In some way, he also made me feel that he meant the compliments he paid me. He didn't slobber all over me like a lot of the boys in school. It made the relationship more precious. It felt like I was working to keep the relationship; he wasn't someone I told to jump and he said how high.

I never liked to think about the fact that he was married and so much older than I, old enough to be my father and a doctor just like my father because that would bring up issues of projection. Was I projecting my dad on Dr Sowande? Was I trying to bring back my father by dating Dr Sowande? I hoped not. I don't want to have sex with my father and that is what I did with Dr Sowande and a lot of other things. Even though he was married, we didn't have any difficulties spending time together. Being a well-known and respected surgeon meant he was away from home a lot; his wife expected it and didn't seem to find it odd that he spent nights away from home. He spent a lot of nights with me, usually at the

Protea Hotel. This time I was meeting Dr Sowande at The Eko Hotel where he was attending a three-day Conference of Medical Practitioners from all over Africa. It was the first day of the conference and the conference attendees were all lodged at Eko Hotel. Dr Sowande figured he would be done by 4pm and we could spend the rest of the day together, far away from the conference and the attendees.

I had been waiting for a little over an hour when he walked in dragging a metallic grey Samsonite luggage. He was tall, broad shouldered and heavily built; yet he didn't look like he had an ounce of fat on him. He was light skinned, his cropped curly hair a light brown with sprinkles of grey. I glanced at him and continued fiddling with my phone. I was bored and getting irritated; Dr Sowande and I have been exchanging steamy messages but he stopped responding when he started addressing the conference; so I was slouched in one of the black couches in the Hotel reception, exchanging messages with my friend Lolade while Aidan checked in and went up the stairs.

When he came back down thirty minutes later, I was slouched in a different couch, even more bored and annoyed. I had just sent Dr Sowande a message threatening to leave.

"Same girl, different couch" he said smiling and sitting down in another sofa in the same circle as the one I was lounging in.

"Scuse me?" I said in a steely voice. I assumed he thought I was some "working lady" he could pick up for the night.

"I can see you've changed your relaxing seat, are you playing truant?"

"Truant?" I asked

"The next meeting is starting in fifteen minutes; shouldn't you be there?"

I realised he thought I was a medical doctor, here for the conference.

"Hmm no, I'm waiting for a friend who is in the meeting, is there another meeting after the ongoing one?"

"Oh right, yes there is" he frowned slightly, typically putting two and two together, "yeah there's another one-hour meeting and that's the last one.

"So why are you here and not there" I asked.

"Since I've missed the whole day due to a terribly delayed flight, I'm knackered and I'm not keen on joining the conference today. I could as well start fresh with them tomorrow"

"Oh okay" I was livid. I wondered if Dr Sowande was going to be attending the next conference meeting or if he was planning to miss it. I picked up my phone to ask him about this, when it buzzed as if on cue. It was a message from Dr Sowande; he had intended to skip the last meeting of the day to be with me but had now been roped in by a senior colleague who was not feeling too great and wanted Dr Sowande to fill in for him.

I sighed with irritation, putting down my phone.

"Everything alright?" he asked, smiling with concern.

"Yeah sure" I answered gaily, "so what country was your delayed flight coming from?"

"South Africa, I'm South African"

"Hmm... Is this your first time in this country?"

"This is the second time I'm coming for this conference; I was here five years ago when it also held in Nigeria"

"Did you like Nigeria the last time or did you come in with a stereotype about us and leave with the same?" I asked, raising an eyebrow.

"My Nigerian friends are all delightful, smart, funny and warm people, so I'm not sure what you are talking about" he smiled.

"Ahah" I laughed, "you haven't seen that South African movie that portrayed us as "alien-shagging people then"

He shrugged, "that was a stupid movie, I'm Aidan Zuma" he said, holding out a broad manicured hand.

"Adunni" I answered smiling. He nodded and mouthed my name in his South African accent.

We spent the next hour chatting away like old friends. It was unlike me, I'm not the friendliest of people, but that day I was friendly. I laughed, I giggled, I stared at Aidan; I made friends with my misfortune. We left Eko Hotel to go to Saipan Restaurant for dinner and to escape Dr Sowande who I knew would be bounding down the staircase anytime soon. I switched off my phone so Dr Sowande couldn't reach me. I was happy for him to assume I had gotten upset and left. Aidan wisely refrained from asking about the friend I had been waiting for in the hotel lobby.

I briefly returned my attention to the bustling crowd at the Mammy market who was dancing and shaking their bodies around a boom box, sweat glistering on their faces, the halogen lamps crudely attached to a bamboo stick stuck in the brown earth adding to the heat and energy of the crowd as the loud speakers boomed out something by Kanye West and some excited dancers caught up in the flow of the party, hooted loudly to the music.

I was sitting away from the dancing crowd on a bench inside one of the makeshift sheds scattered around the Mammy market. I sat on the edge of the bench so I could see what was happening around me and as far as the suya man who was making brisk business judging by the crowd around him. He had set up his smoking grill of spicy meat in a vantage point and was surrounded by a crowd of corpers all trying to make their orders heard over the din. The insects danced around the beam of his lantern as his excited customers shouted "Aboki three hundred naira.", "Aboki how much is this one?" and "Aboki answer me now"

After the two-day Medical conference Aidan visited me in Nigeria frequently. Our romance was ferocious and consumed me like an inferno. I thought about him feverishly, every day and every hour. Our days were spent eating expensive dinners, sleeping in and taking part in dangerous high risk sports. I missed classes and travelled to South Africa every month to see Aidan; with Aidan I went bungee jumping, sky diving and deep sea swimming in the shark infested waters of KwaZulu-Natal beaches.

The more dangerous the sport or entertainment the more Aidan loved it. I put it down to his medical profession and his being fully aware of the inherent risks to our lives. I gradually became an adrenaline junkie like Aidan.

I loved him too much to say no to the crazy things he wanted to do. He was crazy in bed too; he wanted us to try everything, we had sex everywhere; elevators, roof tops, inside cars on quiet streets and in lit swimming pools at night.

At the height of our romance, we paid a flying company that flew us around the coasts of South Africa for an hour while we enthusiastically joined the 'mile high club'. It was exhilarating and frightening all at once.

Initially I couldn't get past the presence of the pilot in the cockpit but Aidan's insistent tongue visiting crooks and crannies of my body I didn't even know existed, gradually broke down my defences and I relaxed into his firm embrace. In the last twenty minutes of the flight, we made love looking at the twinkling lights of the Cape Town metropolis.

Over the one year we dated, my grades fell; I was scarce in school and barely arrived back in town in time for exams. We dated into my final year and I still couldn't bring myself to care about my grades no matter how hard I tried. You would think Aidan being a medical doctor would care about me missing school but he only huffed and said "Education is overrated" Foolishly, I believed him. I was consumed with Aidan, with his beauty, his intense loving and his dashing smile. He loved custom made suits and travelled in and out of London to buy custom made Saville Row suits, shirts and designer shoes. These trips yielded a lot of gifts for me; perfumes, designer dresses, shoes and trinkets and as far as I was concerned we were the perfect couple.

On my many trips to Pretoria where Aidan lived and worked, I met his friends, his colleagues, his cousin who lived with him and his best friend. His best friend was odd; he was taciturn and unfriendly around me although Aidan insisted Katleho was boisterous and friendly. I put it down to the animosity I'd heard so much about between Nigerians and South Africans in South Africa. Normally I wouldn't give a damn about what Katleho thought of me or his hostility, but for Aidan's sake I tried. When I mentioned Katleho's coldness to Aidan, he froze for a minute and asked what Katleho had said to me exactly "Nothing at all, he doesn't even talk to me" I shrugged. "He's just cold and off-putting; I can't imagine the fun loving friend Katleho you talk about"

"I'll talk to him about it" Aidan replied tightly.

Aidan was an orthopaedic surgeon at the Living Spinal & Orthopaedic Hospital in Pretoria. When I visited him there, he seemed well loved and respected. The nurses fawned over him and were friendly with me. An old nurse even held my hand once and said to me, "I love when I see real love at play, real love... you brave thing" I found her touching. I look back now and see all the signs; Katleho's hatred, the old nurse's words, Aidan's love for daring sport... it all added up later... too late. By the time I realised that Katleho didn't hate me, that he didn't hate Nigerians; it didn't matter anymore.

I shook myself out of my reverie and headed for one of the stalls where I could see Toni and his friends chatting and drinking what was probably their tenth glasses of beer.

Bolaji suggested that we dance and before I could point out that we were both rather tipsy, he grabbed my hand and we set off to join the milling crowd. Nneka, another girl who had been standing with them dragged Toni into the dancing crowd while Bolaji and I pitched ourselves at the edge of the party, far from the suya man, his barbecue smoke and the vibrating music boxes.

I swayed in time to the music, letting it wash over me. It felt good to dance; the last time I danced was with Aidan at the Bacchus club in Lagos. I switched with Nneka and danced with Toni briefly then I danced with Bolaji some more, I was having a good time.

Nneka came back again and dragged Bolaji away, and I giggled involuntarily at what looked like a beer induced romance.

"What's funny?" Toni asked, dancing haphazardly in front of me.

"You! You can't dance to save your life can you?"

"I'm doing a great job. Can't you see me? Fantastic dancing right here"

"Can we switch partners for a while?" someone said to Toni.

Toni looked up at the guy at the same time I did and turned to me to check if I was averse to it. I shrugged and Toni nodded at the guy and said "she thinks my dancing is crap anyway, I hope you can do better" and twisted away to foist his dancing on a girl who's drunkenness was obvious.

I looked fully at my new dance partner and he reminded me of Aidan, yet he didn't. He was slim and dark unlike Aidan who was light skinned broad-chested; but his face was beautifully sculptured just like Aidan's yet they were also as different as night and day. Aidan was becoming a ghost I couldn't lay to rest.

"You dance beautifully" he said taking my hand "it's easy to see why you think your friend is a bad dancer, I'm actually worse than he is, as you will soon find out. Will you teach me?" he asked with a tentative smile.

"There is nothing to teach" I shrugged and continued to dance, although more slowly.

"No?"

"Just dance" I smiled slightly "not like me of course" I said hurriedly as I saw he was trying to copy my dance steps, "if you dance like that, you would look very gay"

"Ah okay, we don't want that" he answered dropping the hands he had raised in the air.

We danced for about fifteen minutes not saying a thing to each other and when the song changed and got a little faster, he met me tempo for tempo and the beer induced haze I was falling into started to clear, the cold air and vigorous dancing woke me up.

"I'm Mahmud" he shouted over the loud music leaning towards me.

"Adunni" I raised my voice slightly.

"Yoruba?" he asked with a doubtful look.

"Yes, Yoruba" I knew what was coming next; I have heard it many times.

"You don't look like a Yoruba girl"

I shrugged, some people say I look Ibo because of my very light skin, which also frequently earned me the name 'Oyinbo' as a child, meaning white, but I am tall and slim with the narrow features of the northerners, their long limbs and straight nose. I am difficult to place in that pigeonhole of how Yoruba girls look.

"And how do they look?" I asked him. He shook his head from side to side and smiled without saying anything.

"Another beer?" he asked.

"Hmm", I hesitated scanning the crowd for Toni and Bolaji, neither of them was anywhere around; I shrugged "Okay"

We walked towards the sheds as a dancing competition began on the dusty improvised dance floor. An excited couple dashed out of a shed hand in hand to join the dancing competition, dropping empty bottles with half dry ice dew on their green bodies. We sat on the still warm wooden bench and drank straight from the icy bottles of beer that Mahmud had acquired a short minute ago; my mind drifted briefly to Jay who was probably fast asleep by now.

Mahmud started telling me about himself, I listened half-heartedly. He had studied Engineering at the Imperial College; he was from Minna, he played a bit of polo and had a horse he loved silly; like a lot of the rich kids who had come to the camp, he had been expecting a posting to Abuja and had been surprised to get a posting to Jos. Someone at the NYSC posting office, had drunk one too many glasses of something and thought what the heck, I'm going to screw all these rich kids over this time. He talked, I listened. He had a Northern accent dulled by a British one and a voice that rolled over my skin. His voice gave me tingles or maybe the beer I was drinking did. I was enjoying our largely one sided conversation. I was also drinking nonstop. I knew I would pay for it in the morning.

We returned to the dance arena and our shadowed corner and spent another thirty minutes dancing; intermittently interrupted by the self-appointed MC selecting his best dancers from the lot crowded around the halogen lights. I was lost in random thought when Marvin Gaye came alive with the song that engineered his murder. I leaned into Mahmud and danced till the party broke up late in the night.

Day 6 NYSC Camp

BECKY

My father, my drunken yet strangely religious father and my even more religious, scarf wearing, cowering, abused, but still wicked mother. I imagined them both at home; where they usually were in the evening, after my mother returned from her shop where she sold cooking oil in wholesale quantities; vegetable oil, sunflower oil, extra virgin olive oil and so on.

My father would sit in his favourite spot, in the sunken couch squarely in front of the large TV, in a faded lace trouser and a once white singlet, his bible closed with a stained mug sitting on it.

He preferred to study the Old Testament and would repeatedly nod his head as if some new understanding was coming to him while making copious notes in a large notebook; his beer mug beside his notebook. I have never understood how anyone could drink and read the bible at the same time like my father did.

The note taking and nodding would reduce as the drinking progressed and by the time the mug had been refilled five times, the note writing would have stopped completely and he would instead be "humming and haaing" over the bible like he had discovered some weighty issue that wasn't there the day before. Two more refills and the bible was set aside, demoted to the lowly role of tray for the beer mug; with bloodshot eyes, he would now sit despondently for the rest of the evening, occasionally staring at the TV and the large clock above it; impotently timing my mother who in his opinion was intentionally taking her time at the market and making oodles of money which he saw little of.

"Daddy, good evening" she would call from the kitchen as she entered the house through the backdoor which led into the kitchen from the yard, unloading whatever shopping she had done on her way back from the shop. We never used the front door of the house; except for guests, who were invariably some elder or pastor from the church. They were the only people who visited my parents, probably the only people who were welcome anyway.

"Good evening you too. You decided to wait and close the market gates yourself today hey?" he would ask, his voice dripping with sarcasm.

My mother's shop was in a shopping complex; a mall of sorts, made up of various rectangular shaped shops, selling any and everything, with a few hairdressing and barbing salons thrown in.

"I went to the market, so I could make soup" she would reply.

"We are grateful that the good Lord has placed it in your heart to feed us" more sarcasm.

She would not reply.

This would be followed by an hour of silence, while she slaved over the kerosene stove in the corner of her narrow kitchen, her ministrations interspersed by voices from the TV.

He would fall asleep in his chair, his loud snoring evidence of his sudden deep sleep and she would wake him up with a tired "food is ready"

They never ate together, he would sit at the dining table and wolf down whatever she placed before his designated chair, while she returned to a wooden table and chair in the kitchen to eat the same, but more slowly.

As if on cue, Caleb would come in, a pile of books cradled in his arm. I can't imagine a Caleb without books. I know his escape is the books he reads; with the books, he can be anyone, go anywhere, away from the dreary painful lives we live, to a clean, better magical place where he has two loving parents and no fighting.

I started stealing library books for him when I noticed how much he loved the books I brought home. A straight 'A' student, Caleb wanted to be a doctor and even though I had no idea how he was going to achieve that without a scholarship, I knew if there was anyone who stood a chance of getting an academic scholarship, it was Caleb.

With a cursory glance, mother would silently point at the red flask on the plywood covered kitchen cabinets, "your food is over there".

I think she was a bit nicer to Caleb than the rest of us, but none of us begrudged him this. In addition to being the youngest, winning him the protection of his older siblings, there was a kindness in Caleb that invited kindness from others, his gentleness coupled with his sheer brilliance made him easy to love.

Father would ignore Caleb and focus on the remnants of his meal, meticulously giving attention to the periwinkle and crayfish in his soup. He had stopped hitting Caleb by the time Caleb was 12 years old because he was rather tall for his age and growing like a weed. Despite the lack lustre meals,

Caleb continued to grow like sugarcane in perfect climate. By the time he was 16 years old, he was 6ft 2 inches with wide shoulders that strained his clothes, he looked much older than his age and although father still threatened to slap him, there was no spirit in his threats, they were like empty coconut husks, worthless and without effect.

My father was afraid of our gentle giant and would keep out of his way, sparing him malevolent looks from afar, his hatred of his son disturbing to see.

I like to think my parents were happy once, even in love. There were a few grainy pictures in the house, of them smiling. It was their wedding day and they stood together on the stone steps of the Methodist church where they were wedded. Mother smiling happily, father's smile a little bit more uncertain. He was wearing a grey suit, a white rose in his pocket, his left arm bent in a crook to accommodate my mother's slimmer one. She was wearing a long white A-line wedding dress, with slim sleeves that stopped at her wrist. She was also carrying white flowers; carefully held over her belly, in an attempt to hide my growing presence.

My mother was already pregnant with me when she got married to my father. She mentioned it to me once and said "those were the days of sin and ignorance, before the Lord in His infinite mercies called us out of the miry clay".

Not long after the happy picture on the Church steps, my parents joined a more 'serious' church, 'The Church of the Holy Saints of Heaven' where they found a more intense brand of religious conviction, in all its entirety and power. They also found judgement and a 'holier-than-thou' attitude to go with it.

They left the Church of the Holy Saints of Heaven and tried a few more churches of a similar ilk, before settling at the current 'less intense but still intense' church. However, they never let go of the sense of judgement and holiness they had acquired at the Church of the Holy Saints of Heaven. It followed them everywhere. My parents had a strong sense of holy hierarchy, your level of holiness determined how they relate or didn't relate with you. God help you if you were below them on the hierarchy which was where most of their extended family fell and curiously their children too.

Father fought bitterly with his sisters and brothers, and disowned his parents in a long winded letter which he posted to them. His siblings then refused to have anything to do with him and subsequently us. He never spoke to his parents again till their death and did not attend their funeral. I have no idea why he disowned his parents but I won't be surprised if it was something ridiculously trivial. My father was well known for making a mountain out of the proverbial mole hill, he is God's pettiest creature.

My memory of my uncles and my aunts told me my father was different, his brothers laughed, they tickled us and told us funny stories; they came, candy in hand; his sisters spoke kindly to my mum and played with us. This was all before he decided they were of no use and were out to destroy him and his destiny. I still wonder what he thinks his destiny was exactly, as nobody ever saw a manifestation of it.

My mother's family abandoned them shortly after I was born. I heard it whispered by his sisters that he beat up his brother-in-law the day before their wedding and although this was forgiven and settled in a family meeting; my father continued to misbehave outrageously. During one of the bitter fights with his sisters, I learnt that he had slapped his mother-in-law when she visited them to help care for me when I was born.

This last act severed any relationship between him and his in-laws who also refused to have anything to do with my mother. My mother in line with her religious beliefs stuck with my father, despite his abuse and belligerent behaviour and together they were a sad, angrily pious and unfortunate pair.

Although my parents found religion and found it hard, it didn't seem to help them much. They didn't find whatever it was other people found that gave them hope, peace and strength; that thing that makes Elder Jeremiah soft spoken and easy going and gave Sister Hannah the strength to lift her voice in happy praise, day in day out.

The truth is I never saw my father laugh; he was too busy being angry with the whole world, while going around with a chip on his shoulder the size of Mount Everest. I still don't know the cause of his anger and bitterness but as far as he was concerned, nobody understood him and everybody was out to get him.

The relationship between my parents must have deteriorated quickly after the happy grainy photograph on the stone steps of the Methodist church because he has been beating my mother for as long as I can remember. Once, I watched him smack her head down repeatedly on the hard cement floor.

Abraham and I watched many fights and beatings from behind the door of our shared bedroom, he would beat my mother till she fainted and sometimes he would keep beating her even then. He beat her through four pregnancies that I remember, two of which she miscarried.

I don't know when father started beating us kids but my first memory of my father was of him hitting me for spilling my food. I must have been about three years old. He hit me hard with his open palm and when I turned for solace to my mother who had been spooning food into my mouth she went "hush Becky, don't cry, daddy will get angrier now" The shock that my mother would provide no protection, dried my tears that day and many times in the future. I learnt quickly that my mother's presence did nothing to reduce the abuse I suffered from my father, I was there to deflect his rage from her to me.

The slap that day to my three-year-old left cheek was the beginning of many forceful, open palmed slaps, one of which dislodged two milk teeth from my young mouth. By the time I was six years old, the slaps were supplemented with his plastic bathroom slippers, which he hit me with, at every opportunity; over the head, across my arms, down my legs and frequently on my back accompanied by shouts of 'Witch, Destiny destroyer, Demon child'. Whenever he hit me with the plastic slippers they stung like many bees. I would cry and rub the skin where he had hit me running away as fast and as far as my legs could carry me. The things he said when beating me make me think that perhaps he had no intentions of marrying my mum but the unplanned pregnancy had forced his hand. I, the destiny destroyer had forced him into a marriage he didn't want and contributed to destroying whatever destiny fate had planned for him.

When I think about it, I'm not convinced fate had anything especially great planned for my father; if it did, it would have been a waste of greatness on him; only because my father is a lazy man with a big ego. He lost jobs like a conscientious lady changed underwear and each time his bosses were to blame. He lost a job for reading the bible loudly at work, another one for being late to work repeatedly and another for slapping the tea girl.

I was eight years old, when my father lost his last real job. It was at an insurance company; and he was sacked for being belligerent to his female boss. I still cannot imagine my father reporting to a woman. I think the fact that he lasted three months in that job was a big achievement for his angry, sexist self.

He came back home the day he lost his job with his face like thunder on a tropical rainy day.

"Good evening sir" we chorused, quickly getting up from where we were sitting like ducks in a row in front of the TV, watching a silent cartoon programme.

He mumbled his reply, his face speaking to us in more ominous volumes and Abraham and I began to make ourselves scarce. Rachel who had never taken to this gruff father was toddling away as fast as her little legs could carry her although stupidly to mother; to stand behind her while pulling mother's wrapper to cover her chubby baby face. In her young mind, if she couldn't see you, you couldn't see her.

"Daddy, welcome, hope your day was peaceful" mother said greeting him, still oblivious to the rage he had come in with.

"Pshew" he hissed in reply.

"Ahah. What is the matter?" my mother asked, she was holding 3 month old Caleb.

"I left that stupid job" he growled.

"You left that stupid job?" mother repeated in disbelief.

"That is what I said. Is there wool in your ears?"

"There is no wool in my ears, but why would you leave your job?"

"Because I wanted to, because I can, because I don't have to work with stupid people" he finished angrily, sitting down in his favourite sofa and kicking off his shoes aggressively.

Abraham and I watched from the doorway of our room, a safe distance from the drama we could sense was about to unfold.

"Hmmmm, did you leave your job or were you sacked?" Mother asked tightly.

I wished she could stop asking him questions; that she would just accept whatever story he had decided to tell, but I knew from experience that this wouldn't happen; she was just starting.

"What kind of question is that? I'm telling you I left the job and you are asking me if I was sacked, why and how did you make the leap from I quit to I was fired? Are you stupid?"

"I don't understand what is happening, that is why I am asking, nobody leaves the house in the morning perfectly happy and comes back in the evening having left the job because they can. It doesn't make any sense"

"Who told you I was perfectly happy at the job? I have been tormented in that job since day one" he replied holding up his fore finger for emphasis, "since day one, that Jezebel that calls herself Director of Claims has made my life miserable; that sinful child of Satan who will go straight to hell has talked to me anyhow since she was transferred from Abuja"

"So they didn't sack you, you left?" Mother asked again, a muscle in her cheek was working, and the fingers on her left hand were drumming the dining table.

"Yes I left, I don't have to take that nonsense from anybody, and I will go and find another job in a company where all the executives have not sold their souls to the devil"

Mother quietly walked into their bedroom to put Caleb in his Moses basket. Anyone who has never lived with my parents or seen their fights would think it was over but I knew better, this particular storm was just brewing.

She returned to the living room and my father, "So since you left by yourself you can return by yourself tomorrow right? Because I don't think you should just quit your job like that. You can go there and be the light of God in that dark place" she gritted through her teeth, her eyes tiny slits, her voice angry and mocking.

"What did you say Biodun? What did you say?" he repeated, "Are you ordering me to go back to a job I quit?" he thundered "who do you think you are? Hen? Answer me, because I'm not sure who you think you are, or who you think you are talking to. Who do you think you are?" he got up menacingly.

She took a step back, "I am not ordering you, I am advising you" she answered, "and you cannot be quitting jobs because you don't like your boss or you think the devil is in the job. As a good Christian you should not back down for the devil, please go back to that job. After all, the bible says in

Job 22 verse 29, when men are cast down, then thou shall say there is a lifting up" she finished a little more boldly.

"SHUT UP. Is it only men that are cast down? What about women? Useless entity that you are. Are you not cast down? Answer me, are you not cast down?" He screamed at her "it is a woman like you that is making my life miserable in that place; ordering a whole man like me about like I'm her maid, and you are here quoting bible at me. Idiot upon idiots"

Rachel began to cry in fright. I wanted to go over and drag Rachel out from behind mother who won't protect her from a beating if things got ugly and into our shared bedroom where Abraham was already safely ensconced under the bed; it would mean walking into Father's line of vision and having his anger directed at me.

"Please, please, please oh. Don't shout at me and don't call me names. Useless man. I am not cast down. You are the one that is cast down because you keep getting fired from your job. You think I don't know they fired you? Hen? Instead of you to tell the truth and let the devil be ashamed you are here lying to my face. Mama Siji supplies vegetable oil to your colleagues and already told me you were sacked this morning. Nonsense"

I made a dash for Rachel, the situation was deteriorating even faster than I expected and she was standing there peeking at our enraged father and sobbing. As I dragged her away, father glowered at me through his bloodshot eyes and for a moment it seemed he was going to address me, I lowered my eyes and the moment passed. I hurried into the bedroom and he turned his anger back on mother who for the day was representing all the evil of her conniving gender.

"So you already know. Your fellow witches have told you. I was sacked this morning and you have already heard. I knew it" he paused, "the only news you are interested in is bad news, other women pray for their husbands. They pray day and night but not you. You are busy bewitching yours. Watching out for bad news and glorying in it. You want to be the one making all the money right? Mrs Money maker. Hiding behind the word of God to perpetrate evil. I will deal with you today"

The name calling and screaming raged on and on and shortly he slapped my mother, she slapped him back, he started beating her, he punched and kicked her methodically while she screamed and gave as good as she got. I ran downstairs to get the neighbours to come and rescue my mother from her husband who was about to beat her to death again. The neighbours who had come to mother's rescue many times in the past were not keen, especially as she never seemed grateful afterwards, neither did she carry herself with the humility or timidity of an abused wife; so they took their time and my father had the chance to beat mother even more than he had ever done in the past.

By the time the neighbours arrived, my naked bleeding mother was holding a knife to my father's throat and whispering to him in a breathless voice, that the next time he raised his hands to her she would cut his throat and leave him to die like a goat. He never beat mother again. I added coward to my father's long list of negatives.

I don't know if he stopped looking for work or kept looking but never found another; to be honest I don't see how he could have explained the multitude of short employments to any recruiter or employer and his belligerent and angry attitude which usually followed a servile ingratiating one wouldn't have helped; so father stayed at home and read his bible and drank beer from a stained mug. We became solely dependent on my mother's income from her cooking oil business.

Having lost his source of income without hope of getting another and not having enough intelligence or wherewithal to start a business, father turned the full wrath of his bitterness on his children. He hit us at every opportunity he got and we also learnt to hide; to lie, to pre-empt and gauge his moods, to stay away and one by one to leave home and not return.

I have thought about it for many nights and I still don't know or understand why she never stood up for us, or why she never left him. After holding the knife to his neck that day, I thought things would get better for her and for us; that she would leave him even and take us with her, but she stayed and brought home the bacon while he battered and abused her children. It remains one of the reasons I hate my mother so much. She won freedom from his violent beatings for herself alone and yet did not lift a finger to save us from him. She did not leave or stop him, she let him carry on beating her children. He could hit us as much as he liked as long as he didn't hit her; all was well with the world.

JAY

I woke up the morning after the swearing-in day feeling much better. Visitors were allowed into camp on weekends and Yomi and I had agreed he would visit on the first Saturday in Camp. Since getting to camp, every phone conversation and chat with Yomi reminded me of his imminent visit and the discussion we had previously agreed to have then.

Although I craved his visit I was also dreading it; even though we talked every day we had agreed to leave all baby discussions till Saturday, when we could sit down and talk about it properly.

I climbed down from the iron bunk bed, careful not to wake Adunni who was snoring loudly, oblivious of the hostel noise and the girls milling around boisterously in various stages of undress, banging buckets against metal beds as they went for showers and returned with droplets of water on their shoulders and arms, the hairs at the nape of their necks wet and curling from the heat of their showers.

We were all settling into a norm that agreed with the military time table the soldiers were running and even though we had been told that there would be no early morning drills on Saturday, a lot of people still woke up at 4am to their now standard morning routine. I took my shower along with a hundred other girls in the fenced yard of our hostel. The bathrooms had been abandoned to those who had the guts to go into its fetid interior and those who lacked the nerve to take their showers in the open, shaded only by towels slung over washing lines, five feet high.

The air was brisk and a cool breeze blew hard as I returned to the hostel with my bucket and wash bag in my left hand; thinking about all the things I wished I could tell Adunni, but couldn't and didn't.

I couldn't tell Adunni the whole truth; only a form of it; why I have a love-hate relationship with my unborn child and wished it away; or why Fola hated Yomi so much. I couldn't tell her that although I was four when my mum left, I remembered. I remembered the blinding row before the slamming of doors and the zooming off in her car; that I still felt abandoned and that Fola was not the only one with residual pain.

I couldn't tell her that all I had for a long time was Fola because Dele and Richard were in boarding school in Switzerland and dad was too busy for us; those things wouldn't come out, no matter how much I tried. They would not be explained; presented before another for analysis, understanding and even judgment. I didn't hate my mum; she lives in Spain with her Spanish lover who she met when Dad was on a diplomatic posting to Spain and later left us for. She must have a new family surely, I would wonder. I don't hate her, I am indifferent to her but not to the feeling of abandonment she has left me with.

This feeling that the ones I love will always leave. I can only remember her vaguely; the smell of her Chanel perfume, her orangey red lipstick and her ringing laugh but it was enough; more than enough for me to know I loved her; I loved her when she was mine. She doesn't feel like mine anymore, just a woman who started calling me when I turned eighteen; although that might have something to do with my dad. She called me a few times during my University days;

we didn't say much but I was polite. Fola wouldn't talk to her at all. He was the one with all the rage in him and any mention of her brought a dark cloud to his face. He was old enough to feel the pain when she left and young enough to care. He didn't have another life outside of home like Richard and Dele; a life they could turn to; so he felt the devastation of her desertion the most.

Despite his own sense of loss, Fola did his best to help me fill the gap my mother left. I think he did as good a job as she could ever have done, considering she is someone who abandoned a four-year-old child, not much of an expectation there. He made sure I wasn't bullied in school; that I wasn't picked on. While I sailed through our British International School years on the strength of Fola's presence, I was Fola's window into our social group. My bubbly friendly personality made me a lot of friends while Fola's taciturn nature made him few. His big unsmiling frame made him even more unapproachable; a little frightening, but with me tagging along with him, my friends became his friends. I was his mother in a lot of ways and he was mine. Fola and I grew closer and closer as we went from children to teenagers to adults. More than my father, Fola was a constant reassuring presence in my life as far back as I could remember; till I met Yomi. Since I started dating Yomi, I have frequently felt like I was betraying Fola. Even though I kept telling myself it's a ridiculous feeling, I couldn't shake it off and sadly I know why.

Before Yomi, I had dated a few guys briefly and none of them did anything for my sense of abandonment; I still felt alone, abandoned, in need of Fola and his emotional protection. Yomi on the other hand filled me with delirious giddy happiness, a sense that life could be benevolent towards me, that I deserved a good thing and I'm important enough for a loved one to stay. In a sense, I understand Fola's rage, his abject anger, I loved Yomi helplessly and it infringed on my relationship with Fola, it overshadowed what we had. My sense of betrayal of Fola was almost as consuming as the love I felt for Yomi yet I was stubborn. I refused to let go of this love I had, it was all I could think of. I did not want to think of the hurt in Fola's eyes, or his jeering smile at Yomi or the many horrid things he said to Yomi and me.

On a day that changed everything, Fola cornered me on my way out of the house to Yomi's place "You think he loves you?" he asked, grabbing my upper hand painfully, "he is a man; he is here for the honey and will soon be gone. You are going to let yourself be a notch in his belt?" he asked in a whisper.

"Listen to yourself Fola, you sound like a bad B movie, 'Here for the honey. Notch in his belt.' seriously bro, you need better lines and no I'm not a notch in his belt" I replied, "I wish you would try to like him, he's a great guy and you will agree with me when you get to know him"

"I don't need to get to know him" he snarled, "You think he is a great guy hey? What do you know about men? All I see is a guy trying to get into your panties and that is not my definition of a great guy" he answered, sneering.

Fola's hypocrisy knocked the breath out of me and set my anger alight. I cannot count the number of girls that have trooped in and out of Fola's apartment; the one night stands and two week girlfriends. He would nonchalantly shrug and say "they don't mean a thing, surely you know that" that was always his response 'they don't mean a thing'

"Yomi is not trying to get into my panties and if he is, it wouldn't be the worst thing in the world" I replied angrily, wrenching my arm away from his painful grasp and rubbing at the dent his fingers had made in my arm. I knew that would hurt him like I had pushed a serrated dagger into his heart. "He loves me and I love him as much as I have ever loved anyone. If all I am is a notch in his belt then all well and good. It's real and totally within the realms of normalcy"

"So now you are having sex for the fun of it, for your sense of normalcy?" he continued still blocking the door that led to the garage "that is what you crave now? Normalcy?" his eyes grew darker and stormy.

"I'm not even sure what you are talking about Fola" I started to walk away; I was not going to fall into that trap. Fola had started again; his rage was coming to the fore.

"Answer me when I talk to you! Are you fucking that bastard?" he screamed spinning me around, his fixation with my sex life rising like a monster from the sea.

"Okay. Yes, yes. I am fucking him if that is how you want to see it. It's all sex... fantastic mind blowing sex and he is not a bastard" I screamed back at him.

Fola slapped me. I was shocked and reached for my cheek, the sting of the slap coursing through me to my toes. I ran off to my car and with shaking hands got in and drove off to Yomi's Victoria Island apartment. I cried all the way; by the time I got to Yomi I was calm. My brown skin hid the force of Fola's slap and I tried to apply some makeup to hide my now swollen eyes.

Grabbing my envelope clutch I headed into Yomi's place, he was already home and his face filled with concern when he saw mine. He tried to get me to talk about what was wrong, but I refused. I curled up in the coolness of his 500 count Egyptian bed sheet after a very hot shower and willed my mind to go blank. My gentle Yomi, my kind thoughtful Yomi quietly crawled into bed with me and held me close. He made love to me and it eased some of the pain in my heart. I had missed my morning pills two days in a row and Yomi didn't wear a condom.

When I got back home the next day, I tried to avoid Fola but failed; he was waiting for me. He apologised profusely, following me to my room. I tried to close the door as I didn't want to talk to him; I was weary of him, of his protectiveness and choking love; but Fola started to cry and I let him in to talk, to explain himself, to apologise for slapping me; I still hate myself for letting him that day.

***

"I wish I could sleep for ten more hours" Adunni groaned from her bed.

"Get up lazy bones, you need to get washed before that open space outside becomes a river and it's getting there already, so hurry madam"

"Okay, okay" she groaned jumping down from the bunk bed more carelessly than I had done earlier this morning.

When Adunni got back from a suspiciously quick shower she started telling me about last night; there was excitement in her voice, she had met a nice Fulani boy.

"He is from Minna and not bad looking at all" she announced, dropping her bucket unceremoniously and shoving it under the bunk bed.

"Well I never, tell me more, this is not your beer goggles talking right? I'm not going to see him today and think what the heck is Adunni talking about?"

"I wasn't that drunk when I met him; he is good looking and has a gorgeous voice" she replied.

"So you like him?" I asked clapping happily.

"I don't know yet, but he might be worth the attention, something to pass the time in this boring place" she shrugged, towelling droplets of water from her body.

"I can't wait to meet him then"

"Toni likes you" She said, shifting the conversation from her to me abruptly.

"Me? Like me how?"

"Like you the way a boy likes a girl or the way some girls like some girls these days"

"That can't be right, I don't only have a boyfriend I'm pregnant. How do you like a pregnant girl? I think you are mistaken Adunni"

"He doesn't know you are pregnant and I'm sure he likes you or he believes he does"

"Why are you telling me though?"

She shrugged and I stared at her dully

"Yomi is coming today"

"Oh, how superfantasticaliciously lovely for you"

"That's not even a word Adunni"

"Whatever, who cares, bet you are excited"

"Yes I am" I replied brightly. She frowned slightly and for a moment it seemed that she could see beyond my smile, to my confusion and worry.

We stood in the narrow space between our joined bunks and the next set of joined bunks and continued our conversation while we got dressed and talked about my relationship and feelings for Yomi. I watched myself as I fell into that 'girl in love' ritual of Yomi said this and Yomi said that, then Yomi did this and Yomi did that. As I talked about my lover and friend, I couldn't stop my heart from swelling with pride, or stop the joy from suffusing through me; my adoration for him creeping into my voice. Talking about him to Adunni made me more aware of how much I loved him, how much I missed him and how much I wanted to hold on to him; but this baby, this baby ruins everything was my fevered thoughts. My phone beeped, Yomi was on his way from Abuja.

***

Through some unfortunate circumstance of unusual efficiency, a public-address system was installed in the administrative building on the second day of camp. It then quickly became a tool for psychological and mental torture, constantly having something to say in its screeching, far reaching mechanical voice; from announcing visitors and the program for the day, to reminding errant youth corpers of camp rules and the penalties attached to a breach. Every morning it also played its part in the morning devotion that kept us on our feet for about an hour; and that Saturday afternoon it disrupted the nap I was trying to snatch from the hot afternoon and the lull in chatter and traffic in the hostel. I closed my eyes again, willing sleep to stay; to ignore the rude screaming of the P.A system and hold me, but it refused and packing its light bags it fled.

"Jay, visitors have started arriving, according to that blighted loudspeaker" Adunni said to my turned back. I dragged myself out of the fog sleep had left me in, cocking my ear at the same time for the emotionless voice of the PA system.

"What" I croaked, my voice still heavily laced with sleep.

"They just announced that the gates are now open for visitors to come in, and have since announced someone's arrival on the P.A. system"

"Oh great"

"Yeah, I just hope the rest of the day is not going to be spent announcing every arriving visitor; I might just top myself" Adunni warned peering at me from the top of the Genevieve Magazine she was reading.

As if on cue, the P.A. system crackled and spoke "Adijat Mohammed, you have a visitor, Akeem Mohammed is here to see you" it crackled and repeated the announcement once more before falling silent.

"Yep, we are definitely screwed today" Adunni announced. I laughed.

Now fully awake, I hopped off the bed and proceeded to brush my teeth, swash a mouthful of mouthwash, and reapply my makeup. I painstakingly applied my pink MAC Cosmo lipstick, Yomi's favourite.

At a few minutes past 3pm, the PA crackled again in its familiar grating voice and announced the arrival of Yomi Balogun to see Jadesola Savage.

***

I broke into a short run on seeing Yomi in the milling crowd; he stood a head above most, his white linen shirt sitting easily on his wide shoulders. I could not help the wide grin that spread across my face as I thought of his easy smile, his charm, the kindness in his voice, his teasing. I jumped into his arms winding my arms around his neck; he twirled me round and kissed my cheek and my neck. I was beaming.

"Honey, I've missed youuuuuuuu" I smiled, now shy.

"Have you now, honey?" he said, smiling.

"Come and meet my friend quickly"

"Okay"

I introduced Yomi to Adunni before we headed towards a black Range Rover Evogue. His car was the only one parked within the camp gates; all the other cars were outside. The soldiers at the gate were beaming at us as we got into the car.

I settled into the soft leather seat, cider wood fragrance wafting up from the air conditioning vents while Yomi started the car.

"I don't think they will let me go out of the camp" I said pointing at the soldiers at the gate, "you are supposed to visit, not take me out of camp"

"Don't you worry; you have a special exit pass from the Camp Commandant; I have spoken to him"

"Oh wow, thanks darling, so where are we going?"

"We are going to lunch and anywhere else you want to go. I have a room at the Rockfield Hotel so I can be in town till tomorrow; spend time with my baby" he smiled.

"That is super" I gushed reaching over to hug him again as he drove towards the camp gates; all my previous apprehensions forgotten.

"Bye, bye oga. See you soon oga" was all the shouts we heard from the soldiers at the gate. True to his word, I was let out of camp and now it was just us - the baby, Yomi and I - mine and Yomi's new family, if I let it.

"Darling, how are you?" Yomi asked with emphasis, his voice mellow as he drove through the Jos metropolis.

"I'm fine" I sighed happily and launched into a long story about my stay in camp so far. I talked about Adunni, our hostel for the last six days, and my different roommates and what made them fascinating to me. I was like a river running down its course, I couldn't seem to stop, so I just talked on.

Yomi listened attentively, nodding and smiling. I was mindful not to talk about the morning drills, the jogging and the marching. I did not mention the long hours of standing on Friday and the rain that beat us mercilessly. All of these things would alarm him, set him off, make him worry and I didn't want him upset, we were happy; however temporary it might be.

"So camp has been perfect?" he smiled.

"Yes, yes, it's been fabulous"

"Doesn't sound like the NYSC camp I was in or like any NYSC camp I know for that matter" he continued.

"Its fine, I'm telling you and Adunni is a good friend; she's got my back and all"

"So no marching, no drills, no standing for hours, no jogging no running, nothing?" he asked quietly; a little too quietly.

"There's all that, but nobody is making me do any of it. I have a medical exemption based on ill health so I just lounge about and watch people break a sweat" I replied instantly and he relaxed visibly; that was when I realised he had been as tense as a coil for the last twenty minutes.

"And you never told me you did your National Youth Service, I thought you skipped it" I said lightly.

"No I did not skip National Youth Service, I served in Lagos. It was fun but tough. There was a lot of standing, marching and running in the scorching sun and that is why I am concerned about you"

He has managed to bring it back to me again, he is relentless "Seriously Yomi I am fine"

"And the baby too? Is our baby fine?" he asked.

"Of course, we are both fine"

"Come home" he replied turning into the Rockfield Hotel car park. "You don't have to do any of this; you don't have to be in this dusty town, gadding about in that camp, eating crappy food and sleeping in appalling conditions"

I shrugged, not saying anything.

"If you come home now we can plan our lives, we can decide things and get on with it"

"It's just two more weeks and you have me to yourself forever, just two weeks Yomi" I replied following him into the Rockfield Hotel lounge.

"Two weeks might not be a lot to you, but it's a lot for the baby you are carrying; are you even thinking about the baby at all" he said as we walked into the hotel restaurant.

My excitement was fading and my sense of dread and trepidation coming back in a rush. I held back the urge to heave.

He greeted the receptionist behind the desk who had quickly replaced his bored look with a perky one the moment we walked in; I could only nod at him weakly.

My thoughts ran wildly round my head and I was no longer able to relax. I followed Yomi up the stairs to the room he had booked; I am going to tell him everything, I'm going to blurt it all out and face his anger and disappointment. I can't keep this up anymore. It's doing my head in and I feel half-crazy right now, I thought.

In the room he waved at the overstuffed paisley covered sofa while he moved to the fridge to rummage around. By the time he decided what he wanted from the fridge, orange juice and cracker biscuits, I had consciously arranged myself on the paisley two-seater sofa in a seemingly relaxed pose.

"Darling, I'm trying to understand your reasons for remaining in this useless place for another two weeks, but it's tough" Yomi continued pouring orange juice into two glasses. "Apart from the fact that I miss you no end, there's the baby to worry about, I frankly can't stop worrying and thinking you are jumping and prancing around"

"You sure are going on like a broken record" I replied rudely, "I have not jeopardised the baby's life in anyway; it's hardly more than the size of a pea right now"

"Still you never know" he insisted, ignoring my rudeness.

"The doctors say until you reach the twelve-week mark anything can still happen anyway" I blurted.

Yomi froze, "and what do you mean by that? Something might happen doesn't mean it will, otherwise you and I wouldn't exist right? Lots of babies survive past twelve weeks unless you don't want ours to"

Then he paused for a minute and I could see the moment the thought crossed his mind, it was like a light bulb had suddenly been switched on in his head, "Wait a minute, you don't want something to happen to this baby do you?" he asked, his voice now beginning to rise, his agitation sudden and obvious, "You know what is suddenly funny?"

I waited

"Our roles are oddly reversed, I'm the concerned one, you are the one who thinks a pea sized baby doesn't have to survive beyond twelve weeks" he was now grinding his teeth, "are you telling yourself it's just a pea sized thing and so doesn't count? Are you trying to convince yourself to get rid of this baby? Is that what you want? Is that what you are saying?"

"That is not what I am saying Yomi, I'm only saying we shouldn't get our hopes up over this baby"

"I will get my damn hopes up when I damn well feel like it, don't be telling me what to do with my hopes" he swore at me "it's my baby too and unlike you I'm happy we've made one and would love to be a dad to the baby you are carrying. As far as I can see you are not happy about the idea of motherhood or are you? You want to stay a young frivolous child without a care in the world. Well your reason to care is in there, so you might as well grow up while you are at it. Yes

Jay, grow up. This baby is going to survive past twelve weeks no matter how much you cling to some useless statistics".

I felt helpless in the face of his rage, I couldn't help thinking about how life could be as ironically harsh as it could be unreasonably benevolent and now with my own help was choosing to screw me over in a most fantastic fashion. My helplessness filled me with rage; a rage that was as impotent as the helplessness that caused it, so I screamed my impotent rage at Yomi "That's fine then, get your hopes up, dream about your baby that I am conveniently carrying, I'm not important. It doesn't matter what I feel or what I think as long as your baby is fine yet I'm the one that needs to grow up. The world is not your oyster Yomi, you don't always have to get what you want. You know what? Screw you and your baby talk. Did we plan this? Did we ever talk about a baby before all this happened? Is this what we want right now at this moment?" I screamed, now crying.

"Baby stop" he grabbed my hands gently, "don't do this, yes I agree, the world is not my oyster and I'm sorry I said you should grow up. Of course I'm thinking of you, I know your emotions are out of kilter right now and you have probably been sick a few times in the last week; that is exactly why I am asking you to come home. Come home with me where I can take care of you, watch over you. You are more important to me than any baby but the baby is important too"

I wrenched my hands out of his grasp "Well you haven't been acting like I'm important. It's all about the baby now, baby this, baby that" I continued relentlessly, "I don't want to come home, not to you with your non-stop talk about the baby and how we need to plan our lives around this baby that we didn't even ask for, do stuff, blah blah blah. It's all moving too fast. What if I don't want any of the things you have been going on about? Have you stopped for a minute to think about that? Have you? Oh no, you haven't, I bet you haven't" I finished as Yomi flopped into the sofa, the fight drained out of him.

"You don't want the things I want?" he asked dully, "do you even want this baby at all? Or all you see is an unplanned pregnancy?"

"Yes Yomi, all I see is an unplanned pregnancy" I replied cruelly "and frankly I don't want to keep this baby. I mean what if you leave me, how do I cope then?

"Leave you?"

"Yes" I cut in "people leave all the time you know" I knew I was being irrational; letting my fears and my past take charge of me.

"So that's the issue? You think I'm going to leave you? Jay I'm not going to leave you. Now or ever"

"Well we don't know that" I replied impatiently, "this baby is not part of my plans; it's not what I want. I don't want this baby AT ALL"

Yomi sat staring at me, saying nothing, trying to control the tears that were standing in his eyes waiting to spill, "If that's what you want, then its fine. It's your body and I can't make you keep a baby you don't want. I guess what I want doesn't matter right now, I'm just the sperm donor; I'm just the idiot who got you into an unplanned, unwanted pregnancy. I'll live, even though my baby won't but if the thought of me leaving you is the only reason why you want to get rid of the baby, then what can I say? I can't stop you from punishing our unborn child over your insecurities" he finished hoarsely.

"Yomi stop. Please stop. Don't do this please, I'm begging you, please don't make me keep this baby, please don't make me" I begged, desperate tears now coursing down my face, all my rage suddenly gone like a mist. I fell on my knees and laid my head in his laps letting the sadness and crying take over my body. "I cannot keep this baby, I cannot; I cannot be a mummy now" I kept whispering.

"Come baby, come" he pulled me off my knees, gently cradling me in his arms; his kindness to me in the midst of his own pain is my undoing. I howled like a child. Yomi lifted me easily and set me on the bed; he pulled the duvet over me to my midriff and sat on the edge of the bed, rubbing my back gently.

My crying reduced to sobs and hiccups; I was tired from crying so much and started to feel drowsy. As I fell into a tired sleep I was aware of Yomi lying behind me, his hand rubbing my back; I knew he was crying silently, but I felt a sense of relief; I don't have to keep this baby.

ADUNNI

Earlier today, I watched as Jay jumped into the arms of a well built, dark skinned, afro sporting guy; winding her arms around his neck. He twirled her round kissing her lips and neck. In a breathless voice and eyes that shone with pride and considerable joy, Jay introduced him as her Yomi. He said hello in a voice that was both soft and gravelly.

For the brief moment when I said hello, I realized how gorgeous they looked together, Jay and her Yomi. All the sadness left her shoulders; she looked happy, light and free and gazed at him in utter adoration. His smile was that of a happy man who had found the rest of him. She said something to him and they went off to his car, oblivious of everyone else. I watched as she climbed into the black Range rover and left camp.

I decided to sit on the raised pavement in front of the Medical building from where I could watch corpers and their guests roam around; a few were having a sort of picnic on the parade ground, eating, lying in each other's arms; and some brave souls who had no guests were also having solo picnics; lying alone on pieces of cloth or towel, listening to their iPods, enjoying the weather and the muted noise of the afternoon.

Effiong headed towards me with purposeful strides; I let him come.

"Expecting any visitors?" he asked, flopping down beside me on the pavement.

"Nope" I shook my head, still concentrating on the colourful groups of guests and corpers.

"Me neither" he volunteered "no girlfriend to visit me and my family don't miss me that much, so I figure I should visit with you"

I smiled back, saying nothing.

"You are such an enigmatic lady; you don't volunteer much information, do you?"

"Well I don't have much information to volunteer that's why"

"And why is that? I have met very few ladies who are not dying to tell you their life stories or what they think about a large number of random things"

"You are not a nice guy and you haven't met a lot of nice girls either" I replied.

"You are probably right on the second observation, but I'm a nice guy, a nice guy who wants to hear all about you, what you like doing, what the best part of University was and how you are finding the NYSC experience."

"In one breath you complain about girls who tell you their life story, in the other you ask for the exact same thing from the only girl who doesn't want to bore you with her life story"

"Isn't that life? So shoot" he said, now tugging at the grass blade growing in the crack in the pavement.

"Why don't you go first? That way I know what kind of thing you are interested in hearing"

"I think the only ailment troubling you is "over-cleverness" he replied raising one brow, "I'm happy to go first, unlike you I don't have a lot of skeletons struggling to fall out of my closet"

Even though I knew he was joking, the statement struck home and stung, I winced inside and thought "nice shot Effiong, nice shot."

"Okay so I'm a doctor, recently graduated and relieved, sometimes I wonder what adolescent madness and arrogance caused me to choose a life in Medicine but that's all water under the bridge. I have four sisters, two ahead of me and two after me so I'm an only son and also a middle child. I bet Sigmund Freud would have something to say about that. I had a swell childhood, mixed gender boarding school at ten, first girlfriend at eleven, first kiss and breakup at twelve and that's me basically, I think I have covered the important milestones in childhood"

I burst into laughter, amused at his self-deprecating narrations, "tell me more about each of these milestones"

"Well, I was a troublesome kid and caused my sisters a lot of grief so my parents felt the best way to get me in hand was to ship me off to boarding school and so I ended up miles away from home at the Federal Government College, Abuja, at the tender age of ten. The first term was the toughest but I settled in quickly and by my second year bagged myself a girlfriend as a result of my awesome penmanship. I wore her down with letters; unlike the other boys who didn't want any evidence of their feelings or shall I say wants, lying around, I was happy to put in black and white all the wondrous things I felt for Ada.

She agreed to be my girlfriend in another scribbled note; eleven years old and I had a girlfriend of my own; my life was perfect. After two terms of exchanged letters, hurried meetings after dinner in reading rooms and disused classrooms; two terms of spending my pocket money on ridiculous gifts of candy and gum which left me painfully penniless, Ada agreed to a kiss and so my first kiss happened. It was brief and almost non-existent but for a twelve-year-old me, it was everything. I walked on cloud nine for the rest of the term, no amount of form master threats, senior's punishments or terrible food could take away from that"

I smiled at him and how much he enjoyed laughing at himself.

"Unfortunately, she broke up with me the next school term, she got a better offer from someone who had more money to spend on candy and gum; someone who had the money and the right connections to get her flowers and expensive chocolates from out of town. Poor girl figured my cheap candy and gums couldn't buy her love and broke up with me in another scribbled note. Considering how much I thought I loved her, I moved on rather quickly to be honest; to the next girlfriend and the next girlfriend and the first sexual experience which shortly led to my first pregnancy scare which was in my last year of boarding school. Since then it has been me and my condom everywhere. I was frightened into safe sex. I think all boys should be frightened into safe sex; there is nothing like the fear of your life being over at sixteen to get you to practice safe sex forever.

"Whoa. You do have a lot of cheeky firsts"

"Yes I like 'firsts', the first class I attended in Uni. was Mathematics 101, first exam was Chemistry 153; first paid job was as a lesson teacher teaching chemistry to secondary school students; that supplemented my meagre allowance as a university undergrad. First time I saw you was on the bus that brought us to camp...."

"You saw me on the bus?" I interrupted him.

"Of course I saw you, didn't you see me?"

"Well yes but not properly till we got to camp, what I saw on the bus was the back of your head"

"Well I saw you properly when I got on the bus and watched you for ages through the driver's mirror. I think I freaked the driver out a few times because he kept catching my eyes in the mirror; it was so funny I almost laughed out loud but I didn't want him dropping me in the middle of nowhere so I kept my mouth shut. I did want to climb into the back seat and smack the guy sitting beside you though"

"Smack him? Why?"

"Because he was staring at you almost as much as I was, that's why"

I couldn't help giggling.

"So now your turn" he said turning to me, he has meticulously pulled out all the grass blades growing through the cracks while he was telling me his story.

"It's getting dark here, and the insects are getting more aggressive, they've been going for my arms for the last half hour" I replied.

He stared at me intently for a few seconds, his eyes filled with disappointment.

"So we are not going to talk about you?"

"No... not right now.... But we will, the moment we grab two seats in the dining hall; it's me or these blood sucking insects and right now they are winning"

"Okay let's go" he got up from the pavement and dusted his white shorts, I did the same. We walked in concert to the dining hall.

***

When my father died, I was fourteen and his death was the most devastating thing that could have happened to me; I haven't stopped dreaming about him. On good days, we laugh together in my dreams; he is the young dashing dad I had, his white shirt is dazzling, and his hair is dark and curly.

On bad days, it is an emaciated person I see, skeletal, rasping, bald and pitilessly ravaged by cancer; that is who I see calling my name, reaching out for me; he would fade away before I got to him; on these days, I would wake up in tears, the tears rolling down the side of my eyes and pooling in my ears.

Shortly before he died, my mum stopped taking us to visit him; later when I confronted her she said she wanted our memories of him to be of the laughing, kind person he was. She is wrong, I remember both of him; the exciting, laughing, kind person she wants us to remember and the sickly wasted him she did not want us to see or remember. I remember my dad angry at dying. He did not reconcile himself to death, to leaving us. This is perhaps why he remains such a force in my mind, I know he did not want to leave us, he did not want to leave me; he was taken.

The cancer ward where my father spent the last three months of his life receiving chemotherapy and valiantly fighting the death that smacked away the puny hands of treatment like a giant swatting a fly, was a short walking distance from my school as both were owned and operated by the same University of Lagos.

So one day after school, I skipped my Home Economics after school practice and sneaked off to the hospital. I knew my mum wouldn't get there till about 4pm after dropping off my siblings and getting them lunch; she no longer drove straight to the hospital after school. She had lost a lot of weight too and always looked drawn and tired.

"Adunni, what are you doing here? Where's your mum?" my dad asked, he was propped up on the bed, his face a stretched mask over bone.

"She's dropping the others at home; I told her I had Home Economics practice. I wanted to see you"

He held my hand in his warm dry one and smiled weakly at me, "my darling angel, my cheeky Adumdum, I am delighted to see you" he smiled weakly, ever his charming self, his teeth shinning white in his now bare boned face.

I nodded and sat in the chair by his bed, drawing it closer to his bed, "are you taking care of your siblings for me?" he asked.

I nodded again, I couldn't bring myself to speak, a nasty lump sat firmly in my throat, making it difficult to respond, "And mummy? Are you taking care of mummy too? Are you being nice to her, no sassing? No giving her trouble?" He persisted.

I had gone to bed one day a sweet child and woken up the next day a truculent angry moody teenager who answered back and hated the whole world; he knew I was giving my mum a tough time.

As far as I was concerned, the only person who understood me was here, sick and dying. I didn't see any reason to listen to anyone else or cut anybody any slack they didn't need; but I wasn't going to tell him that; even while sick my father could get very angry very quickly and tell me off.

"Mummy needs you to be nice to her till I come back okay?" he continued, squeezing my hand.

"I am nice to mummy, and everyone else but when are you coming back?" I asked; somewhere in my young mind I suspected the horrible answer to my question.

"Soon love, I'm coming back soon, cos I'm going to beat this thing" he replied staunchly; "the doctors are saying good things, they are all my friends and they are working hard, tirelessly to get me out of here, so you and I can hang out like we used to"

"But you look so tired" I replied unwilling to believe the doctors here were doing enough for him. I had seen them walking around slowly, clip board in hand, they were not running towards him or surrounding his bed working diligently. What was daddy talking about here?

"See that juice bag over there?" He pointed at the red drip bag hanging over him, its wire snaking down into the back of his left hand, it looked ugly and deadly, like a parasite taking blood from him rather than giving it to him.

I nodded again.

"That juice is making sure I get my energy back so I can be out of here in no time"

"That's not juice, that's blood and it is disgusting" I replied darkly wrinkling my nose.

"Oh dear. My Adumdum is losing her sense of humour, daddy needs to come home soon to restore it. Of course, its blood I know you are smart enough to know that"

"Okay" I nodded and the tears rolled down my face, I don't know how I knew, but sitting right there by his bed, I realised my dad, my handsome dashing, loving dad with the funny anecdotes and the impromptu trips to ice cream stores and family weekends in Abuja, was not coming back home. My heart broke into many tiny pieces, shards that pierced what was left till I felt the pain physically and my knees weakened and my stomach churned angrily.

"Come here ducky don't cry." he hugged me close, "now you are making me cry. We are both cry-babies. Cry baby Adum" he tickled me. I tried to laugh but my smile wobbled before it could become a laugh.

"How's your drama club going, are you having fun?" he asked. We proceeded to discuss school and the classes I enjoyed and the ones I hated and all the after-school activities I had signed up for. I didn't tell him I had dropped out of many of them in the last two months; instead I made up stories about how much fun I was having in school.

A few minutes to four I got up to leave, "mummy will soon be here" I said.

"Okay ducky... I'm glad you came Adum"

"Me too"

"Adunni" he called after me as I got to the end of his bed and signalled me back, I turned back and he dragged me close to him "I need you to know that I'm proud of you and I will always be. You are strong and beautiful and you are going to do great things"

I nodded and hugged him before I left. I cried all the way home. It was the last time I saw or spoke to my dad. He never came back home and my sense of humour probably died with him too.

Sometimes I wish I had sneaked out of school to see him a few more times, to snatch more moments with him, but at the time I couldn't, it felt like too much. I no longer wanted to associate the smell of the hospital with my dad...for me, the smell of the hospital was not of drugs and antiseptic cleaning fluid, it was of death, despair and sadness; it was a smell of fear and lost hope. I wanted to think of my dad as happy, laughing, eating, lying on the sofa snoring after a particularly long night shift, doing the normal things fathers did.

I also clung to the hope that he wasn't lying and was indeed getting better and so there was no need to sneak in to see him, he was coming home soon... stupid child that I was.

***

I turned over in my bunk bed and on to Jay's bed to avoid my bed which had grown warm with my body heat, I laid quietly for a minute, luxuriating in the coolness of Jay's bed and the stillness of the hostel; everybody was either sleeping, outside somewhere or in the fellowship hall adjacent to the Mammy market.

The fellowship hall is home to a rather well organised non-denominational Christian fellowship in camp called NCCF. I believe it's well organized because they even have printed programme pamphlets, a hat-wearing guy thrust one at me yesterday. How they got the colourful pamphlets designed and printed in this backwater totally beats me but evidently they did and each week of camp had been meticulously planned and jam-packed with programmes; 'Standing in the gap' on Tuesday, 'Bible study' on Wednesday, 'Prayer meetings' on Thursday and 'Drama Night' on Friday, were some of the events advertised in the pamphlet and I found it both inspiring and sad. While providing something for the religious faithful to do with the little spare time they had, it was an ardent testimony to the prolific and viral industry that religion has become in this country. Everywhere you go there is a church or a fellowship, there is singing and the sound of tambourines; loud speakers turned outwards and blaring at you angrily, forcefully sharing sermons and testimonies with you. There are Wednesday services and Friday vigils in addition to Sunday services.

After my dad died, all my faith died with him; it wasn't helped by the fact that all I heard during the first year after his death was "God knows best" "God loved him more" "He has gone home to rest" Words that only filled my young mind with angry questions, 'gone home where? This is his home and we are his family and he has left us. How can this god love him so much that he takes him away from his young family, what kind of god is that? Surely loaning him to us for say twenty or thirty more years wouldn't have hurt this god that loves him so much? Oh, and if this god was going to take him, did he have to do it through something as degrading as cancer? Did he have to suffer? I had no answers to my questions and no patience to look for them. I settled drowsily into Jay's rapidly warming bed, hugging my random memories to myself and listened to the clamorous music floating into the hostel from another mushroom fellowship in the next hostel, something called "Sisters in Faith"

Day 7 NYSC Camp

BECKY

"I basically hate these rich kids and how they strut around camp"

"Tell me about it" Adesuwa replied, "They act like the sun and the moon shine out of their bottoms with their designer jeans and sunglasses. Have you seen how they spend money in the Mammy market?"

"No, I don't go to the Mammy market"

"My sister, you should visit the Mammy market sometime, they spend money the way you would use rain water, without any care. Some of them don't even eat the food provided by the camp"

"That's impossible" I said

"I am telling you, they eat breakfast, lunch and dinner in the Mammy market" Adesuwa said nodding.

"I can't imagine it"

"One day I will be rich too, I am tired of poverty life" Adesuwa sighed.

"What do you know of poverty life?" I asked

"Plenty my sister, plenty" she said.

This new thing of Adesuwa calling me her sister is starting to grate on my nerves.

"Welcome to my world then, my father lost his job when we were kids and he never got round to getting another one, so with one income coming from my mother's shop, our meals soon became very meagre" I said.

"Well, there was eleven of us kids so there was rarely ever enough food to fill our stomachs, it was like my mum couldn't stop having children despite the fact that she sells tomatoes and my father drives a bus" Adesuwa said.

"It wasn't that our meals were lacking in quantity, but rather in quality" I continued, "we made and stored large amounts of the maize meal Ogi and ate it almost every day with boiled beans or Akara and sometimes by itself"

Adesuwa nodded in agreement, "We drank Ogi too like mad people, and lunch? Lunch was always eba, day in day out, eba with okra everyday"

"Lunch was always eba or semolina with us too and dinner was whatever we could rustle up, things like eggs, milk, meat and fish were luxuries" I added.

"What eggs? What meat?" Adesuwa asked, "We ate those things on festive days and some festive days we didn't even get them. I'm not impressed with my parents at all, especially as my mother still always managed to find money to buy 'aso-ebi' to wear to someone's birthday, wedding or burial but no money to put fish, meat or eggs in her children's food; and don't let me even start on my father – he beat the living daylights out of us regularly and he didn't need a lot of reason either" Adesuwa said.

It felt eerily like Adesuwa and I had rather similar childhoods, hungry, deprived, abused and saddled with irresponsible, uncaring parents.

"My father was like that too; to be honest I'm not so crazy about my parents either. I don't know why people like that are allowed to have kids. I have always wondered if mother worried about us at all. She would leave the house every morning after the customary breakfast of ogi and moinmoin or Akara and never return before 6pm. Sometimes we would drink the garri instead of making eba solely because we had no vegetable soup to eat the eba with. I quickly learnt to go foraging in search of the vegetable called Gbure; they cooked well and went down well with eba" I said.

"You were smart enough to forage, I was too scared to enter the bushes" Adesuwa shrugged.

"Initially, I was afraid too and would stay largely on the edges of the bushes, but then Bala, a gardener in one of the better houses on our street noticed me foraging a few times and showed me where to go and how to find good mushrooms that could pass as meat in a stew; delicious oyster mushrooms. I always kept an eye out for the mushrooms when I went in search of vegetables especially because Rachel my sister had taken a liking to them and eaten better when she had them in her soup to fish out and eat in between morsels of eba. The mushrooms also made me feel like I was providing some sort of balanced diet for my younger ones so I encouraged Rachel and Abraham to eat them by telling them it would make them grow tall and strong"

"You are a good sister, my older sisters were too busy fighting amongst themselves over boys, dresses and the few powders and hair accessories they had to even feed us younger ones" Adesuwa said.

"I almost killed my siblings once though from my foraging attempts" I said quietly, still upset by the memory of our close call with death.

"Really, how?" she asked

"One day I went foraging, I had only managed to pick a small bowl of 'Gbure' vegetables in over an hour and I was starting to wonder if there were other foragers frequenting the same area" I said.

"Were there?" Adesuwa asked.

"I foraged in a short stretch of forest on the way to the local market, I wouldn't put it past the market women to pick all the wild vegetables there to sell cheaply in the market"

"Okay" Adesuwa said.

"Just when I was giving up, I spotted a row of beautiful oyster mushrooms, I was elated and hurried towards them; they were growing straight out of the soil rather than from a dead log or sick tree trunk where I usually found them. On closer look, they looked slightly different, like oyster mushrooms but with a slight hollow like a funnel. I ignored the warning voice in my head and told myself these were definitely oyster mushroom. I had picked oyster mushrooms from this forest enough times to know and if they were not oyster mushrooms they were probably in the same family and just as edible and delicious. I went ahead and picked them along with some more vegetables and hurried home to cook lunch.

When I got home, Abraham had a scowl on his face and Rachel had been crying. "We are hungry" he said, like his face wasn't speaking volumes. I apologised profusely and promised him that lunch would be ready shortly"

"You were gone for looooooong. I'm hungry" Rachel whined, her eyes filling with fresh tears.

"Let me give you a little garri to drink; it's not a lot so you have to let it soak, okay?" I begged her as I began to quickly rinse the vegetables for cooking.

"Can I have garri too?" Abraham asked,

"No you can't, there won't be enough left to make eba for all of us" I replied as I poured water into the handful of garri in a chipped ceramic bowl. I placed the bowl on a higher shelf so that it would swell up and give Rachel more to scoop into her mouth; hopefully filling her hungry stomach while I cooked.

"You have mushrooms" Rachel said in a singsong voice, her delight evident.

"Yes Rayray, that's why I was so loooong, I was getting you nice mushrooms for your lunch"

"Okay" she replied happily, walking off with her bowl of garri, I watched with half an eye to make sure Abraham didn't beg it all off her.

"Thirty minutes later and the vegetable soup was ready, a little watery but looking good. I decided to check it for salt and splashed a little of the sauce on my palm and a piece of mushroom fell into my palm, I licked it all up hurriedly before it could burn me; it tasted delicious, I thought proudly. Five minutes later and I was in the most excruciating pain ever; it was as if someone was scrubbing my insides with sharp stones. I knew immediately it was the mushrooms. Fear and nausea washed over me and I could feel my bowels moving angrily as I rushed off to the bathroom where I quickly stuck my fingers down my throat and forced myself to throw up. I threw up repeatedly until there was nothing left of the ogi and Akara I had for breakfast"

"Wow that is scary, what did you then do?"

"I realised this was a race against time and I had to think quickly to win this. The biting pain in my stomach was still there, dull but there and my vision was starting to blur. I rushed back to the kitchen looking around frantically till I found the plastic keg of palm oil. I have seen palm oil being used in a Nollywood movie to neutralise the effect of poison, so I guzzled it down in the hope that it was not some theory made up strictly for the entertainment of a gullible audience. Thankfully it wasn't and a long twenty minutes later, my stomach had settled down a bit, my vision was no longer blurred and the nausea was reduced. I threw out the pot of vegetable soup into the gutters that ran along the fence outside our house"

"Oh my God, did that truly happen to you Becky or are you making it up?"

"I swear to God, it happened to me. I still get a sinking feeling in my belly when I remember how close I had come to death and how close to death I had brought Rachel and Abraham just because I was desperate and impatient. If a tiny sliver of mushroom and sauce could cause so much pain, I can only imagine what would have happened if I had actually eaten the mushrooms in a meal or given it Rachel and Abraham. Nothing can ever make me eat a mushroom again"

"I think you have totally turned me off mushrooms now"

"Some years later out of curiosity, I checked online for the name and mycology of the mushrooms I ate and I found out that I had eaten the Funnel oyster mushrooms and would have died the most painful death ever; bleeding through the nose, vomiting blood, sweating profusely and yes the sharp pain in my stomach like sharp knives would have gotten many times worse"

I did not bother to tell Adesuwa that after pouring the vegetable soup into the gutters I had watched dispassionately as Baba Ashiru's dog 'Riro' sniffed the soup cooling in the gutter, took a few licks of it and ran off, that the big lick was the end of Riro. He died howling and vomiting blood. Baba Ashiru blamed our other neighbour's wife who he insisted was a witch.

"We thank God that didn't happen to you" Adesuwa said, referring to the symptoms I had described.

"Yes, thank God"

"That day I had to go to the local grocery shop on our street to beg for a loaf of bread. Luckily for me, it was manned by a young girl called Aina who kindly gave me a big loaf of bread after I told her we had no food and my parents were away. I hurried home to share the bread with my siblings; Abraham wolfed it down gulping water as he went, no questions asked. Rachel on the other hand glared at me doubtfully and demanded to know the whereabouts of the vegetable soup and mushrooms; bread was not the lunch I made her wait for and she wanted to know why"

"You were practically raising them" Adesuwa sighed.

"That I was"

I told Rachel, "Rayray the vegetable was bad, the mushrooms were bad mushrooms and they spoilt the vegetables and made it taste bad, so I threw it away"

"You threw it away?" she asked, "but I wanted to eat the vegetables" she replied, her voice trembling.

"Yes I know love, I know you wanted to eat vegetables and I will make you vegetables on another day but not today; from now on we won't be eating mushrooms, you have eaten enough to make you grow big and strong, if you eat anymore mushrooms now you might grow too big and become a giant. Do you want to become a giant?"

"No I don't" she shook her head, "so I have eaten enough mushrooms to grow big and strong?" she asked again.

"Yes you have, you are a good girl, just finish your bread now and we can play games"

"Okay" she said and went off to finish the bread she was clutching.

"That story is just humbling, I hope and intend to be a much better parent than my parents, even if it kills me"

"Me too"

***

The very next day, like some demon was taunting me, I saw the funnel oyster mushrooms again; perhaps it was talking about them the day before that made me spot them but I saw them and they looked exactly like the ones that almost killed me, beautifully designed and odourless – a beautiful angel of death on the narrow path beside our hostel walls.

I went back into the hostel and got a cellophane bag, wore it over my hands like a glove and returned to carefully pick the mushrooms that were again growing straight from the soil and not on a dead log or dying tree. Closing the bag around the six little stumps, I walked away, delighted with my find and convinced they would come in handy someday, may be soon – a little sprinkle in someone's food or drink would yield thrilling results; or if I could get access to the camp kitchen? Maybe not, again mass death would draw attention and there is nothing ingenious about killing a lot of people in one fell swoop, I thought to myself, enjoying the beauty of my thoughts.

I slipped the bag of mushrooms into the raffia handbag holding my bible and study book and continued to consider all the people I could "bless" with these mushrooms. I was lost in the beauty of my thoughts, when I walked into him.

"Watch it lady" he said, his accent Northern but tinged with something else, something foreign.

"I'm sorry", I replied automatically as I took a better look at his face; he was made on one of God's showing-off days and the result is a face chiselled from granite with features perfectly defined and flawlessly symmetrical, laughing eyes and a row of shiny white teeth, arranged unvaryingly like corn on a cob, perfectly aligned, his mouth a symmetrical shield around them. His limbs are long and seem loosely attached to his slim frame, his fingers also long and shapely. Despite his long limbs I wouldn't describe him as very tall, 6ft at most. He is so dark, he's almost midnight blue, and he is unbelievably beautiful. I absorbed all of this in a fraction of a second and quickly replaced my scrutiny with a nonchalant gaze, stepping out of his way.

He smiled a knowing smile, knowing the effect of his looks on women and even some men and had probably seen this many times, the scrutiny, the realisation, the sucker punch in the stomach, the insouciant gaze followed by the weak smile.

"That's okay....take it easy okay?" he said.

"Yes, thank you" I replied feeling odd as I clutched my raffia bag and turned to go into the hostel for the "Sisters in Faith" fellowship starting in fifteen minutes by my bedside.

I love Dr Effiong and can't imagine that I am falling in love with someone else at the same time. Sister Becky, guide your heart jealously it is the well spring of life, I admonished myself as I scraped the bottom of my shoes on the door ledge before entering the hostel.

JAY

The rest of the weekend was spent in cautious conversations. Yomi and I like two adversaries circled each other, waiting for the other to strike first. I kept my thoughts in check and we both avoided talking about the baby for the rest of the weekend. We ate, swam, watched movies and did all the activities that would otherwise make for a relaxing weekend but we were both tense and unhappy. On Sunday, Yomi did some work on his laptop and I slept for hours and swam till I was hungry; then I had some grilled chicken and lettuce and mango salad by the pool side.

Then it was Monday morning and time to get back to the camp. I got dressed slowly, thinking about Yomi and how kind and good he is despite being raised by a cold nasty woman.

I remember the first time I met Yomi's mum, it was like meeting a shark with the heart of a crocodile and the eyes of a snake.

She smiled at me coldly, the smile not reaching her eyes "Hello Miss Savage. The last time I saw you, you were this high" she said hitting her knee with the side of her hand.

"How is your dad?" her cold smile was frozen in place.

"He is fine"

"I can't imagine anyone leaving such a lovely, lovely fellow, so dashing and warm" she continued and I knew she was referring to my mum; it was like a kick in the guts; an unexpected and swift kick.

"That's not necessary mum" Yomi interjected her, "let's go upstairs Jay" he put his palm in the small of my back and propelled me upstairs.

His parents had invited us to dinner, primarily to meet their son's girlfriend but it felt more like I had put my head in a snake's mouth. The animosity from Mrs Balogun was hard to believe or understand and the evening was filled with many more jabs and thrusts from her.

Yomi tried to rescue me a few times but it just fuelled the flames of her anger more; the angry dragon in her wouldn't be tamed; it kicked and bit and watched me with malevolent eyes.

"So you went to Unilag?" she asked.

"Yes ma"

"But why? All your brothers schooled abroad"

"Fola didn't"

"But Dele and Richard did, right?" it wasn't a question.

"Yes" I mumbled.

"I wonder why you were sent to Unilag then"

"She wasn't sent to Unilag mum. You make it sound like a punishment, her dad wanted her close to home and Unilag is a good school" Yomi answered.

She huffed in disagreement and continued picking at the lettuce and tomatoes on her plate.

"What did you study?" she asked again.

"Mechanical Engineering"

"Very good" she nodded, as if she was granting her approval, albeit reluctantly.

"So what is the plan now? Are you planning to work or just be a woman of leisure? That would come to you easily"

"What would come to her easily?" Yomi asked with a steely gaze.

She smiled bravely in response.

"Whatever Jay decides to do, I am sure she will do very well, she strikes me as a bright young lady" Yomi's father cut in dryly, "do pass the salad bowl this way Yomi" he smiled and that particular storm blew over.

"How is your darling dad?" she asked a few minutes later, now smiling a little less coldly.

"He is well, thank you ma'am"

"I hear he owns a fishery in Epe now and is actively involved in running it?"

"Yes he is and loving it"

"How entrepreneurial of him, I cannot imagine him as a fish farmer, your ever so dashing father; you know I once worked with him?"

"Oh I didn't know that"

The air was so tense you could cut it with a knife.

"He was debonair in his day; his sharp suits and dapper style were legendary in diplomatic circles and he wore these hats" she tapped her finger on the table trying to remember.

"Homburgs" I volunteered.

"Yes, and he had them in different colours to match his suits"

It was awkward to hear my dad being discussed so familiarly and passionately by this cold woman.

"He still wears them" I replied, too drained from her attacks to mention that although he wore Homburgs most of the time, my father also sometimes wore Panamas and Fedoras; after all to most people hats were just hats and there was no distinction between them.

"Yes his elegance was sartorial" Mr Balogun said in a toneless voice, his eyes angry. I was confused by the whole experience; if only I knew why.

A few hours later we were getting ready to leave when Yomi's brother Bamidele breezed in. I had met him a few times before and found him charming and funny although rather distracted. He had a stressed hurried air about him and always seemed to be rushing off somewhere; either on his way back to the hospital where he worked as a doctor or rushing off to play tennis or something.

"Hello everyone, did I miss dinner?" he grinned, leaning over to greet his mum "hello mummy"

"Don't hello mummy me young man. You work too hard in that crummy place and yes you have missed dinner. There's a plate waiting in the kitchen somewhere if you go in and talk nicely to Mama Julia" Mrs Balogun was smiling affectionately as she spoke to Bamidele.

"Hello gorgeous, I can see you are still with this ugly man? Such a terrible thing. You should leave him for me" Bamidele said hugging me affectionately.

"You know Yomi is not ugly, he's lovely and handsome" I smiled, happy to see Bamidele, who was a like a ray of sunshine in the otherwise stormy and ominous room.

Yomi who had been moodily silent for the last half hour, turned from the bar where he was having a quiet discussion with his dad, "Stay away from my woman young man" he said pointing one finger at his brother jocularly.

"She's too lovely for you bro, way too lovely"

"The Savage women have a thing for doctors, don't they love? Lots of love for doctors, so Yomi do be wary of this one, they can be a treacherous and fickle lot" Mrs Balogun suddenly chipped, smiling distantly. Her final dagger delivered, she got up and sailed out of the room.

"That's enough from you. You don't know where to stop do you?" Mr Balogun thundered at his wife's retreating back "insulting your guest is a new low even for you"

There was a brief deafening silence, Bamidele hurriedly walked off in the direction of the kitchen.

"Let's get out of here babes" Yomi said, his face like the clouds before a heavy storm, dark and angry, "I shouldn't have brought you here, mum is never going to change"

"It was nice meeting you again Jadesola" Mr Balogun said, holding my hand in his large palms, "I think you are a lovely, lovely lady and Yomi is lucky to have you"

"Thank you sir, it was lovely meeting you again too" my voice shook as I answered.

In the car, I was silent, staring out of the window, too ashamed to talk, too furious to cry. I just sat and stared, my mind in a jumble. I don't remember ever feeling so ashamed in my life, eighteen years gone and she could still do this; what kind of mother did I have? Did she have sex with every Tom, Dick and Harry while she was married to my dad? Which doctor did she love that Mrs Balogun knows about?

"Jay, I am so sorry about how this evening has gone, I have no idea what got into my mum, she is not the easiest person on a good day but today she has pushed the boat out, I am so sorry" Yomi begged turning to glance at my face as he drove.

"It's not your fault love" I replied, still staring out of the window at cars driving in the opposite direction towards Lekki, "it's not your fault my mum loves doctors and obviously loved them while she was with my dad"

"You don't know that Jay. Please don't listen to my mum"

"Please Yomi, let's be real here. I spent all evening wondering why your mum was so cold and unfriendly, and she was kind enough to tell me. She hates me because of my mum the slut" I was crying now, the tears streaming down my face, I wiped at them with the back of my hand and reached blindly for the tissues in the box compartment between Yomi's seat and mine.

"Don't say that Jay, don't ever say that about your mum; and please don't cry. I can't bear to see you cry honey. Please stop crying. This is all my fault; I should have warned you about my mum but I was hoping she would love you as easily as I love you. I can't imagine anyone in their right minds not loving you. I'm so sorry Jay, please let's put all of this behind us please"

"Put all of this behind us?" I asked incredulously, "your mum hates me"

"My mum does not hate you. She has probably had issues with your mum in the past but that is between them. My dad loves you, Bamidele adores you and most importantly I love you with all my heart. My mum doesn't count; you are not going to spend your life with my mum"

"What's the point?" I replied tiredly still crying into the wad of tissues in my hand, it is the shame that hurts the most, the knowledge that I know so little about my mother and that there are other people, strangers who know so much more about her, unsavoury things that they can use as weapons to hit me with, to hurt me. How does one go through life this naked? Never knowing when another story about your mother is going to strike. She of the red lips and clicking high heels and swishing dresses; my attractive, vivacious and unashamedly fickle mother.

I cried harder.

Day 8 NYSC Camp

ADUNNI

Jay came back to camp that Monday morning, just before the bugle calling us to morning devotion went off. She was already dressed in her white vest and green khaki pants, they have been washed and crisply ironed. I enviously imagined the hot luxurious bath she must have had at the hotel where she spent the last two nights and the quiet sleep on soft clean sheets in a room that was devoid of sweaty talkative women and the smell of illicit cooking. Still she looked drained, like something a bored cat has been playing with, all tired and run down.

"Hello darling"

"Hey stranger, welcome back to reality"

"I know right. It was kinda hard coming back here" Jay climbed her bunk and sat on the edge, her booted legs dangling over the side.

"I don't know why you bothered to come back, I'm getting tired of this camp, I need a hot bath and a few night's sleep in a room where there are no women chattering, snoring and laughing in the middle of the night".

"You sound fed up" Jay replied swinging her legs back and forth as much as the little space between the bunks could allow.

"Tell me about it. I can't wait for this to end"

We complained to each other for a few more minutes while I got dressed. I made a quick job of it as there was no motivation to spend ages looking at a hand mirror when everything was likely to go to pieces in a few minutes of running around the parade ground.

It was our second Monday in camp and the inter-Platoon games were starting. Football, volleyball, long jump, cultural dance displays, theatre plays and a beauty contest were some of the competing events planned for the two weeks left of camp, but not even the thought of all these activities and the possibility of the fun they represented was enough to distract me from the fact that I was getting tired of camp life, the noise, the food, the dust, all the bodies cramped together in what was gradually becoming a small space in my mind and the constantly shouting soldiers and their infantile whips.

I could only hope for the two weeks to pass quickly. I could already feel my health flagging and I was worried about what this could mean for me. I was a little bit more tired at the end of each day and finding it harder to get up in the mornings. The food we were forced to eat was not helping either. I saw and ate the most peculiar mishmash of food. An assortment I don't think is served in any home I know of. That Monday morning, Jay and I ate a breakfast of boiled yam, fried eggs and boiled plantain all dumped together in a chipped ceramic plate with flower designs. After the hiccups of the first few days that sent me running into the bushes, my stomach quickly resigned to the tests and tribulations of camp food and began to present a stoic façade to all the crazy food I ate while I avoided the bushes and the toilets as much as I could, controlling my bowels with a will I didn't know I had.

The camp toilets were a no-go zone, you could smell them from a hundred metres away and you could hear the green flies from fifty, buzzing around purposefully. My first visit to the toilet was also my last. The toilets were full and overflowing, every inch of the toilet seat, toilet cover, the flushing handle and toilet base was covered in faeces in different stages of drying. There were fingerprints of excreta on the walls, on the doors, everywhere, it made you wonder if people came to the toilet without any forward plans for how they were going to clean up afterwards, and what did they do? Wipe their bottoms with their hands and transfer to the walls? Wipe their bottoms on the walls and doors directly? How did they get their bottoms on the walls, doors and toilet covers? Did that effectively clean their bottoms to their satisfaction? This was supposed to be a female toilet and yet there was faeces maniacally smeared everywhere you looked; you were stepping in it and inhaling it. I ran out of the toilet the first day I went in, my desire to empty my bowel completed removed for another twenty four hours. The next time around, I made for the bushes and continued to visit the bushes as infrequently as I could manage.

After presenting our stomachs with their share of the morning's trials, Jay and I quickly headed to the parade ground, we preferred not to wait for the soldiers to come screaming and shouting for us to get away from the Mammy market.

"Hi girls" Becky, one of the self-appointed leaders of our Platoon called out to us, crossing the dirt path to Jay and me.

"Hello"

She was not only a self-appointed leader of our Platoon, she was also the self-styled leader of the mushroom fellowship in the second female hostel and every day they would meet to sing and clap energetically like their lives depended on it.

"Are you guys looking for the cultural troupe?" she asked smiling, tall and heavy set, her white vests were neatly tucked into the white shorts sitting firmly in the middle of her ample waist and she had her hair in neat straight cornrows running from the front of her head to the back of her skull. Her fore head was wide and her eyes were set close together in her face, she was not particularly pretty but she looked strong and sturdy; like a well fed, well trained horse, like someone who could take care of herself in all circumstances.

"No we are not" Jay replied, a very blank look on her face "should we?"

"But you guys signified interest in joining the troupe when it was announced on Wednesday" she countered, still smiling.

"No, we did not, you are confusing us with some other people" Jay replied shaking her head, she pulled me and we started to walk on.

"Unless of course listening to an announcement now means signifying interest" I smiled to dull the barb of my sarcasm.

She stared at me keenly for half a minute before falling into step with us; "Very well, why don't you just try things out? Our Platoon needs to win something in the inter-Platoon competition and the cultural dance competition is a good place to start. I haven't seen either of you at volleyball practice or drama practice. You need to participate in something and not just 'make friends'" she cupped her fingers in inverted commas".

It felt a bit like she was scolding us even though she was smiling lightly, I could feel the dislike she was trying hard to hide.

"Thank you, we will think about it, no need to make us feel guilty you know" Jay replied.

"No, no, no, that is not my intention, I'm just saying be a team player, do something for your Platoon, we need to have a perfect dance ready for the competition on Saturday and we are counting on everybody in the Platoon to pull their weight. We already have a good volleyball team and the drama practice is well underway, so if you want to be good team players, the dance troupe is practicing over there" she pointed at a building of classrooms on the way to the camp gates.

"Okay, okay, just chill, we will go there and see what we can do, I don't see how we can add value, but we will go" Jay replied in a testy voice.

"Moral support then. Give them moral support, I personally look forward to seeing you there. It's that building over there, see you guys there"

"Let's just go" I dragged Jay away.

"I personally look forward to seeing you there" Jay repeated in a mocking voice, "That is one nasty lady; so forceful, with her weird smile and all that; trying hard to be nice and not succeeding much" I was surprised at the vehemence in Jay's voice. She had been tetchy since she came back to camp. I suspected a lover's quarrel and placed a soothing arm around her waist.

"I'm not even sure she was trying to be nice, with her inverted commas and everything but that's okay, we won't let her get to us"

"You saw that too didn't you?" Jay asked.

"Yes I did, she's a silly girl"

"Cow" Jay added.

I noticed Becky almost as soon as I arrived in camp; stomping around with a forced smile sometimes with a tall skinny girl with very big teeth in tow. Becky's heavy build and stride coupled with the loud voice of her friend who said everything at the top of her voice meant that you noticed them everywhere they went together.

Every time our Platoon met which was every day, Becky's voice could always be heard offering one insistent opinion or the other; she wanted everything done just so and anyone who disagreed got her unpleasant smile and keen stare.

I don't think a lot of people liked her; with her pushy nature, eerie smile and dark unsmiling eyes that looked at you intensely as if she was memorising you, not just your face, but also your thoughts, your secrets, your soul before cruelly stripping you of everything, peeling off your skin to confirm what she already knew was underneath, eyes that do not know how to smile, they watch, they learn, they file away, cruel eyes; Becky had cruel eyes.

Having given our word, Jay and I went off in search of our Platoon's cultural troupe. Two detours later, one to the Press room to flip through the newspapers that were delivered daily and another to briefly watch a football match that was just kicking off, we found the dancers in one of the classroom-like buildings, as promised. Becky was already there and waved us over like old friends; we ignored her.

A dance routine was going on; sixteen people in four rows of four; six men and ten women dancing in unison to music from an iPad on the window. An assorted group of on lookers stood at the back of the building with Becky; although she was no longer waving us over, she was smiling at us lazily like a cat to a mouse.

A coach stood in front of the dancers, watching their steps and clapping in rhythm.

"You have to move in unison. Listen to the song, learn the rhythm of it and let yourself do the steps you have learnt to the rhythm" the coach shouted, "If you have to look at the feet of the person beside you or in front of you, you have not learnt the rhythm of the dance and you will keep missing your steps. Watching the next person's feet will always leave you one step slower than the rest, you can't afford to do that" he said, clapping and walking round the dancers.

"Ikemefuna, join me, let's do the steps again, the rest of you watch" he ordered, "it's not difficult, but you have to concentrate" he signalled to the guy manning the iPad who quickly restarted the song they had been practicing to. The coach and Ikemefuna turned their backs on the rest of the dance crew and began to dance.

"He dances from somewhere inside him"

"That's right" Jay said "the dance seems to flow out from the centre of him through his finger tips and his toes, to every part of his body, he is in tune with his body"

"Ikemefuna is the same, their rhythm is beautiful; they are like a musically married couple"

"Excellent musicality"

"Jay that is not even a word"

"Yes it is, make up your own words and stop vetoing mine"

"So now you are Wole Soyinka?"

"He started somewhere"

Ikemefuna and the coach stopped dancing as the song ended and the coach beckoned to the group again "Now do it. Put your mind to it, concentrate and follow the rhythm. We have to win this competition and I'm counting on you guys"

The dancers moved back to the space in the middle of the room and Ikemefuna joined them, all eyes on him now, as they began to dance to the music from the iPad.

"These dance steps look simple; why can't they get it right? They are so clumsy" a girl sitting on the window sill behind me muttered in irritation.

"You will be surprised at how hard to master these steps can be" Becky suddenly replied from beside us, startling Jay and me. Jay shifted away from Becky's looming presence till she was practically leaning into me.

"I don't think so" she replied, "I mean just look, its two-one-two-two-one-one" she slapped her hand against the wall in a beat "and they turn around when the song pauses then they move into a circle and spread out a bit and repeat those first set of steps"

"You should join them then, why give instructions and pass judgements from the side-lines" Becky replied.

"Nne, thank you" a guy with a thick Igbo accent clapped his hands in agreement with Becky; "My sister, by the time you join the dancers you will realise it's not easy. What we need you to do right now is join this dream ensemble and stop critiquing from the fence line"

"Christie, it's true, you will be surprised at how difficult these dances are, they are usually much more difficult than they appear, and I personally respect their efforts" Lucy an extremely skinny sinewy lady who I had failed to notice before also chipped in.

"Okay then, I will join the dancers, I don't see the big deal" Christie said jumping off the window sill and joining the dancers who had briefly taken a break to listen to more suggestions from their coach.

"For someone who was convinced of how easy the dance is and said so loudly, Christie is proving to be a bad dancer" I whispered a few minutes later.

"A disjointed, uncoordinated, no-idea-what-her-limbs-are-doing-half-the-time kind of dancer" Jay added "It's always provocative to me when I meet people who have a totally different and better impression of themselves as opposed to what the world can see, on one hand they are oblivious of their shortcomings and probably go on to do great things solely because they are ignorant of how badly they started out or they go on and make a total fool of themselves because they are unaware of how bad they are at this thing"

"Unfortunately Christie falls in the latter category, she is not going to win any dancing medals for our Platoon; her flailing around is so appalling, the rest of the room is laughing behind their hands; look at them turning their faces towards the window to laugh" I added in agreement.

"Except for one person" Jay pointed surreptitiously "can you see how he is watching her?"

"Nne, I can see you are enjoying the dance" he called out to her "I can see it's just as easy as you said. Keep up the good work" he was the guy who had earlier challenged Christie to join the 'dream ensemble and stop critiquing from the fence line'.

"Ahhhhhhhh. You know I am suffering here" Christie said bursting into laughter and prancing in and out of step with the rest of the dancers "Okay, I accept, you win, you got me, dancing is hard work"

"I think she needs to stop and get out of there before she hurts anyone, she certainly has no idea how horribly she is dancing; she thinks she is suffering but in actual fact the rest of the dancers are the ones suffering"

"Well she can't see their baleful looks" Jay said.

"Got you how?" he replied "I don't even see how you are suffering, your dancing is implausibly enthusiastic and irreproachably heartening. To be honest you are the one who has got me, because your zest is catching" he continued, grinning at Christie adoringly.

"Did he just say 'her zest? Implausibly enthusiastic? She sounds like a fizzy drink. He definitely has the corniest hookup lines this side of the Atlantic and is not afraid to use them in front of an audience"

"The way he is grinning and staring hungrily, I just want to howl, like oh lawd stop now people" Jay said.

"Are you sure my zest is catching?" she grinned back, her T-shirt stuck to her sweat streaked body, "Is it catching you yet?" she continued.

"Yes gorgeous. Your dancing is catching me, everything is catching me. In fact I am joining you" he responded leaping into the group and only marginally avoiding the feet of the hapless dancer he had leaped behind.

"I'm Uche" he introduced himself as they both danced out of rhythm, she grinned back at him and their clumsy dancing continued.

"And so a clumsy match in heaven is made" Jay said giggling "that felt like watching a bad Bollywood movie"

"Yes it did, and all Bollywood movies are bad"

"Not all. I've watched some good ones, I grew up on Amitabh and his awesomeness"

"Jay, please stop"

"Stop? You never watched Amar, Akbar, Anthony?" she asked finishing in a singsong, "I don't think it's even possible to say that movie title without singing it; surely you must have watched Mahd? Or Sholay?"

"It's obvious to me that the TV raised you and although it has done a good job, there are side effects" I replied, turning away to face the window. I leaned my elbow on the window sill, a small breeze hitting my face pleasurably. Effiong sauntered into the room just then, a buxomly lady with dewy skin hanging on his arm.

"Alright, let's rest a bit" the coach announced to the dancers who were all breathless; Christie and Uche were now missing from the more dedicated group, probably off to do more exciting things than awkward dancing.

"Dr Effiong and Dr Emma are here to show us some dance steps from Akwa Ibom"

"Is he in our Platoon?" Jay asked nudging me with her elbow.

"Effiong?" I asked without turning.

"Who else?"

"No he is not, he is in Platoon two"

"So we are stealing skills from Platoon two"

"Does she have to hang on his arm like that? Like a trophy wife?"

"Firstly, she is not his wife, talk less of a trophy one and you Adunni sound annoyed" Jay said.

"No I do not"

"Yes you do, annoyed and jealous"

"I am definitely not jealous"

"No? You are not jealous of those curves? That Kim Kardashian kind of curves?"

"No I'm not, I don't care actually"

"Well, say hello to Effiong, he is glancing here a lot and has quickly disengaged himself from Emma"

I did not respond; I continued to stare at the view of people from the window.

"No I don't want to say hello, he's a silly boy, coming here to show off his Kim Kardashian wanna-be"

"Adunni, you sound so irrational, if I didn't know you I would surely say you are jealous" Jay insisted smiling.

"I have no reason to be jealous" I muttered as I turned from the window and set off for the Mammy market. Jay fell into step with me after a few minutes and there was a companionable silence between us. At the Mammy market, we eyeballed different bukas, withdrawing our heads at the same time and turning down the bukas without having to consult each other. Sometimes I feel a kindred spirit with Jay that I do not understand, we are so different yet so alike. I also feel protective of her but I blame this on her small frame, a monster would feel protective of Jay and her wide trusting eyes.

We decided to have lunch which proved rather uneventful. My appetite was poor but I forced myself to eat, the rice sat like a huge lump in my throat and I pushed every spoonful down by guzzling the cold Sprite that I had requested with the rice.

We returned to the hostel and Jay and I got on our beds and just talked; starting with inane camp related topics till we started talking about our life experiences. I was again cautious what I talked about while Jay went on to chronicle her life from when her mother left. Just like my father's death is a marker in my life and everything is either before father's death or after, for Jay everything is either before mummy left or after.

An hour later and Jay had moved well beyond the sadness of an abandoning mother to the happy story of meeting Yomi, she proceeded to explain in detail again how she met him and how he made her feel, how simple it all was and yet how terribly complex.

BECKY

Lying on my bed, I let thoughts of Dr Effiong fill my mind, "If I don't talk to him, will he know how I feel?" I reasoned with myself, "I have to be pragmatic about these things, men are funny creatures; they walk around like they see, when in actual fact they are blind. I am going to talk to Effiong, not just follow him around like I am lost, I am not lost. I love him, I have found my soul mate, the one who will make this useless life's journey easier and he deserves to know that it is he. Secondly, if he knows, he can deal with those two girls properly, I have also noticed one Emma following him around, she is a doctor but a brainless one. She is married but removes her wedding ring on some days and wears it on other days. This camp is full of immoral women, women without scruples or depth. If you are going to wear a wedding ring and be faithful, do so, if you are not going to wear your wedding ring, then don't; you should be decisive and not dilly dally like some bit of lukewarm water that gives no proper satisfaction to its drinker, I sighed rolling over in my bed to reach for the raffia fan lying on my travel bag under my bed. The room was stifling and even though I was probably getting more breeze than most of the girls in the room, I was still covered in a thin sheen of sweat from the hot and humid weather.

After the morning drills is a good time to have a conversation with Effiong, most people return to the hostels to sleep after breakfast, so everything is usually quiet around the clinic and administrative building and Effiong is always at the clinic at this time, I reasoned. Convinced I now had a perfect plan, I got up, wore my shoes and headed to the camp dining room to make an early start on the lunch bell that was set to go off in another fifteen minutes.

I ate a quick lunch of rice and fish stew; there was a generous amount of fish in my stew and this was mainly because over the last week I had mindfully cultivated the kitchen staff. Half of the camp turned up their nose at the camp provided meals choosing to buy and eat food from the Mammy market but I did not have that luxury, with what money would I make these purchases? So with much speed and thoughtfulness I made forceful friends with the cooks and their assistants; a few remained unfriendly but those I ignored and their serving spoons I avoided.

With my heavy and very satisfying lunch sitting comfortably in my stomach, I walked quickly to the clinic. The customary free books were there in the bookshelf in the front of the administrative building, many of them now tatty and dirty. I riffled through quickly and picked one I had not read but the beginning and end of which I could easily predict and took up my position on the ledge in front of the clinic to wait for him.

He was predictable and my wait was short. He showed up a scant twenty minutes after I sat down on the ledge, a stethoscope hanging from his neck and a rumpled khaki cap, the standard issue one sitting prettily on his head. He came out talking to another doctor, a walking handover.

"Okay, take care, send me a message if you need me, otherwise I'll be back here tomorrow" Effiong said, his shift was ending.

I got up and climbed up on the ledge where he was standing shaking hands with his doctor colleague, I quickly dusted the bottom of my white shorts to get rid of any stuck sand while waiting for him to finish the pleasantries.

"Thanks man, have fun" the other doctor said, turning to walk into the clinic to begin his shift.

"Hello" my voice is raspy because my throat is dry, I'm not sure he heard me.

"Hello" I repeated, licking my parched lips and swallowing hard.

"Hi, how are you?" he replied.

"I'm Becky.... I've wanted to say hello to you for a while and to thank you for doing such a good job in the clinic"

"Oh" he shrugged, "I've just been doing my job, nothing special"

"I'm sure you are just being modest..." I smiled, I could feel the sweat in my palms, "so where are you going now?"

"The male hostel" he smiled, I was encouraged by his smile.

"Okay let me walk with you then, I'm also going back to the female hostel"

"Okay" His smile is shaky, distracted.

Walking along the ledge we both headed towards the hostels in silence; I was desperately racking my head for something to say.

"So have you been enjoying camp?" I asked.

"Somewhat"

I didn't know what to say in reply so I smiled, my smile was nervous and blank because I was trying to think of something to say at the same time, I knew I looked strange.

"Camp is good, it's a good place to meet people and get to know people" I suggested.

"Hmm"

"I'm happy I'm meeting you in camp here, this is part of why camp is good" I tried again.

He said nothing, we were now walking through the Mammy market and very soon would have to part ways, he turning to the left to go to the male hostel and I to the right to the female hostels. I desperately thought of a way to make the conversation last longer.

"It's very hot today"

"Not so much"

"Do you want to sit in the Mammy market and have a cold drink?" I asked.

"No, I'm sorry, I need to get to the hostel and get some things done, some other time perhaps" he smiled faintly and walked away hurriedly, like he couldn't get away fast enough.

I stood in the middle of the Mammy market and watched him go. I continued to watch him till he was two blurry white pieces tucked into one another with white blobs of shoes attached to brown sticks.

I could not believe what just happened; I felt like dropping into the dusty sand in a prostrate heap and sleeping away the fatigue that was suddenly creeping into my bones. I wanted to wallow in self-pity just this once, for once I wanted to dwell on the questions in my head, questions like 'will anything ever work out for me? Will I ever be truly happy? Will anyone ever love me in return? Am I so unlovable? So un-endurable that he must walk away so quickly, with such irritation?'

More than one week of trailing this arrogant fool around, like a lost puppy, like a child beggar hoping for a dirty brown coin and he walks away from me the first time I talk to him. I have never seen him walk away from those two whores. If it was that gangly yellow piece of skin called Adunni he would have all the time in the world, he would be smiling and grinning happily; his treachery was almost unbearable.

The sun hit my eyes where I was standing lost in my own thoughts and that was my cue; I purposefully picked myself up because even though I was standing I knew I had fallen;

so I picked myself up and walked briskly into the hostel, forcing a spring into my legs and swallowing the acid taste in my mouth.

By the hostel fence, Adesuwa was smiling and flirting with one of the camp officials, one of the more neatly dressed ones; he was smiling back and caressing her arm. I averted my eyes and continued inside, stupid girl; despite her usefulness to me I was convinced that Adesuwa's pendent breasts also served as her brain.

Day 9 NYSC Camp

JAY

By day nine of camp we were largely settled into the daily soldierly routine forced on us. One hour of spiritual devotion from 5am to 6am while standing in fields that were wet with morning dew, followed by drills, exercise and marching practice till 8am; some nasty Platoon leaders pushed their Platoons particularly hard and you could always see the exhaustion and misery carved boldly on their faces from a mile off. At 8am, Adunni and I would exhaustedly return to the hostel for our second shower of the day after which we would go in search of breakfast at the Mammy market; breakfast was as usual a mix of many things.

The hours after the drill till lunch time was ours to do with as we pleased; so on a lot of days, Adunni and I would return to the hostel to read and sleep.

That morning, the hostel was gratefully empty of girls, they had all gone off to practice their volley ball, drama, cultural dancing and whatever activity they were all involved in. I was contentedly halfway through Denise Chong's '*The Girl in the Picture*' when I was distracted from my reading by a voice, "Excuse me" her hair is a pale gold.

"Yes?"

"Are you Jay and Adunni?" she asked pointing a finger with chipped purple nail polish at me and then at sleeping Adunni.

"Yes, why?"

"There is a guy outside looking for you both, he said his name is Toni"

"Thanks, but how did you know where to find us?"

"He described you girls and you two follow each other around camp like Siamese twins; so, it wasn't exactly rocket science figuring out who he was describing" she shrugged and walked away, her missive delivered.

"Thank you" I called after her.

"You are welcome" she called back without pausing in her stride.

"Hey sleepyhead, your friend Toni is outside" I shook Adunni and jumped off the bed.

"Okay" Adunni mumbled, frowning with her eyes still half closed "my friend Toni, but you are the one in a hurry to go outside"

"Well yes, I'm not going to enjoy any reading with that racket from the next hostel so we can as well go and see what fun the Mammy market has to offer"

The Sisters in Faith fellowship were having another loud meeting in the next girls' hostel.

"Fun or food?" Adunni mumbled.

"That too. You have no idea how hungry I get, it's like a 'I'm going to die if I don't eat right now kind of hungry'"

"That's normal considering..." Adunni said as she got off the bed and started to brush her long black hair into a ponytail.

"Not according to google and the comments on Netmums, I'm supposed to be too sick to eat anything" I countered

"Have you been googling things?" Adunni asked.

"Of course I have, who doesn't? Google knows every-thing and has generously let me know that based on what I am feeling, I am either pregnant with a monster or not preg-nant at all and what I most likely have is a malignant stomach tumour that is going to kill me in a horrific and sudden way"

"You see what I mean? You should never google your symptoms or anything to do with how you are feeling, there are sinister imaginative lunatics waiting online to answer every question about your medical condition; trust me the people online answering questions have issues, they are seri-ously basic souls" she said

"I know that, but I can't resist google you see" I said.

We found Toni waiting outside our hostel, leaning against one of the metal poles holding up the roof of the hos-tel; and together we all wandered towards the Mammy mar-ket.

Booths selling mobile phone recharge cards have sprung up all around and in the Mammy market, the iron feet of their colourful umbrellas entrenched in the red soil opposite our hostel and held up by big rocks sitting at their base. They stood like sentries to the Mammy market, their colourful covers blowing in the breeze. There were probably enough phone recharge card sellers here to keep the whole of Plateau State supplied with call credit.

Vying for space with the recharge card sellers were the photographers, they were also in the camp in huge numbers and proof of their expertise hung from cloth lines tied to crooked poles in front of their wooden makeshift studios. The pictures fluttered in the wind rebelling against the pegs holding them to the clothes line and reminding me of the photo grounds at Unilag. I must have taken a hundred pictures every school term. The photographers would call out to me with what was akin to love whenever I drove past on my way to or from class.

One of the photo booths seemed emptier than the others so I ducked in to take a closer look at the photographs; many of them were pictures of girls at the Mammy market, on the parade ground during drills or just sitting down, all wearing some variety of the Youth Corper uniform - white on white, white on khaki and so on. A few of them had been caught unaware, the expression on their faces shifting from thoughtful to happy to closed. It made me wonder if anyone had taken a picture of me without my knowledge and with this on my mind, I started to go from shed to shed searching the faces in the pictures, looking for myself. I wished finding myself was something I could do this easily, by just going from one wooden shed to another.

"Hey" Toni said putting his hand through mine, "what are you looking for?"

"Hey you too, I'm looking for me, where's Adunni?" I looked around him.

"She just went off with Mahmud now, so I'm in charge of you from here on"

"In charge indeed" I said

"So you are looking for you, what makes you think they have taken your picture?" Toni asked

"I don't know I'm just checking; something tells me they have; I have made too many eye contacts with those camera-carrying stalkers" I said.

Then I found it, a picture of me, I was leaning against the wall, my hands folded one across the other with my fingers stretched to hold my sides, under my breasts. It was a half frame picture and it stopped at the waist band of my white shorts; to the ordinary eye I looked content and happy but I knew I was none of that when that picture was taken. I stared at it critically, I was looking far off in the direction of the parade ground as if an ongoing event had caught my interest.

I could see the faraway look in my eyes, the thoughtfulness, I was not watching a football match, I was thinking about my life, my future, and the bundle of cells snuggling under my white vest growing rapidly and making my waist wider.

The photographer had caught me in one of my more pensive moods; I yanked the picture off the rope.

"Good afternoon Aunty, you like it? You look very pretty in that picture" the photographer said, somehow materialising beside me.

"You shouldn't take people's picture without their consent, it's not nice" I answered him.

"That's why we are paparazzi nooooooooow" he wheedled "and you like the picture"

"Just take" I thrust a hundred naira note at him "And don't take my picture again without asking me, I have a good mind not to pay for this invasion of privacy"

"Aunty are you a lawyer? The picture is two hundred naira oh. Pictures cost hundred naira outside; here, it is harder to print so we charge more"

"You can go and take two hundred naira for pictures you took with consent not for this one"

"You shouldn't be angry Jay, that is how these guys make their money" Toni said, "and it's a nice picture, I would have bought it for you if I had seen it earlier"

"Thank you, but its bit creepy of these photographers to take your pictures without telling you and put them up on ropes out there, just like that"

Any observant person could have taken a good look at that picture and wondered if I was pregnant, I just want to finish this camp and be gone; I thought nervously.

"Let's leave this place Toni"

"Okay, if we sit on that bench over there, we can see everything happening around without having to be in the middle of it" Toni said pointing at a shed with a lone wooden bench in it – the bench was four round logs tied together with raffia rope and balanced on two squat planks, but it looked sturdy enough.

"Can I see the picture again?"

I handed it to him silently.

"It's a nice picture, can I keep it?"

"Why? What for? How do you plan to explain that to your girlfriend? Oh, this is the picture of a stranger I met in camp and I liked it and took it off her?"

He shrugged, "you are not a stranger, you are my friend and I don't have to explain anything to a girlfriend I don't have"

"Well in future, there will be a girlfriend to explain to and how awkward that will be, anyway I think it's weird to give you my picture"

"So in future, I will bring out my album of pictures, not like I have one, go through it and explain to my girlfriend of the future why I have each picture? I don't know what kind of relationship or girlfriend is going to require that kind of explanation but hopefully I won't be the guy in a relationship with that kind of girlfriend"

"Right"

"And it's just a picture, you are making such a big deal out of it"

"Okay, here. You can have it, it's just a side view anyway"

"The side view of a pretty girl watching a football match?"

"May be"

"You look a little preoccupied in the picture though, like your mind is somewhere else, I wonder what was making you so thoughtful"

"You got all that from a picture? That's a little bizarre, maybe I should take the picture back"

"Oh come on, don't be touchy, you are too lovely to be touchy"

"You would be touchy too if you were in my shoes"

"Well I get that; my sister was touchy during her pregnancy too" he replied smiling at me now a slight glint in his eyes.

"What? What did you say?" I stammered, trying to mask my surprise.

He smiled, "you are pregnant, right?"

"How would you know? Do you go around assuming every girl is pregnant? If you want to call me fat or bloated just say so. Don't go calling me pregnant just because..."

"I don't think you are fat or bloated, I think you are pregnant and gorgeous and cool; I am jealous of the lucky guy"

Silence. I leaned against the wall of the shed for support, my knees weak, my mind reeling from the fact that a lot of people must now know that I am pregnant.

"You seem shocked that I know"

"Of course I'm shocked. How long have you known?"

"Well I didn't know initially, not when I told Adunni I like you, she must think I'm an idiot liking a pregnant lady. I sort of figured it out after you fainted on the parade ground. I have four older sisters, all married and all have been pregnant one time or the other so when I looked closely enough I realised it"

"Everybody has probably figured it out then"

"As long as the camp officials have not figured it out and nobody is telling them you are fine, twelve short days and camp will be over"

"Yes"

"So I guess it's a No to me then"

"If I said yes, you would date a pregnant woman?" I asked incredulously

"You won't be pregnant forever" he shrugged, "I like you very much"

"That's very touching Toni, but you are right, it's a No"

"I see..." he paused, "friends then?"

"Yes friends" I smiled back.

"So have you and Adunni always been friends?"

I appreciated the fact that he was changing the topic.

"Funnily no, we weren't friends in Uni, just acquaintances, we became friends here and I feel like I've known her forever"

"Yeah Adunni is cool, aloof but cool"

I smiled. We sat on the bench and just talked, comparing notes on our university days and the mutual acquaintances we had till my bottom felt numb, but I was reluctant to get up, the sun was shining brightly, a beautiful, powerful orange ball of heat, free owner of its own destiny.

"My bottom is numb"

"I'm so sorry, let's go and find lunch, would you like to eat lunch now?" he asked.

"Yes sure, let's do that"

After a lunch of chips and fried fish we returned to our bench where we sat down again for another hour till the bugle went off, a loud round sound.

"Is that the bugle?" Toni asked.

"I'm afraid so, the games are about to start"

"Oh yes. Would you like to watch the football match? I want to"

"No I'd rather not, I'm a little tired, I think I should go in and lie down a bit, catch my breath and all that"

We both got up at the same time almost bumping into each other, he turned and he kissed me; first on my forehead then on my mouth, his lips were soft.

"I'll walk you back to your hostel Princess"

"Thank you" the tears filled my eyes, he reminded me of Fola, my darling awkward loving giant. I suddenly realised that I missed him very much.

The lump forming in my throat was growing and the tears in my eyes threatening to fall so I walked as quickly as I could towards the hostel; I did not want Toni to see my tears.

At the hostel gate, I paused only briefly when he said "See you later Jay, or tomorrow if you don't come back outside today" he patted my shoulder, the second time today.

My hands were trembling as I reached for my phone; I have to speak with Fola today, right now.

His phone only rang for a second before he picked it up.

"Obafolawe" I whispered

"Jay? My Jady Jay"

I giggled through the tears rolling down my face.

"Are you still mad at me?" he asked.

"No, I am not; I cannot stay mad at you"

"But you stayed mad at me for so long"

"I know, I'm not mad at you anymore and I want you to know that"

"I miss you terribly; it's horrible without you, everything is boring and my awkwardness has doubled in the last three months; I don't remember how to talk to people anymore. When I came back from Kuala Lumpur, Bolanle said you had already left for camp; I called you so many times Jay" he said everything in a rush.

"I know Fola, I know, but I couldn't bear to talk to you"

"I'm sorry Jay, you know I am.... You mean the world to me, be my friend again; please be my friend"

"We will always be friends; you are my brother and my friend, but I need you to accept this, accept the future this way"

"Why? Why should I accept this?"

"Because you have to, because I want you to, if you love me you will accept this"

"Okay" he replied; like all the fight was gone from him.

"Thank you, I'll see you when I come back from camp"

"We don't have to wait till then, I could fly into Abuja this weekend and drive down" he replied.

"No, no Fola, that's not a good idea, let me come and see you when I come back to Lagos"

"Okay sweetness"

"Bye Fola"

"Bye"

I walked into the hostel to screams of "goalllllllllllllllllll" from the football field, one lucky Platoon had already put one in the net.

ADUNNI

Bolaji's Platoon nine team beat the Platoon three team, two goals to none in the sixty-minute game with spectators standing four men thick and in some places six men thick, round the football field to watch the game.

Mahmud and I by some luck of timing had front row positions to watch the match and walked away at the end of it covered in fine brown dust.

We walked into Toni as he entered the buka that had become Jay's and my favourite 'canteen' in the last few days.

"Where is Jay? I thought she was with you?"

"She was, but she didn't want to watch the football match so she went back to the hostel"

"I should go and check her then"

"Leave her be, she wants to rest and is probably sleeping"

"Okay, what are you guys eating?" I asked turning to Toni and Mahmud in turn.

"The usual, rice. Rice will soon start growing on my head" Mahmud answered.

"You can't have eaten more of that stuff than I have, it's always rice or noodles, rice or noodles. Camp needs to end mehn" I replied.

"You guys don't eat yam?" Toni asked, "There is yam and eggs, there is eba, there is bread and Akara; there are options unless you are fussy eaters"

"Those options are somehow jare" Mahmud said pushing the roughly hewed wooden bench serving as a table aside to walk to the other end of a similar bench serving as a chair.

We silently ate hot plates of white rice, fried eggs, and fried fish with cold drinks; our hunger superseding conversation. We were still at this important task when Bolaji and David wandered in with two girls; Nneka and a dark girl with kinky un-permed hair.

"Fine girl Adunni" Bolaji said smiling at me.

"Hey you" I said smiling back at him; he was still visibly basking in his Platoon's recent win and here to remind us of it.

They joined our table, dragging extra chairs to form a tight circle.

"You guys, meet Azy" Bolaji introduced the kinky haired girl.

"Azy, meet my people" Bolaji said.

Expectedly, Bolaji began to rehash the football match we all just watched.

"We are going to win this tournament" he said nodding at the end of his narration.

"Well you guys are on track" Toni replied.

"Our team is very okay... very, very okay... except for Jubril who can't seem to kick a ball" Bolaji said frowning.

"The one that lost that first goal?" David asked.

"Yes that one, na stupid guy" Bolaji answered.

"Yes, yes that Jubril guy didn't do well at all, still the fact that you guys played well today is no assurance that you guys will play the same way later this week. I mean look at the way Kareem kept making those wrong passes to T-man" Toni said waving his hand in dismissal of Kareem's footballer skills "If he continues like that, he will definitely finish you guys"

"No, no, Kareem is not so bad, it was T-man that was off, but you know on that third pass I got that ball because I just knew what Kareem was trying to do there" Bolaji added.

"You are just a show off Bolaji, but we still like you"

"Don't mind him Adunni, he can't help himself"

"I'm a machine" Bolaji said, laughing.

"I'm telling you though, if you guys play like that in your next match, we will whoop you" David said turning to Bolaji "Your defences are not great, your saving grace is that you people play a fast game, your team is full of runners. You can only try that nonsense with Platoon three because all their players are slow. If you are unlucky enough to play with the greatest Platoon in this camp, my Platoon eight, we will show you what football is, not this child's play you have been doing. Playing football like women" David finished.

"Here we go"

"Whao, whao, whao, what kind of talk is that?" Nneka asked "what do you mean they were playing like women? Have you seen the girls playing volleyball and how well they play?"

"I don't know why you have to look for women trouble with that kind of statement" Toni grumbled, "Don't mind him, what does he know? That's why he never scores with the girls... he's always talking nonsense" Toni said.

"And you score with the women all the time? ... Because you don't talk crap? What exactly do you talk?" Nneka asked Toni.

David burst out laughing "I'm not the only one putting my foot in my mouth today; anyway, my pretty lady please forgive me, no insult intended but we are going to make these boys here cry" he said pointing at Toni and Bolaji one after the other.

"We shall see" Toni answered.

"Yes, we shall see, it all ends on Saturday, that is when we will know who has made who cry" Bolaji added thumping the table and getting up.

"Adunni, I hear you are the Miss NYSC candidate from your Platoon" Bolaji said.

"This is the first I am hearing of that and no I am not"

"Why not? You would win" Toni said.

"Yes she would, left to me" Mahmud added.

"Ahw, thank you guys but I don't want to compete in a beauty contest"

"Nneka here is representing the great Platoon nine so watch out, she intends to win and she will" Bolaji warned, Nneka smiled at him.

"Let's go" he said turning to Nneka and Azy who both got up obediently and followed him.

"Okay guys, see you later" Toni also got up and smoothly navigated around the roughly hewed benches and the jutting splinters waiting to tear clothes and skin.

I leaned back against the wooden wall of the buka, Mahmud smiled at me.

"Hey Miss NYSC"

"Hey you too and its Miss Adunni"

"You should contest, aside from Adanma in Platoon four, I don't see anybody giving you good competition"

"Oh please, there are loads of very beautiful girls in camp, Nneka is gorgeous and she is competing"

"Her mouth is too wide and you are way prettier"

"You are mean and you have been looking at a lot of girls"

"Just to confirm that you are prettier" he said and winked, "can you imagine I almost didn't come to this Orientation Camp? I was going to blow it off and just stay in Abuja. I would never have met you. Imagine that. One never knows what one is missing until one sees it... or her" he smiled, his eyes wrinkled at the side, his teeth starkly white in the rapidly darkening bukateria.

"Flatterer"

"I am serious Gimbiya, you are so breathtakingly beautiful and yet so chilled and mysterious. I have never met anyone as exciting as you"

"You are exciting too"

"I'm not exciting, I'm a bumbling guy with nothing to offer, but my adoration and dedication"

"I like what you have to offer"

"Come and sit here" he tapped his left lap, "I want to hold you a little"

"Just a little?"

"I want with all my heart and soul to hold you, to run off home with you after camp and make you live with me forever and ever, you are my kwazazzabo Gimbiya"

"Oh wow, this is escalating very quickly, I know Gimbiya means princess, what does Kwaza... something mean?" I got up and climbed into his lap, he wrapped his arms around me and I laid my head in the crook of his collarbone.

"Kwzazzabo means gorgeous, you are my gorgeous princess" he lifted my head up and kissed me, his hand under my jaw caressed me; he kissed me again, harder.

"You smell wonderful Gimbiya, like green apples and freesias, I could stay here and inhale you for like a decade" he sniffed my hair breathing in deeply.

"I'm not sure I would smell good if I sat in your lap for a decade"

"You would, trust me" He planted small kisses on my head.

"The buka woman is looking at us" I whispered into Mahmud's collarbone.

"We should give her something to look at then" he said, holding my head, he kissed me again long and hard.

"That's enough Mahmud, don't be naughty"

"Let's get out of here"

"Where to?

"Somewhere with no audience"

Hand in hand, we left the buka for one of the empty shacks dotted around the edges of the Mammy market. Mahmud started to kiss me hurriedly all over my face, one hand in my hair and the other running over my back urgently.

"Mahmud, we should stop now"

"Why?" he asked, his eyes already dark with want.

"Why? Because we can't take it much further so we shouldn't get worked up"

"If by worked up you are referring to me getting a boner, then it's already too late; Come on babes, be adventurous, come here" he pulled me close and rubbed against me till I felt the boner he was speaking of.

"There is nothing adventurous about a raffia roofed shed" I pushed him away gently, "I need to go now anyway, it's getting dark and the mosquitos are biting, I'm wearing shorts and my legs are becoming a buffet dinner for them"

"Do you want to go into the hostel and get changed into trousers and come back out?"

"Darling, let's call it a day okay? See you tomorrow?"

"You are being a tease Adunni and it's not fair"

"No I'm not, you are taking things too fast"

"I believe in living in the moment and I love you"

"No you don't, that's your boner talking; will you walk me to the hostel?"

"Of course pumpkin... and I do love you, it's not my boner talking"

Mahmud and I had hung out a few times since the first night we met at the Friday party; mini dates and I enjoyed every one of them. He was witty and boisterous with the self-depreciating sense of humour I always like in men; he had me laughing every time we were together and I would forget all my sadness and fears.

He had kissed me on our second mini date and declared with a grin "Now we are an item and you can't listen to any other guy here; tell all the bastards you have found your bastard"

Day 11 NYSC Camp

BECKY

It was the turn of Adesuwa's Platoon to present a play to the rest of camp, as part of the drama competition - their interpretation of Zulu Sofola's *'Wedlock of the Gods'*. Adesuwa somehow landed the role of the main protagonist Ogwoma who was given out in marriage to a man she neither knew nor loved.

I bet Adesuwa's loud shrill voice was instrumental in landing her the role, and on getting the role, she rehearsed and performed her part and a few others frequently and intensely till I knew the play by heart. I began to wonder if anybody else in our hostel would bother to watch the play; after all Adesuwa had already acted it all out for our listening pleasure.

When she first told me her Platoon was performing 'Wedlock of the gods', I said to her, "that is a rather heavy piece of work you are taking on, I hope you guys are not biting off more than you can chew"

"Why would you think that? We can do this very well, Obioma who will act as my lover and Nonso who is my father in the play are both Theatre Arts graduates; moreover Obioma produced this play as part of his final thesis in his final year in Uni"

"I get that, but you guys have just one hour to perform it"

"It will be enough, Platoon eight is performing Hamlet"

"I thought the rule was that each Platoon should perform a piece of drama that portrays African culture and tradition either present or past, or something in that vein?"

"Yes, they are performing an African interpretation of Hamlet" she replied.

"I see, I take it all back then, if Platoon eight can make an African interpretation of Hamlet whatever that is, then you can also give Sofola a good go in one hour"

"Yes we will and you must be there in the front row, cheering me on"

"I will"

"Malik has promised to be there too to cheer me on"

"Malik? Who is Malik?" I asked.

She smiled, suddenly shy, "he's a camp official that has taken a very strong liking to me, you might not have noticed but we hang out a lot, he wasn't here when camp started but he joined us a few days ago, he is here on secondment from Abuja"

"Right, good for you"

So come 2pm I was sitting firmly in the third row in the hall, right behind the judges and camp officials in the first and second row, waiting for the play to begin.

"Is this seat taken?" someone whispered, tapping the white plastic chair beside me.

"No it's not" I turned to see who it was and my heart skipped a bit; I looked around quickly noting that the plastic chair beside me was not the only empty seat in the room.

"Why?" I asked, his reason for choosing this chair was lost to me.

"Because I want to sit down here?" he said smiling.

"Of course, sorry, yes you can sit down" I wanted to hit myself, for giving him the impression that I did not want him to sit beside me.

"Thank you" he smiled at me, he of the perfect-like-corn-rows-on-a-cob teeth, he with the laughing eyes that say life is good and everything is therefore amusing; he sat down and stretched his legs out in front of him. Adonis who I walked into a few days ago was now sitting beside me, it could only be destiny; I suddenly felt sweaty and clammy.

"I hope they will start on time today" he said.

"I hope so too" he was talking to me. I swallowed hard to wet my drying throat and mouth.

"If they don't, they will get marked down, I hear the judges mark down those who don't start and finish in their allotted time" he continued, oblivious of my discomfort.

"Hmmm" I wanted to say more, I wanted to cock my head to one side and laugh coquettishly, but I had no words and I was frozen in my chair.

"I'm Mahmud by the way"

"Becky" I whispered "Becky Oni" I said a little more loudly above the rushing sound in my head.

"That's a pretty name" he turned and smiled at me, rubbing one hand along his thigh like something had bit him and he was trying to assuage the sting. Nobody had ever told me my name was pretty.

"So, do you know anyone in the play? It's more fun to root for a Platoon's play when you have friends in the play"

"Yes, my bunk mate Adesuwa is in the play, she is acting the lead role of Ogwoma she is very good at it too"

"Okay, good... Ah, ah, here they are, the play is about to begin"

"Good evening Camp commandant, RSM, esteemed judges, fellow youth corpers, all and sundry. Welcome to the Jos National Youth Service Corps Orientation Camp, batch 'A' drama competition. This is the Platoon four drama performance and today we will be performing a play titled '*Wedlock of the Gods*'. Today we will take you on a walk through pre-colonial Nigeria, arranged marriages, traditional laws, gender politics, levirate and the devastating effect of the interlinking of these cultural practices on love, woman rights and family dynamics. We hope you will enjoy this classic performance from Platoon four, thank you" the narrator bowed and left the stage to a smattering of applause.

"What is levirate?" someone behind me asked, I had no idea what the narrator meant and so I didn't turn around.

"It is when a man marries his brother's widow" Mahmud turned round to answer the question. He is not only devastatingly good looking, he is bright. I sank lower in my chair, hating destiny's sense of humour.

The play began and in no time, I forgot about the Adonis beside me and became enthralled by Ogwoma's passion and pain and her rapid descent into disaster and tragedy as she ran back into the arms of her childhood lover while in mourning; pushed by her vicious and forbidding mother-in-law Odibei; her strident voice constantly questioning and judging the confused and sad widow, ably portrayed by Adesuwa.

"Your bunkmate is a very good actress" he whispered.

"Huh? Yes she is, she's the one acting the widow" I whispered back.

"Yes you said so, will you be acting for your Platoon too?"

"No, I don't act, I'm not a good actress"

"You don't know that, bet you are better than many"

"I'm not honestly, I'm playing volleyball for my Platoon though"

"That's fantastic, I like a girl who is not too dainty to hit a ball"

"Hush. You are disturbing the rest of us" a girl whispered from the row of chairs behind us.

"Sorry" Mahmud whispered back. We went back to watching the play which ended in tragedy as I had known it would. Knowing didn't mean I wasn't angry though. I was angry with Odibei, with Ogwoma's parents who pushed her into an arranged marriage; selfish, nasty self –centred parents; just like mine who should die horrible deaths.

"There are just too many people who shouldn't be allowed to have children or even live"

"Oh, oh, someone is angry" Mahmud answered. I didn't realise I had spoken out loud.

"It's true though"

"Well you can't take away people's right to have children or live just because they are nasty people" he replied.

I don't know, we should be able to, I wish I could; mentally unstable adults who are too selfish to think of the well-being of others especially their children shouldn't be allowed to live, starting with my parents and other idiots like Ugwoma's parents and that evil woman called Odibei – I don't say this out loud though, I only smiled at Mahmud in acquiescence.

"Do you want to go outside and walk a bit, get some fresh air?" Mahmud asked breaking into my reflections.

"It's nine pm, the bugle goes off at ten pm" I spluttered trying to think, my mind was in a whirl.

"That gives us an hour to stretch our legs, let's go"

"Okay"

We got up and left the hall with the rest of the now exiting crowd. I wanted to kick myself for ever thinking Dr Effiong was the real deal; when all the while Mahmud was waiting to get fresh air and stretch his legs with me.

He held my hand and we left in the direction of the dining hall. I could feel my heart beating a strange uneven throb in my chest. This is it so help me God; destiny, if this is another joke like Dr Effiong, I swear I will take it upon myself to find you, you figure out the rest.

Day 12 NYSC Camp

ADUNNI

I was jarred out of a dark formless dream by the loudest din imaginable, screaming and crying girls running out of the hostel in various stages of undress.

Fear rushed through me, every hair on my body stood on end and I could feel the blood pumping through my veins as I leaped down from my bunk and landed on the hard floor with a thump at the same time as Jay, we stared at each other in disbelief at the chaos around us.

"What is going on?" she screamed.

"I don't know. Just hurry let's go" I screamed back over the growing noise.

A loud crashing sound spurred me on and I forced my feet into my white running shoes with shaking fingers. Across the room, a bed bunk fell into the next bunk and the second bunk groaned loudly under the weight of the first one and began to totter and shake, it swiftly gave up and fell on to the next bunk with a loud clang, that bunk also began to lean, it was obvious what was about to happen; I made a wild dash for the door, Jay behind me crying silently.

Unfortunately, fifty other frightened girls had the same idea, we were all running for the door. There was a tedious dread sitting in my stomach, cold and unmoving yet biting, what was most frightening in all of the pandemonium was the unknowing.

"Why are we running? What is chasing us?" I asked Jay.

"I don't knowwwwwwwww" Jay shouted above the din.

"Why is it so dark?" I asked again, knowing that Jay did not have the answers but asking anyway.

"The light bulbs are probably gone, let's run Adunni; I'm so scared"

A keening scream came from outside where I could see a big crowd forming, dark shapes streaming out of the other hostels and all running steadily in the direction of the parade ground.

Oh Lord of heaven, I am done with this camp business. Give me all the inquisitive worrying sisters and mothers of this world, it is better than this nonsense.

I grabbed Jay by the arm and continued to push towards the door, the urge to get outside into open and hopefully safer space was overwhelming; the bunks were now doing exactly as expected, falling like a pack of dominoes, the noise was deafening. I glanced at Jay for a brief second and grabbed her by the arm "Jay, don't fall, hold my hand, you must not fall"

We finally got out of the hostel door in what felt like the longest journey from our bunk to the hostel door and followed the mammoth crowd towards the parade ground.

Just then the bugle went off and the soldiers came running, blowing their whistles and wielding their whips and leather belts. They ran into the hostel we had just come out of us, switching on the yellow light bulbs which stupidly none of us had thought of switching on as we escaped the dark rooms by the light of the full moon.

"Two weeks in this hell hole and I have never been so happy or relieved to see the soldiers and their whistles and whips" Jay said, sighing.

"You can say that again"

They have become our shepherds and guardians and like sheep we looked to them for help, comfort and answers. It was a humbling thought as we all stood in small circles on the parade ground asking each other what had happened and finding no one to provide answers except hopefully the soldiers who were still in the hostels investigating the cause of the stampede.

"Attention" the RMS screamed, appearing from nowhere, he put his whistle to his mouth and blew it for almost half a minute till we were all holding our ears.

"Everybody into their Platoons" he screamed.

"Is he mad? How can we find our Platoons? It is 2am and we just had the most frightening horrendous experience. What Platoon? Surely you can talk to us without us standing in lines"

Nobody answered, then slowly and dejectedly with no reason or understanding, like the sheep that I now realised we all were, we began to shuffle around trying to make sense of the horde we were in, to fall into our Platoons without knowing which way was the beginning or the end of the line. The soldiers came and pushed and shoved the confused crowd around, like one would control a difficult herd of cattle, they corralled us into our Platoons; soon some order was restored and we were all standing in lines, facing the RMS.

"This morning there was a stampede" he boomed, the anger in his voice was apparent.

"You don't say" I muttered quietly.

"A stampede without meaning. People running without knowing what was chasing them, beds been pushed to the ground and windows been broken from people jumping out of them. Ten people are now in the infirmary with injuries, with four others on their way to the hospital with broken arms and legs."

A loud rumbling noise ran through our ranks in response.

"Quiet" the RMS screamed again "You have nothing to say to me... Are you animals? Are you sheep? That you run without knowing what is chasing you? You are supposed to be graduates, leaders of tomorrow yet you stampede like untrained wild animals"

There was a hushed silence; we shuffled our feet, some stared at him in disbelief and indignation, others hung their heads in shame.

"Are you not better than animals? Than a mob of wild men? Educated men and women, the future of our nation who have spent the last eleven days learning to espouse a life style of discipline, alertness and team playing, leaping out of their beds to the sound of an unknown noise; and without waiting to find out, to verify the cause, direction or implication of the noise begin to run like brainless cattle.... Executing a survival of the fittest race like mere cave men. We are not yet sure what started this stampede, but we have been led to believe it was a scream from one of the hostels – I will not be surprised to hear it was a loud scream from an idiot having a bad dream" he boomed.

We all gasped at this, at the possibility that we jumped out of bed and ran for our lives with nothing on our heels but someone's bad dream.

"I will inform the State command and the National Office of this unfortunate incidence and let them deal with you as they see fit. In the meantime, listen to me with wisdom, I will not tolerate a mob mentality in my camp. This camp is not about winning alone or surviving alone, it is about winning together, surviving together. It is why everything here is done in teams and I will not tolerate any thing otherwise. We are a team, protecting each other, not each one to himself, fighting to stay alive alone. Left to me you will all be reposted in six months' time to other camps to redo these three weeks of service because I don't think you have learnt anything. You are the worst set of Youth corpers I have ever had and I am disappointed in you all. You are hereby dismissed to think of your shameful behaviour of this morning. Be back here at 5am sharp. Anybody caught in the hostel at 5:10am will be expelled and on a bus out of here today. Exercise and drills will be for double the time this morning, you lot obviously need it. I am ashamed of you all" He finished angrily.

"I feel like crying, I am so tired, so tired of everything, I just want to go home" Jay moaned.

"Anyone who gets expelled from camp will be going through this hellish experience in six months' time in another camp somewhere else in Nigeria for another three weeks and the RSM is keen to expel someone today, is that what you want?" I asked.

"I don't care"

"Neither do I, but getting a job without this compulsory service is near impossible hence why we are all here" I replied.

"I'm just tired, I don't want to be a patriotic youth anymore" Jay said.

"Patriotic? We are not patriotic youths, we are products on an assembly line and this is the final bit of our journey before we are finally chucked into the job market ready for purchase by fat cat companies who are spoilt for choice. It is the one thing that seems to work in this country and when I say work, I mean the one thing you can't really boycott"

"Three weeks of living hell" Jay said, climbing slowly into her bed.

"Yes three weeks of living hell but it will end, just about 10 more days" I said the words without believing them myself. I was as tired and discouraged as Jay was, but right then someone needed to be the ray of sunshine for both of us, so I said the words and tried to get myself and Jay to believe them.

For once the hostel was quiet, everybody was subdued and discouraged, and one by one they crawled into their cold beds and fell into a drugged sleep that was summarily interrupted by the tyrannical bugle at 5am.

We trudged back to the parade ground again at dawn to a glaring, frowning RMS whose face looked like an angry mask.

"Attention. A search of the hostels has shown up a remarkable find. A small boa constrictor was found in one of the girl's hostels"

A ripple of shock and surprise ran through the crowd.

"Quiet. Cowardly lot... Is the boa constrictor a biting snake? The poor thing was more afraid than you lot. It was hiding under a bed"

There was more murmuring and someone shouted, "Witches. Someone turned to snake"

"Stop that stupid talk right now. I will not tolerate any meaningless folklore in this camp. A constrictor is a non-venomous snake, if you don't provoke it, it won't attack you and I am convinced someone brought that thing into the hostel; so if you are here and you like to have snakes for pets, be warned that no pets whatsoever are allowed in this camp; and if you brought it in to cause this stampede then you are an animal yourself. In fact I will be keeping an eye on that particular hostel from now on, I expect better from the mothers of this our great nation. You will still have double drills and exercise sessions today. Anymore hanky-panky from you and I will ask the drinks company not to bring in any free drinks today. I don't need drunk idiots on my hands. You are dismissed to your drills"

As promised, exercises ran for twice the time as promised and the soldiers were merciless and unsmiling, my bones screamed and my muscles wept... I was stoic... this is camp.

"May God punish who ever brought that snake into the hostel either as a pet or a prank; stupid, devious girl, may all the demons of hell know your name and worry you" Aina, the girl beside me cursed repeatedly as we sweated through the drills.

BECKY

Johnny came to me by luck. I was on my way back from school on a hot afternoon when my stomach began to rumble. I knew I had eaten too much of the mangoes from the tree outside the east wall of my school; but it was difficult to resist. Lunch was never something to look forward to in our house, so I had eaten my fill of the juicy yellow mango fruits; nine or ten mangoes.

Now my stomach rolled and a sharp pain ran through me, twisting my guts with vicious persistence, my bottom began to quiver and I dashed into the dense bush that ran beside the road. I ran for a short minute, heart in my mouth, mentally begging my sphincter to hold on for just a few seconds while I ran in to the bush, far enough not to be observed from the dusty road.

Lifting up my skirt, I hurriedly pulled down my grey faded panties and the already tired elastic band holding it up gave way, no matter I bent my knees, spread my legs and let rip, empting my bowel of its disagreeable watery contents in a spray that hit the grass and shrubbery between my legs; forcing me to spread my legs wider to prevent the brown smelly liquid from hitting my legs too.

It was over in a minute and I reached into my school satchel to tear pages from my Agricultural Science notebook. Agricultural Science was not my favourite subject; Mrs Hassan who taught this class in a husky, bored voice was also not my favourite teacher. We had a mutual hatred that ensured her classes were unpleasant for both of us. Mrs Hassan preferred to be nice to the light skinned girls with long hair, especially if they went on or pretended to go on holidays abroad and brought back colourful gifts which she received with a wide grin and effusive thanks. She liked the geeks who wore glasses too just because they made her look good with their grades; everyone else fell between the cracks of her attention, she did not care if you lived or died.

I ripped the notebook from the middle, being careful to tear it out in joint pairs to prevent the whole book from falling apart, you learn how to tear your notebook to sit tests from a very young age, test writing papers were not provided by the state schools.

I wiped myself as best as I could and gingerly stepped away from the brown mess that I had created, stepping out of my expired panties at the same time. I lowered my school skirt, checking it thoroughly for brown stains.

I picked up my school bag to go and that was when I saw him, curled up in a crushed square of grass; head tucked into one of the curls of his brown and mottled body; he seemed to be sleeping. I froze in fright, and turned on my heel as silently as I could, never taking my eyes off the serpent, my heart was thudding in my chest. One vigilant step after the other I put space between myself and the spiral danger; then I ran as fast as I could till I was clear of the bush.

By the time I got to the front of the house, I was calm and feeling brave, I continued walking, past our house and further on to the gated mansion at the end of the street; I needed to talk to Ahmadu about this; if anyone would know what to do, it would be Ahmadu.

"Ahmadu good afternoon"

"Good afternoon Becky, is everything okay?" Ahmadu spoke with a thick Northern accent that meant he pronounced 'afternoon' as 'Aptunoon' and 'everything' as 'eperytin'

"I want to show you something"

"What? Don't waste my time oh, I'm a very busy man" he was smiling.

Ahmadu was a security guard at Chief Koleosho's empty mansion where one of his wives used to live. She was rumoured to have died of cancer without having any children and so the house stayed empty. Ahmadu lived in a small gatehouse built into the walls encircling the house and sold bread, cigarettes and sweets from the small window of his gatehouse. He was friendly and would always say hello to me, his hellos increased day after day, in proportion to my growing bosom.

"Just come with me, I promise you will like this" I answered.

"Okay" He got up and followed me.

When I entered the dense bush in the same place I had entered it a short half hour ago, Ahmadu stopped, "what is this Becky? Where are we going?"

"Come Ahmadu, are you afraid?"

"Afraid of what? You want me to follow you into the bush, I will follow you, no problem" he was grinning, probably hoping I was inviting him to a tryst.

I got to where the snake was and I was gratified to find that it was still there, completely oblivious of us or perhaps aware but intent on ignoring us.

"Look at that Ahmadu"

"Ahhhhh. Becky. Na snake be this. Better food, make I kill am for you?"

"Food? You eat snakes?"

"This na boa constrictor, e dey sweet well, make I go bring stick I go kill am now"

"But I don't want you to kill it, it hasn't hurt you, it's sleeping"

"This one is harmless, e no dey bite person, if you no vex am e no go fight you, in fact na pet rich people dey take am do, this one now still small, e fit still grow well"

"Pet? Like keep it in the house as a pet?"

"Yes, yes, na good pet, e no dey cause wahala, e dey chop rat, rat no go dey for house, but we go kill this one"

"No we won't kill it, I want to keep it as a pet"

"Why you wan keep am? Where you go keep am? Your mama go gree so?"

"They won't know"

"Chei Becky, you be craze pikin oh, you wan keep snake in the house where your papa and mama dey and you no go tell them? I no dey oh"

I shrugged, "it's my snake"

"Your snake? As na you find am? Okay make I help you catch am?"

"Yes please"

"You go give me something oh"

An hour and a few gropes of my firm breasts later, I became the proud owner of a boa constrictor. I named him Johnny. I had no clue of Johnny's gender, but he was still Johnny. I kept him in a big box under my bed, and whenever I was home I let him roam around the room. When I needed to go out, I would put him back in the box; I fed him mice and lizards and chicken. I caught the neighbours' chickens and fed them to Johnny, especially the chickens owned by Mrs Aina, our next door neighbour. Mrs Aina is every hoity-toity, she thinks we are a trashy lot and treated my siblings and I like shit even though everybody knew she was having an affair with our fat landlord. I fed Johnny once a week and

Mrs Aina lost all her chickens, every single one of them to Johnny and me; Johnny grew fat on chicken. I loved Johnny.

Sometimes my room smelt because Johnny sometimes did a poo in his box while I was away in school and my father would complain about my hygiene and the smell wharfing from my room. He would promise to whip me mercilessly if I didn't do something about my evil smell.

Johnny who started out at about 30 inches grew very quickly and my room became too small for him to explore. One day he managed to get out of my room and ended up in the living room, my useless cowardly father saw Johnny, peed his pants, screamed the house down and got the neighbours in, together they killed Johnny before I returned from school giving me more reasons to hate the vile creature I called father, like I needed more reasons.

He insisted that we all fast and pray for thirty days to protect ourselves from further manifestations of the devil in our joyless home and to "send back to sender' any evil gifts from our spiritual enemies, ironic considering the devil already lived with us and we called him father.

So in camp, when I saw another brown snake with dark brown saddles along its back curled up under a tree and this time I was yet to empty my bowels, I carried it lovingly into the hostel; it felt like a reunion, a homecoming. I knew Johnny had sent it to me, if only for a brief moment to let me know everything was alright. I knew I couldn't keep a snake in this crowded room of baying women but I could use my temporary pet to pass a message, to teach Marilee a lesson and this I have now done.

***

For two weeks I thought hard about how to punish the idiot called Dariye. He's the one who issued mattresses on the first day of camp and rudely informed me not to disturb him for a better mattress; his sneering face, rude voice and the shame he caused me have all stayed with me. Seeing him around camp naked from the waist up and shamelessly showing off glistering rippling muscles, a leery grin permanently etched on his face didn't do anything to soothe the rage I felt.

As the camp handyman, Dariye did his repair jobs out of a shed at the perimeter of the Mammy market close to the male hostels. You could see him from the Mammy market on days when he chose to work; sawing and cutting wood or screwing things together, his back glistering with sweat, head bent in concentration.

I was convinced he was doing more than taking care of broken furniture and pipes, especially with how girls grinned and smiled at him, stupid cretinous whores with no shame or boundaries.

I went to visit him on Monday with a broken chair from one of the halls.

"Mr James said I should bring this to you for repair"

"Mr James? Who is Mr James?"

I shrugged and thought fast, I had merely made up the name, "the camp official who is like an albino, he wears black framed glasses, very thick"

"Ahhhh, his name is Mr Julius not James oh"

"Okay" I stood there.

"Leave the chair, you can go, I will work on it when I have time"

"Mr Julius said today" I moved closer to his work table where I could see a large hammer lying carelessly.

"Why? Is this the only chair available for him to sit on? He should not disturb me please"

Such a rude fellow. This world is definitely much better without you.

"So you can't repair it today?" I asked again.

"Good afternoon" someone called from behind me before Dariye could give another rude response.

"No I can't repair it. Good afternoon sir" he said in the same breath turning to the new visitor.

It was one of the soldiers, I turned and left.

The second time I went to Dariye's workshop, I walked round the back to avoid the other corpers walking towards the shed and that was when I noticed the manhole which rightly signalled an underground sewage tank; imagine my delight when I noticed that the manhole was only locked down with a big rusty padlock. I noted the man hole for later investigations and proceeded to enter the workshop, a kettle in my hand.

This time Dariye spoke even more rudely referring to me as "Mr Julius' mouthpiece" I smiled and asked if he could repair the broken kettle I was carrying.

"Why do you have an electric appliance in camp? I could report you for this you know?"

"Please don't, just help me repair it please, I hate taking cold baths" I smiled as warmly as I could. There was nothing wrong with the kettle, I stole it off another girl in my room who was too afraid to make any noise about her contraband kettle going missing.

"Ehn, ehn, you like hot baths? So if I repair this kettle what will you give me?"

"I can pay" I replied, knowing fully well this was not the preferred answer, he was responding exactly as I wanted him to, the mention of baths had him conjuring up images in his head; images and imaginations of opportunity.

"You can do better than that oh, you know I can report you to the camp commandant for having this kettle? He repeated, "You know what will happen?"

"Okay please don't do that, I am begging you, if you repair this kettle I will take care of you when I come to collect it"

"You will take care of me abi? Is that a promise?"

"Yes it is" while we were talking I had picked up the hammer that had eluded me in my previous visit and a few large nails.

"Okay come back tomorrow and I will have this kettle ready for you"

"Thank you"

I came back later in the evening, shortly before the bedtime bugle went off, to break the padlock on the manhole and to try moving its heavy concrete cover. After about half an hour of heaving, it did move; the stench that rose from the sliver opening assaulted my nostrils with such force that I literarily reeled back. I replaced the manhole tightly lest the smell should invite the soldiers to lock the manhole again.

***

On Friday, I visited Dariye in his wooden workshop for the third and last time. It was a befitting end to a shitty individual and I hoped that by the time, the sewage tank filled up enough to need emptying, Dariye would no longer be recognisable; poetic justice if I must say so myself.

"Now shitty Dariye swims with the shits. Shit has happened to Freddy. Shitty is as shitty does" I thought, my attempt at rhyming made me giggle and increased the spring in my walk as I returned to the hostel.

"Hello pretty lady who is smiling to herself"

I was annoyed by the sudden intrusion into perfectly enjoyable time alone and so turned with a frown which quickly turned to a smile the moment I saw who it was.

"Mahmud" I exclaimed.

"Yours truly in the flesh" his smile is wide and happy, "where are you off to?"

"To the hostel to wash my shoes, I think I stepped in something bad" I smiled back.

"He crinkled his nose, the smell hitting him at the same time as my response.

"Okay let's talk later?"

"No, I can wash my feet under the tap over there" I said pointing at the knee high water taps outside one of the female hostels. Mahmud stood a distance back, still crinkling his nose while I washed my feet and shoes. I smiled at him warmly, he smiled back not so warmly, a little thoughtful. An ugly thread of fear snaked through me and I hoped he was not wondering what he was doing here with me, waiting for me. I cursed that useless Dariye under my breath, even in death he clearly did not wish me well.

I hurriedly finished washing my feet and shook the water out of my sandals, the cool breeze hit my wet legs, cooling and drying them as I walked briskly back to Mahmud; and walking slightly apart, we strolled towards the green fields.

"Have you had dinner?" he asked as we settled on the raised pavements in front of one of the buildings, the one nearer to the camp gates, far away from everyone else.

"No I haven't, I missed the camp dinner bell" my stomach grumbled in acknowledgement of this fact.

"Let me buy you dinner, what would you like?"

"Buy me dinner?" I asked flush with delight.

"Yes dinner, what do you want to eat?"

Having never bought or eaten any meal from the Mammy market, I had no idea what they had for sale. I thought quickly, there is always rice, every cafeteria in Nigeria that wants to make any money will sell rice.

"Rice and dodo" I replied, getting up from the ledge and wiping the sand from the bottom of my white khaki shorts.

"No, don't worry about coming to the Mammy market. I will buy the food and bring it here, I can't let you trouble yourself that way"

"Oh okay, thank you Mahmud" I smiled at him.

He nodded and stalked off, I relaxed against the coolness of the iron beam beside me and waited for him. The sun was beginning to set in a fiery orange glow, sprinting home as if it was late for dinner and mama would be angry.

After the night we watched Zulu Sofola's 'Wedlock of the Gods' together, I knew he would be back. When I forced myself to look beyond his charming smile and the butterflies in my belly, I saw another Johnson. Here for some sex on the sly; he would run into me accidentally only in the evenings and late at night and in places where people were not likely to take notice of us together, just like Johnson did during my undergraduate days, handsome, sexy, drop dead gorgeous, charm the pants off the ladies Johnson; well he was definitely 'drop dead' now; bless him.

So when he startled me earlier today, I could only smile. Mahmud was definitely here for the goodies on the sly, I could no longer kid myself about destiny's touch. Destiny did not touch girls like me with men like Mahmud unless it was for corner loving; my roommate in Uni called them 'kelekele lovers'. They hang around you where no one can see them with you and dump you as quietly once they have had enough of you. You can almost bet your soul there is a long term girlfriend or a serious love interest somewhere. Why men do this thing is beyond my understanding but here is another one; he doesn't even want to be seen with me at the Mammy market. I can only wonder who he is worried he will run into, all the other girls he fancies? Someone he thinks is prettier and better than me; a slow rage glimmered and glowed in my belly.

"I'm backkkkkkkkkkkk" he called flopping beside me on the ledge.

"Welcome, I was starting to think you were not coming back"

"I would never do that, here" he said thrusting a plastic bowl of food at me and a sweaty bottle of Fanta "I bought you a bottle of Fanta to push down the rice"

"Thank you but can I have the Coke instead?" I asked pointing at the Coca-Cola bottle in his other hand. He frowned slightly and then quickly replaced it with one of his warm smiles "of course you can, I can see you like it black"

I smiled, refusing to rise to his flirtations, and started to eat the food. It was so much better than the dinner I would have gotten from the camp kitchen; not as filling but definitely much better. I could feel the rage again, trying to rise, at the thought of how unfair life is, even here in camp.

"Kiss me" he said abruptly, putting aside his bowl of rice; I smiled and put aside my bowl too, a cold feeling was starting to build in my stomach.

He roughly slipped his hand behind my head and pulled me close planting his lips on mine firmly. His lips were soft and cool, he grazed over my lips and teased my mouth open with his tongue. The cold in my stomach started to heat up; his tongue pushed into my mouth licking my tongue as our lips locked, the heat became an inferno, raging in my belly, down to my pelvis. I leaned into my kelekele lover.

Day 13 NYSC Camp

ADUNNI

Weekends were officially the best days in camp. They were no bugle, lie-in days with the soldiers absent of whips and full of expansive grins and friendliness.

We got out of bed lazily at 6am and had a slow breakfast of cornflakes mixed with powdered milk and cold water; the sun was already overhead and racing west when we got out our buckets to go to the tap.

There was a long queue at the water tank and we waited in line with about fifty brightly coloured buckets and jerry cans and twenty vigilant 'ready-for-a-fight-if-you-jump-the-queue' girls.

A dark heavyset lady wearing what looked like two shorts stomped purposefully past the long queue and dropped her bucket a short distance from the gushing tap.

"Please join the queue at the back" a bespectacled girl ordered her, frost in her voice.

"I was here before" she replied almost as frostily.

"Where before?" bespectacled asked, "please go to the end of the queue and join it, we don't want any trouble here, let's just do this in an orderly manner.

"Are you calling me a trouble maker?" heavyset asked bearing down on the slimmer girl who suddenly looked frighteningly endangered.

"Oooohhhhhh, they are going to disrupt this queue now and none of us will get any water" Jay wailed stamping her feet angrily.

"No they are not" tall Chinyere said.

"She is not calling you a troublemaker, she is merely saying you should join the queue at the back like we all did when we came here" Chinyere said firmly addressing heavyset.

"Yes" someone said staunchly.

"Yes, join the queue at the back now" Ama from our hostel added.

"Anwuli, come and join the queue now" another begged the big bully.

Anwuli knew she had lost the battle, "I was here before oh" she kept repeating as she walked in more sedate strides to the end of the queue that had now grown much longer since she initially came.

"Can the buckets just fill quickly, I'm in a hurry" Jay muttered.

"Yeah, yeah, yeah, it's another Saturday and Yomi is coming, you need to primp and prep for your boo" I replied with a smile.

We filled our buckets ten minutes later and with wet sand clinging to our rubber slippers and feet we hurried back to the hostel courtyard to have our baths. The courtyard is a long grassy strip between the U-shaped hostel that has been converted to both bathroom and laundrette in the last two weeks.

"So you have resolved everything in your mind now hey?" I asked as I reached over my shoulder to scrub my back with my soapy sponge.

"Hmmm"

"Hmm meaning 'yes' or hmmm meaning 'not yet'?"

"Not yet"

"Okay" we fell silent and for a minute faced the business of scrubbing and rinsing down our bodies.

"Jay, I don't want to be a wet blanket, but you know you can't keep postponing this decision? For your sake and Yomi's sake"

"Well I can't decide if I should keep the baby or not"

"I'm not even sure that's the decision you want to make anymore, I think you are keeping the baby, and what you want to decide is whether you are keeping it alone or with Yomi, that's what you need to decide fast"

"How superior and presumptuous of you. I don't know and no I haven't decided if I want to keep the baby, stop telling me what I want or need to decide because you don't know" she snapped.

"You are right, I don't know, I do know that you acting a bit stereotypically like a spoilt child"

"Really? How so?" her voice was cold.

"Apart from the fact that you haven't categorically said why exactly you don't want the baby, I also don't understand why you are still undecided. All I hear is me me, me, me... how I feel, how I am going to feel, how I have felt. It's either you want the baby or not, and it's either you want the baby daddy or not, even if you didn't know before you got pregnant, surely the pregnancy should have helped you put things in perspective a bit – now that I am pregnant, I realise I do not or I do want this baby and so on, ad infinitum"

"I guess you would know, having done this so many times"

"Yes I would actually, I got pregnant in my second year and even though I loved my boyfriend at the time very much, the pregnancy helped me realise I didn't love him enough and didn't want to have a baby with him"

"So you just went and got rid of it"

"If you put it that way... unlike you I didn't wait till it was an adult before murdering it"

"You are an asshole" Jay whispered as if she did not want the world to hear her swearing; picking up her bucket she headed for the hostel.

"I am your friend" I replied. I drained the rest of the water in my bucket over my feet and gingerly stepped out of the puddle onto the hostel pavement and went inside the cool unlit hostel.

"I am your friend Jay" I repeated pushing my bucket under the bunk bed, "but you need to decide what you want to do, with the baby and for the baby. If you are not keeping it, do something early, if you are keeping it then start taking your vitamins and try to be happier"

"Adunni I don't know; I can't decide, I love Yomi very much and I want to have a family with him, but not this baby and not now"

"Why not now and why not this baby? What is wrong with this baby?"

"Adunni just stop, leave me alone, I don't want to talk about it, you already called me a murderer today, I'm not going to stand here and let you call me more names"

"I'm sorry Jay, I'm not here to call you names, you haven't been so happy and I'm just trying to help you see that you need to decide and then live with that decision, it's just what it is"

"If only" she muttered, now fully dressed, she climbed on her bed and plugged her earphones into her ears; conversation over.

JAY

"Hello Sugar" I smiled brightly at Yomi as I climbed into another black Range Rover Evoque.

"Hey" he answered shifting the car into drive and driving slowly out of camp, his eyes firmly on the road ahead.

"How are you doing?" I clicked the seatbelt into place.

"Okay" he said shrugging, "how are you doing?"

"Very well"

"And the baby?"

"Very well I guess"

"Good, would you like to eat something? I noticed a Calabar Kitchen when I was driving down here this morning; we could go there"

"Yes sure" we lapsed into a silence that endured till we drove into the car park of the Calabar Kitchen restaurant. We ate our lunch in continued silence; our conversation limited to the food we were eating.

After our spicy lunch of Jollof rice, grilled chicken and fried plantain, Yomi drove to a hotel, not the one we stayed in the last weekend for which I was glad.

Manning the reception was a heavily made up lady in a red shirt and blue trousers; her orange lipstick sat brightly in the middle of her face reaching from one side of her lips to the other and well out; her eyebrows were boldly drawn on in the shape of boomerangs ignoring her natural eyebrows which had been cleanly shaved off; the eyebrows gave her a surprised look.

Yomi collected his keys from her and headed down the corridor, I followed him meekly.

We spent the rest of the day in the hotel room watching cable TV and getting to know each other's bodies again but the sex was perfunctory, not the excited sex of young lovers who had been apart but of an old married couple who saw each other daily and no longer thought much of sex. I was holding back and I was sure he was holding back too. We went out for dinner but couldn't seem to find any palatable restaurant and ended up returning to the hotel with Suya wrapped in newspapers. We ate in silence and watched more cable TV.

On Sunday morning, we were woken up by the room service breakfast Yomi had ordered the night before. The sight of the scrambled eggs and the bacon covered in an oily sheen had me heaving and dashing for the bathroom. I ate dry toast and glared at the covered tray of food in disgust.

"We need to talk" Yomi said coming out of the same bathroom where I had gone to throw up my dinner in the toilet bowl. A white towel around his neck, his hair dripping into it and another around his waist. He sat down in front of me and cradled my hands in his.

"I love you Jay, I love you so much and will do anything to make you happy"

"I love you too baby"

"I need you to know that I have done something; something that might upset you a little but I hope you will understand I did it for us, for you, because I want you to be happier"

"What did you do babes?" I asked.

Then he said the craziest thing ever, "Jay, I spoke with your mum"

"What?"

"Yes baby, I'm sorry I know it's not what you would have wanted, but hear me out"

"You spoke with my mum" I repeated, all my bewilderment evident in my voice.

"Yes, I think it's time you and your mum built some bridges, I..."

"How dare you contact my mum?" I said cutting him off "How dare you? Who died and made you God?"

"Nobody" he replied, "Jay see, I'm trying to help you build a bridge, you are not happy and one of the things that is eating you up is the fact that you don't know your mum or have a relationship with her, you don't know her story, if you and your mum could repair your relationship, get to you know each other a little, you might feel better about becoming a mum yourself"

"And it all comes back to the baby again, you selfish bastard. Your only focus is you, what impacts you, what concerns you. Two years I have dated you and not once have you tried to build a bridge with my mum, but now that you think it might force me to keep the baby, you go about calling people you don't know"

"Jay, it's not about forcing you to keep the baby, it's about helping you feel happier about becoming a mum"

"Same thing I hear there, asshole. Why would you call my mum? You called a woman I haven't spoken to in almost 20 years without telling me first? Is she your mum? Don't you have your own mum Yomi?"

"Come on Jay, calm down"

"Don't tell me to calm down, you son of a bitch"

"Wow, wow, Jay you haven't let me explain what I discussed with your mum"

"What you discussed with my mum" I sneered, "hello little Mr Detective discussing with my mum, tell me, how did you get her contact details?"

"I spoke with your brother Deji and he said..."

"You spoke with who? Oh my God I can't deal with this, who else have you spoken to on this your fact finding mission? My granddad? My nursery school teachers? My former nannies? What exactly are you looking for?" I picked up my hand bag and started to pack up my travel bag which I had stupidly emptied on a chair in the room.

"Jay...."

"Don't touch me, I don't ever want to see you again" I shouted.

"Don't touch you?" he asked, ice in his voice, "have you ever loved me? Is our relationship even real to you or was it something you did to pass the time while waiting for your knight in shining armour who would make you feel better about your mum leaving when you were four?"

I did not respond, I pushed down my clothes till they fit in the bag and forced the zipper close.

"Why can't we discuss like adults without resorting to screams and name calling? Can't you see I'm trying to help here?"

"Help who? I don't remember asking you for help. Contacting my mum or whoever you have contacted is bang out of order and I don't want to ever see you again. You are an asshole, a stupid egotistical asshole"

You don't want to see me again, you don't want the baby, you don't want to see your mother even though her absence in your life is eating you up; you love me but I can't be a part of the innermost you; help me understand you Jay because I don't and I'm getting tired of playing 'fit the puzzle' with you"

"Well it doesn't matter anymore, I'm sure my mum can help you understand me better since you are now both on speaking terms"

"Jay listen to me, I was trying to help you here, help both of us – listen to this; you are expecting a baby with your boyfriend who loves you and wants to spend forever with you yet you can't bear the thought of having a baby with him. How do you think that makes me feel? Would it suffice to say you have been lying all this while and don't love me at all? I don't know what you want exactly or what you think you need..."

"And that's why you thought, oh wait, let me call her mum who she hasn't spoken to in twenty years; I'm sure she will know exactly what her daughter wants and needs to do. Yomi you are sick, arrogant and wayyyyyyy out of line. You are way out of line mister and you need to know that"

"I accept that but you need to try, your mum wants to talk, she will be flying in this week"

"And I will not be speaking to her, or to you. I don't want to marry you or be with you, you are a sneaky son of a bitch and I don't like your mother"

"Oh really? You don't like my mother? You are not satisfied with calling me names and screaming at me like a fishwife, you had to go for my mother?"

"I don't like your mother Yomi and she doesn't like me either anyway"

"I don't remember asking you to marry my mother; I don't like your brother Fola either, he creeps me out and if I didn't know better I would think he wanted you for himself"

"You bastard. You down and low bottom of the lake dirt sucking bastard. Stay away from me forever" I slammed out of the hotel room.

"Did I touch a nerve?" He shouted after me.

"Asshole" I screamed running down the corridor towards reception where the orange lipped lady was still holding forte with two men similarly dressed.

"I gave your mum your number" he called after me before slamming his room door loudly enough for me to hear as I asked for a cab at the reception.

Day 14 NYSC Camp

ADUNNI

It's our second weekend in camp and as usual Jay left the camp with Yomi the day before and will not return till the early hours of Monday. I was spending my Sunday afternoon lying on my bunk flipping through a month old edition of Vogue and soon the hostel began to feel like a dark room of bad smells and bad feelings, so I decided to watch the football match starting on the parade ground in a few minutes. It was the final match of both the football and volleyball camp leagues and Bolaji's Platoon nine football team nicknamed 'All Star Arsenal' was finally playing against David's Platoon eight 'The Jos Warriors'. Bolaji and David have gone at each other so many times, they probably now felt personally responsible for the outcome of the final match.

I walked into Toni outside the hostel and together we found a good spot to watch the match from; by the front door of the clinic, near one of the two goal posts then we waited for the match to begin. The noise and excitement in the air around the field gave the impression that all of Camp had turned out to watch the match.

The match started after a short speech from the RSM and in the first forty five minutes neither team scored a goal, they both defended their sides fiercely. By half time, our voices were hoarse from screaming, we were covered in dust and I could feel my head aching, but still we rushed over to Bolaji's Platoon bench where the players were already surrounded by a lot of beaming girls offering them lemonade. Bolaji broke

248

into a huge smile when he spotted Toni and me behind the mob of girls "hello people" he called out to us, grinning tiredly.

"Hey you, you are doing great out there" Toni said.

"Yes Bolaji, good game, score a goal for us soon okay?" I added.

Half time ended almost as soon as it started and we all returned to the field for another 45 minutes of 'on the edge of your seat' football which also ended without any goals to either team.

The RSM conferred with the referee for a few minutes and announced through a crackly microphone that the game was going to be decided with penalty kicks. The penalty-kicks started with Ahmadu from the 'All Star Arsenal' who sent the ball into the corner of the net, flashing past the tips of the goal keeper's fingers. The scream and noise was deafening; I jumped and screamed at the top of my lungs. The field quickly went silent as the Platoon 8 player got the ball. The air was still... everything was still... he kicked the ball directly at the goal keeper who crouched quickly and grabbed the ball; a low moan went round the field from the supporters of Platoon 8. Platoon 9 also lost the next kick and in no time both teams had gone through the five penalty kicks allocated to them with no winner emerging – now it was sudden death penalty kicks and whoever lost the first penalty kick would lose the game.

The Jos Warriors had the first go and the All Star Arsenal goal keeper caught the ball. At that moment I felt pity for the 'Jos Warriors' goalkeeper, everything suddenly depended on him; he had to catch that ball or else his team would lose the match. Constantus, the best striker in the 'All Star Arsenal' positioned himself in front of the ball and in a flash he kicked the ball powerfully, leaping with it; the Platoon 8 goal keeper didn't catch that ball.... It went right in.

Constantus pulled his jersey over his head covering his eyes and ran off screaming a blood curdling victory shout. His whole team ran after him also screaming jubilantly. The field broke into an uproar... boys shouting at the top of their lungs... and girls screaming and jumping up and down.... I was screaming too, happy as a dog uncovering a long buried bone.

The goal keeper who lost the deciding ball and the captain of the Platoon 8 football team sat on the football field and wept like babies.

The winning team and their supporters streamed to the Mammy market to celebrate till the bugle went off, one of them carrying the yellow tin winner's cup on his head.

I saw David briefly, walking the other way towards the male hostels, a broken man. I hoped that he would avoid Bolaji for the next few days till when Bolaji's bragging and boasting might not hurt so much, little chance of that though.

We noisily bought dinners of grilled chicken and bread from the chicken stall and headed to the drink stalls to buy cold bottles of beer, Smirnoff ice and Orijin; we were about to do a lot of drinking.

Our Platoon came second in the volleyball tournament and I was pleasantly surprised when Janet ducked into our makeshift bar to give me a bar of celebratory chocolate. I felt guilty eating them considering I didn't do much to support the win.

"Should we go and watch the cultural dance competitions" Toni asked at 8pm, "it's starting right about now" he said draining his bottle of beer.

"If you are not too drunk, I'm not too drunk" I shrugged.

"Me drunk? At all at all, let's go"

The Cultural dance competition was already underway when we got to the administrative hall where it was holding, we were forced to stand, our backs against the cool cracked walls. The hall was warm but not uncomfortably so and beside me, Toni was already getting into the groove of things, humming with restless energy and tapping his thigh in time to the rhythm of the drumbeats and the stumping of the dancers.

Space was a premium in the hall as it seemed nearly everybody had turned out to watch the performances; still it was easy to notice tall gangly Terry, my Platoon leader pushing through the standing bodies, causing a ripple of movement in my direction.

I turned away from his determined progress into the hall and tried to focus on the dancers on the stage in their stiff Yoruba Aso-oke, beads and bells rattling around their ankles.

"Adunni" he called as he finally shouldered his way to my side, "How far? I've been looking for you" he said with a small smile, the women in Aso-oke were leaving the stage and there was a lull in the stage performances while we waited for the next set of dancers to climb the dusty wooden stage.

I eyed him warily but said nothing. What could he possibly want?

"Enjoying the dances?" he continued, undeterred by my silence.

I shrugged in reply, "it's ok, Toni is enjoying it very much, he wanted to come" I was keen to rope Toni into this conversation.

"That's good" he nodded, his smile widening, "hopefully, we will win this one and with your support, we will also win the Miss NYSC on Saturday"

"What do you mean my support?"

"We can almost guarantee a win with that one if you represent us"

"How so? I'm not interested in contesting"

"You know you are one of the prettiest, most elegant ladies in this camp and with the right support and encouragement, you will win it for us" he continued.

"You keep saying with the right support, with the right support, I don't understand the Greek you are speaking Terry and I don't want to contest"

"Just come and see the Senior Camp Director, he asked for you. Na him say make I come find you sef" he finished switching to Pidgin English abruptly as if the mention of the Senior Camp Director had flipped a switch in his head.

"Why does the Senior Camp Director want to see me? I don't want to contest"

"Please Adunni, just come abeg" he wheedled, "he's right outside and wants to see you briefly"

I glanced at Toni who was now in a lively conversation with the girl on the far side, discussing the merits and demerits of the competing Platoons. I nudged him "I'll be right back, keep my space" Toni glanced at me and then at Terry, a question in his eyes but he only nodded, saying nothing.

Outside, the evening air was a welcome contrast to the warmth of the hall, the sound of drums started up again, amplified by the electronic speakers in the hall as we walked away. I could see the Senior Camp Director standing under a tree with some male corpers. As we approached, the corpers said their farewells and wandered off.

"Sir" Terry greeted the official with a quick bob of his head, "She's here"

The Senior Camp Director was a rotund man, although always in some form of sporting gear or the other, they always failed to make him look physically fit in anyway and his belly strained against the pullover he wore determinedly.

"Adunni-Dunni" He said jovially as Terry retreated, having delivered his charge. "How are you, my dear?"

"I'm fine"

"That's good. That's good. Do you know me?" he asked.

"Yes Sir, Mr Adelakun"

"Good, I hope you are enjoying this camp?" His eyes roved across my face down my neck and further downwards; I could feel the irritation building inside me.

"Camp is ok" I shrugged, "Terry said you wanted to see me" I added quickly as he opened his mouth to comment on the short reply.

"Yes, well..." He paused and shifted closer "I've been seeing you around. You and that your fine friend and I always wanted to meet you but you know how this place is"

I watched him silently. Is this going where I think it is? I wondered.

"So when Terry came to me about Miss NYSC and how you would make such a great contestant, I was happy" His smile grew wider and his eyes were flickering between my face and my chest like a weak candle.

"He said you are not keen on contesting for Miss NYSC and I said to him, Terry does she think she cannot win? She will win. She is easily the prettiest girl in this camp and shouldn't worry"

"I don't want to contest for Miss NYSC" I replied.

"We are saying the same thing" he wagged his finger at me, "you don't want to contest because you think you won't win; but you will. You will win because I am supporting you, in fact I can guarantee your Platoon will win the competition if you are representing them" His smile was beginning to nauseate me "All you need to do is be nice to me; if you are nice I will be nice"

"Nice to you? Sir, I don't understand you"

"Come on, Adunni" he pronounced it Key-mon giving me a knowing look "I know you don't have a boyfriend around and a beauty like you shouldn't be so alone here. Date me. Be my girlfriend and life will be wonderful for you and me"

For a moment, I was speechless. My anger boiled to the surface but I quelled it, thinking to myself that isn't really this man's fault; the culprit is Terry who must have thought he was doing me a favour by pimping me for competition points. Mr Adelakun must have been emboldened by my silence because he stepped closer, opening his mouth to press his case. Immediately, I stepped back, raising my hand to forestall any ideas he might have about closing the physical space between us.

"I'm sorry sir, but I can't. I'm not competing for the Miss NYSC title" my voice was chilly "and I have a boyfriend at home, I can't cheat on him"

"You can't cheat on your boyfriend at home? Silly girl. Who is talking about home? This is camp... we are in faraway Jos, enjoy yourself with me, I will show you what your boyfriend cannot show you in a million years, it's not like you haven't been doing these things before"

I could almost hear the click as he stepped on a mine in my mind and it blew up in his face.

"What things? I asked. He began to smile slyly, "what things?" I repeated, "You are a fool, a useless stupid fool. I don't know what kind of girls you have been coming across in your life who have somehow given you the specious belief that you are worth cheating on anyone for, or able to show anyone anything. You can't even keep your body and mouth from smelling but you want to show me a million things, Stupid fool" I turned and walked away in the direction of the still ongoing cultural dance competition.

He was standing there, struggling for what to say as I left. I glanced around but Terry was nowhere to be seen. It was probably better that way. There was no telling what I would have said to him if he was unfortunate enough to cross my path that night.

I was almost at the hall when I noticed there was a lip-locked couple under a tree just ahead. I wouldn't have paid any attention to them as there were usually groping couple in the many poorly lit corners of the camp, especially during events when most of camp was enclosed in the main hall, but the girl's simple cornrows coupled with her corpulent form gave away her identity. I smiled ruefully; Becky isn't such a prude after all. There was no avoiding walking past them though and they broke apart as I came abreast. I wished they hadn't.

Security lights outside the admin hall bounced off the guy's face for an instant and I was stunned. Mahmud. I knew he had seen me too because he froze. I didn't stop walking, moving right past them without a second glance.

"Adunni" he said to my back but I did not acknowledge him. Tears prickled my eyes, I felt both betrayed and vindicated; a golden man with clay feet, beautiful feet but clay... so definitely clay and not that into me after all; just goes to show.

I returned to the hall and watched quietly as the last cultural dance competition was completed and Platoon four was declared the winner. They had also previously won the Drama competition with their presentation of Zulu Sofola's '*Wedlock of the gods*'... I remember watching Adesuwa Becky's wing man, playing Ogwoma in that play; tall skinny talkative Adesuwa who probably says everything that comes to her mind even before she has examined it for veracity and common sense and darkly stout Becky with her gruff nature and menacing smiles; unexpected friendships - Adesuwa and Becky, Mahmud and Becky.

JAY

I got back to camp on Sunday evening in a filthy rickety taxi three hours after leaving Yomi's room, the sun was starting to set, its face in layers of fiery orange and tomato red. Adunni was surprised to see me and said as much but I didn't care to explain myself.

"Wow, you are back, is everything okay?" she asked.

"Yes I'm fine, don't worry about me" I said letting my bag fall to the floor and immediately climbing up on the bunk.

"Are you sure? You look upset" she pressed.

"I'm fine Adunni, please don't worry" I turned my back to her to let her know I didn't want to talk anymore.

"Okay" a few minutes later I heard her leaving the hostel. I waited till she was completely out of earshot before burying my face in my pillow and weeping my heart out. I had held it in since the horrible conversation with Yomi and now I let it all go. I cried for over an hour till I was exhausted and my body had no more tears to give. I felt tired and cleansed and promptly fell into a dreamless sleep waking up two hours later in the dark quiet hostel knowing exactly what I was going to do.

I am going to have the baby, my baby and raise it alone; I can do it. I'm tired of everybody trying to tell me how to live my life, of people trying to be a crutch for me as if I have some undiagnosed condition that makes me unable to do things on my own, by myself; will prove them all wrong. I don't need Yomi or anybody else to raise this baby, it's mine and I am keeping it. Good a thing as my relationship with

Yomi was while it lasted, I know it's over now. It is over for good.

It's time to live with the choices I have made with my life; when my mum comes on Sunday, I will see her and listen to her and understand why she left a four-year-old child and never looked back.

I felt like I had been set free. I jumped down from my bed to make myself a student's dinner. I poured some sugar-coated cornflakes into a plastic bowl, added water from an Eva bottle and two spoonsful of powdered NIDO milk, the baby needs protein, lots of it and starting now baby is getting all the nutrients it needs.

I paused a little and wondered if my nonchalant attitude so far has had any effect on my baby, has he or she been very sad inside there? Poisoned by my sad thoughts and confusion, starved of good food, jerked around and irritated? I don't know.

I touched my belly gingerly, "darling I am going to make it up to you, you and I are going to have immense fun, and we are going to have the time of our lives, best friends and things. I will always be there for you my honey, from now on"

I climbed back into bed my stomach full and my mind at ease for the first time in a long time. All my worries and guilt no longer mattered, all that matters is my baby. I'm not even going to worry about telling daddy, that will work out somehow, if he loves me as much as he says he does then he will forgive me my indiscretion, if not right away, some day. I am an adult, I can do this.

The first thing I said to Adunni the next morning was, "I'm keeping the baby"

"You might as well" she replied "I'm glad that is what you have decided"

"I'm keeping it alone" I continued, she was silent.

"Oh and Yomi?"

"Doesn't matter, I'm keeping the baby alone"

"That's fine love, you are going to be fine and I'll be there for you, I promise" she replied hugging me, "You are a good kid and I'm glad you have decided what you want for yourself, well done you" there was no judgement in her voice, there was kindness, there was appreciation, there was happiness.

"Thanks" I couldn't help the tears filling my eyes.

"Come on, don't be a cry baby, you will be fine"

"Thank you Adunni, I feel like I have known you forever"

"Don't be fooled, it's the camp effect" she replied in a husky voice.

Day 16 NYSC Camp

BECKY

Camp had suddenly taken on a whole new image to me. It was suddenly a place of hope; an exciting, colourful, joyous place where young people meet and get to know each other, build endurance and find love.

The whole of camp looked brighter, more colourful, the water from the tap felt colder, fresher, the air was clean and sharp, even breakfast tasted nicer; I was deliriously happy. I couldn't help smiling at everyone, even though most of them did not smile back but that was okay. I wouldn't smile back at me if I was in their shoes and knew what I was getting on.

Mahmud and I had a meeting planned for the front of the Press building in broad daylight in a place where everybody could see us. I was so excited I couldn't stop the shivers that ran down my arms every time I thought of his handsome chiselled face and his hands on my body.

Mahmud was proving ardent, delighted with me, excited and I was starting to think I might have been wrong in my initial assessment of him; "maybe I'm not a secret lover after all maybe he is just taking his time sharing with the world this beautiful thing that is growing between us" I thought with delight.

"Heyyyyyy Becky wait for me; I'm coming with you" a voice cut into my day dream.

"Adesuwa, you don't even know where I am going"

"Okay, where are you going? Camp is not that big, you are undoubtedly going to the field"

"I am going to the press building actually"

"Well great; I'm keen to hear that radio programme too" Adesuwa said, falling into step with me.

"What radio programme?" I walked fast so she would focus on keeping up and not talk so much.

"The one that's going to be broadcast from the Press room at 10, isn't that why you are going there?"

"No, but what's the broadcast about?"

"It's a Christian programme about relationships, how to find and keep your perfect man. The radio host is going to be interviewing a lady who used to be an understudy of the late Pastor Bimbo Odukoya; worked with her and all that so she is a relationship guru"

"I'm not interested in any 'finding and keeping a man' programme"

"Well, you should be; we all need a man, especially now that school is over; a girl needs to settle down with the right man and I'm not even sure there is any left out there. Malik is nice but I feel that he is not very open, maybe he is married" Adesuwa said.

"Why do you care? Is he your boyfriend?"

"Well, we haven't put anything into words but who knows, it's in the works, hopefully this programme will share some nuggets on keeping a man like him; he is very elusive to be honest"

"I don't need some scam artist telling me how to find and keep a man"

"She is definitely not a scam artist and actually you do need someone telling you how to find and keep a man, we all do because nobody knows it all" she piped.

"So you are going to listen to someone who claims to know it all"

"She knows enough and the fact that you are not dating anyone as I haven't seen anyone around you in the last two and half weeks is proof that you sure don't know it all" Adesuwa replied tartly.

I paused and gazed at her thoughtfully, 'one day I am going to kill this girl, break that scrawny neck and actually enjoy doing it'

"Come on, what are you waiting for?" Adesuwa said with impatience.

I followed her silently.

The press building was rowdy, the front door was wide open but people were milling around, not going in or out, just hanging around the front porch talking and leaning against the wall.

Adesuwa walked in like she knew exactly where she was going turning left into a big room which had been set up with chairs in rows. Black boom speakers were standing in the four corners of the room, wires snaked along the floor to the front of the room to connect to a large ancient radio.

I chose a seat near the window where I could see out to the front of the Press building, it was ten minutes to ten and I expected Mahmud to show up anytime from now.

As usual Adesuwa wouldn't shut up and kept up a one sided conversation till the programme started at 10 and even then she didn't stop. She would pause briefly to gulp air before continuing her meaningless chatter in response to everything the radio host and his guest were saying. I couldn't help but wonder what folly led me to befriend this girl; still I let her words sail past me forcing them to become a soothing background to my rosy thoughts of my near meet up with Mahmud; he was by now almost an hour late. I forced down the pique that was threatening to destroy my sense of wellbeing.

"Adunni" I heard a familiar voice shout, not very loudly but loud enough for me to hear. I turned quickly and saw Mahmud through the open window running towards the Press building. He was heading towards the window I had been watching intently for the last half hour. I only needed to see the shine of her long black hair and her neck to know Adunni was on the other side of the window and she was the one Mahmud was running towards so breathlessly. He didn't look like he even remembered we planned to meet here.

I got up and walked quickly to the window, keeping away from the line of vision of anyone looking in from outside. I leaned my back on the cool wall by the window as he stopped in front of her. She was leaning on the wall in the same place as I was, on the other side of the wall and I could almost feel her long lean back against mine, her coolness and aloofness radiating through the wall to me.

"Hello stranger" Mahmud said in his easy smiling voice.

"Hello" she replied.

"Long time no see, where have you been?

Silence

Have we not been in this same camp?"

Silence

"I feel like I haven't seen you in forever" he continued.

"Leave her alone" I screamed in my head.

"I'm sorry I can't talk right now, can we catch up another time?" she said coolly rebuffing his friendliness.

"I told you, I told you" I crowed silently.

"Haba Gimbiya, are we fighting? What have I done?"

Gimbiya? That is what he calls me – the bastard.

"Please don't Gimbiya me, you haven't done anything, I just don't want to talk"

"Adunni please don't be like this"

"Like how? Why do you want to talk to me, is your girl-friend busy?"

"What girlfriend?"

"You probably mean which one? As it looks like you have many, good on you, you are obviously having a blast"

She pushed away from the wall as if to walk away, I peeped out to see his face and he grabbed her hand quickly to stop her from leaving.

"No Adunni, that girl is not my girlfriend"

"Which girl?" she asked.

Good question Adunni, I hate you but good question, answer the question, you treacherous bastard son of a dirty camel.

"I know who you are referring to, I only hang out with her because she won't go away and she is practically a stalker. She follows me all over camp smiling and trying to start con-versations, so if you saw us talking that is all there was to it, we were talking"

"Poor Becky, so you talk to girls by putting your tongue down their throats? I don't mind you having fun in camp, its camp and that's what most people are doing anyway but this blatant lying is an insult to my intelligence. I saw you and you saw me so this outright lying is just more proof that you are a slimy piece of shit. You should crawl back under whatever rock you crawled out from, that's where you should stay"

"Adunni please understand, that girl kissed me. She kissed me I swear it; if you had waited a little more you would have seen me pushing her away"

Adunni laughed, a cold and mocking laugh, "I think you should stop talking, because you are a very bad liar and you haven't thought your lies through, please just stop. I'm not even mad at you now, I'm terribly amused and a little shocked at your poor lying skills, and do stop calling her that girl, she has a name and I hope she realises quickly what a piece of slime you are, kissing you indeed" she snatched her hand out of his grip and walked away.

My legs felt weak, I was right about him after-all, he was even worse than I had imagined; I held the window for support. I could not bear to let him see me or let him know I heard every word he just said about me, about us. It would have dire consequences for both of us, for him mostly. I wanted to clutch my chest to assuage the pain, the feeling of tightness, the white hot pain, the heat filling my face and causing sweat beads to break out on my forehead.

I watched him as he walked away from the window, a small frown on his face. I felt I was seeing him for the first time; the sleek movement I found beautiful now seemed like the slinking of a gutter snake, and his frowning face no longer looked distinguished, all I saw was the lying ugly face of a traitor.

How could I have deluded myself into thinking we had something? That he was different? That he would look at my fat stodgy body and wide face and like what he saw? How could I have been sooooo stupid to think he wasn't using me? He is a man, they are all users, every single one of them, spineless, lazy, lying users.

He said I was unique, he probably meant I was so ugly there was no one else like me. Becky Oni, you are a fatuous gullible idiot who deserve to be let down every single day of your life and have your face rubbed in it. It's your fault bad things happen to you.

"Becky, Beckkkkkky" Adesuwa yelled, her voice shrill as she walked towards me. I shook my head to clear it of the dark angry thoughts swirling around in it.

"You missed most of the radio programme and it was enlightening. Why are you leaning against the wall alone like that?" she asked, "you won't believe what just happened" she continued without pause, not waiting for a response from me.

"I am sure you are about to tell me" I replied pushing away from the wall in the same way Adunni had done earlier but less gracefully, I probably looked like a truck lurching away from its stop.

"Malik just offered to make sure I am posted to Jos Town and not to a village" she said gasping with what seemed like joy and surprise, "can you believe that Becky?" she asked as we exited the Press building.

"In exchange for?"

"Not in exchange for anything Becky, don't be funny, he just said a nice girl like me doesn't deserve to go to a remote village to suffer poor drinking water and mosquitoes for a year. I think he truthfully loves me and is going to ask me to be his girlfriend which is why he doesn't want me posted to some remote village"

"It won't be because he wants a bit of that stuff you have in front of you there right?"

"What stuff? He is helping me; that is all"

"And if you think this help will be for nothing, then you are dumber than I who just got taken in by a low life retarded idiot" I mumbled under my breath.

"What did you say?" Adesuwa asked frowning, her smile faltering.

"I just asked how ordinary Malik would achieve this posting miracle" I answered.

"He is not ordinary, he is handsome and dashing and intelligent and don't worry he will do it, he has friends in high places and they will do anything to help his girlfriend, he made me promise to let him show me the beauty of Jos throughout my service year, isn't that fantastic?" she finished clapping softly.

"So you are going to be seeing the beauty of his bedroom for a whole year in exchange for a city posting and a relationship that will probably not lead anywhere? I'm not sure that's a good bargain you have made Adesuwa, a bit foolish I think"

"Please don't call me a fool. I don't like it when you use such negative words" She replied in a petulant voice, I like parties and Malik is dashing, I was sure I will enjoy seeing Jos with him"

"You are either utterly artless or asinine or you are a cunning little devil who knows exactly what she is doing"

"I don't understand all this name calling you are resorting to Becky, this is why I find you tiring at times and considering

I'm the only friend you have you truly should try to be nicer to me. Calling me names and being rude won't change the fact that I have been lucky to get a city posting, why can't you be happy for me?"

"You have the promise of a city posting, you don't actually have the posting yet, you know, so let's hold off on the celebration a little"

"Whatever, you are just jealous and you are letting it eat you up. I was going to put in a word for you with Malik so you can get a city posting too but I don't see the point now because you plainly don't care for it"

"Okay Adesuwa, congrats on your city posting, I'll see you later" I said turning away from the hostel gates.

"You are not coming in?" she asked.

"No I'm not, I want to go for a walk to clear my head; it seems I can't rid the world of evil no matter how hard I try"

"Whatever" she flounced into the hostel.

Day 17 NYSC Camp

ADUNNI

I jumped off the rope, taking care not to snag my leg on a trailing length of rope. I had just completed the rope climbing exercise which we all had to complete before the end of the day. The Platoon Commandant was standing there, bellowing at stragglers who were hesitant about getting on the rope.

"Good job Adunni" someone called out from the crowd around the mesh of ropes and frames, I smiled and looked around for the familiar voice – Effiong.

"Hello" I smiled.

"How are you today?"

"Very well, you?"

"I'm fine, you have been like an illusion, and all I keep getting are glimpses of you all over camp"

"Really?"

"Yes really, walk with me please"

"Where are we going?"

"Nowhere in particular I just want to talk to you" after a few minutes of walking silently he stopped and pulled me to the side of the dusty path, "I can't get you out of my mind, I know how creepy and weird this might sound but since I met you I have known that you are a part of my future, my life. There is something, I feel it, I want it. I want to be in your life and you in mine.... Adunni please give me a chance to be your friend"

"We are friends"

"More than friends then?"

"Ah, ah, Effiong, isn't this a bit out of the blue?"

"Not for me no, you have been avoiding me for the last two weeks, it's not fair at all. Adunni, I want to be more than just friends, I want you in my life, your smile, your calmness, you are beautiful inside and out, and yes I know you have a heart of gold behind all that aloofness. You take care of Jay and worry about her like she is your own sister, you are kind and giving and good, I see the goodness of your heart and I am in love with you"

"Oh" there was a lump in my throat. I cleared my throat to shift it, this kind of conversation would normally have me laughing in derision and disbelief but I was silent, touched by the earnestness in his voice and the seriousness in his eyes. I was shocked by the realisation that I liked Effiong. I like the crinkling in the corner of his eyes, I like the honesty that shines strongly from his eyes, I like his gentle smile and very white teeth, and I like his slim hands. I like his quietness, his seeming fortitude. The lump in my throat was now in my belly, I was reeling from the shock of it all.

"I love you"

"Please don't say that, you don't know me" I couldn't keep the coldness out of my voice.

"I love you and I know you, I know your perfume is something floral with smells of jasmine and roses, and your hair smells of coconut oil. You love British artists because I have heard you singing Ed Sheeran and Florence and the Machine. You are not a social media freak because you are not always scrolling through your phone, you love drinking Sprite never Coca-Cola, and you love your noodles very spicy. I

don't know you very well but if you let me, I will know you"
his eyes were serious.

"Effiong, I am happy to be your friend, and I am grateful
for the compliments, but I cannot promise you more, I can't
give you more"

"That's okay for now" he smiled, "can I be your friend,
perhaps with time...."

"Yes you can be my friend, that way you will stop stalking
me"

He smiled, "that's not stalking, I haven't even smiled at
you from outside your bedroom window at 5am, what do
you know?"

"That would be terrible Effiong, please don't do that,
ever" I said laughing.

He slipped his hand into mine and we started to walk
again.

"You are beautiful and ethereal Adunni and you take my
breath away everyday"

"Now you are embarrassing me"

"I'm sorry but it's the truth, you don't know how beautiful you are to me, you are graceful and elegant and you are
lovable, I love your hair and your smile"

"I already agreed to be your friend Effiong"

"And you are witty and smart"

"Thank you Effiong, can we go to the admin building
now? Jay, Bolaji and Toni agreed to run me through the kind
of questions the judges are likely to ask at the beauty contest
and I'm sure they are already waiting"

"You are contesting for Miss NYSC?"

"Yes I am"

"What changed your mind?"

"This and that" I shrugged. No point saying that dirty mouthed Mr Adelakun with his smarmy offer changed my mind. I'm not leaving this camp with some halfwit thinking I didn't contest because I was afraid of losing or didn't think I could win without his 'help' - laughable fool.

"Now I pity the other contestants, they shouldn't bother"

"Yes they should, you are just a flatterer"

"No I am truthful"

"I hear you"

Bolaji, Toni and Jay were already waiting in the designated room in the admin building; after friendly hellos and pleasantries, Bolaji produced a sheave of papers from his back pocket.

"What are those?" Toni asked.

"Practice questions for Adunni"

"Ahhhhh, you look like someone who managed to get expo before an exam, where are these questions from?

"The internet of course, Toni you do know google is your friend right?"

"Okay let's get started" I said quickly cutting off the beginning of another inane argument between Bolaji and Toni, "thank you Bolaji for getting the questions ready, are there answers there too or do I have to make them up?"

"For the questions about you, there are no answers here, but for the others there are suggestions. All four of us are judges today, so we will all sit around this table" Bolaji said pointing at a rectangular table surrounded by five chairs. We will start with the questions that are not about you, as those are the ones that you might find harder to answer" Bolaji explained passing sheets of papers round the table "and you will get questions from each of us starting with Doctor at the end of the table"

"Okay"

Okay Adunni" Effiong cleared his throat, "if you won ten million naira in the lottery today what would you do with it?"

"I would use the money to start a small business sourcing, packaging and selling local food products. This will enable me to help farmers and contribute to sustainable farming in Nigeria and if the business grows I will be able to help my community by hiring people"

"Wow, that is a fantastic first time answer" Toni said.

"I know right, good start Adunni" Jay added.

"Thank you"

"Adunni, if God could grant you one wish what would it be?" Toni asked.

"I would ask that God heal every sickness in everybody and that every man, woman and child be blessed with good health all the days of their lives"

"And that effectively puts me out of a job" Effiong said wryly.

"But it's a good answer" I countered.

Yes but short, World hunger is another good one, why don't you say that you will ask God to eliminate hunger so that nobody is ever hungry again due to poverty or financial deprivation" Bolaji said.

So the questions went on and on; Bolaji must have printed a hundred questions and was intent on going through as many of them as possible.

After two hours of answering questions I was exhausted, "can we take a break now? I'm exhausted"

"Okay but let's take a few personal questions and then we can take a water break" Bolaji answered.

"First question, who is the most influential person in your life?" Toni asked.

"My mum"

"Don't stop there, you have to tell us why" Bolaji added.

"Okay, my mum is a widow who lost her husband to cancer when her children were still rather young yet she single-handedly raised us on a teacher's meagre income. She is a strong, kind woman, a woman with great fortitude and a never ending spirit of forgiveness. She never gives up especially when it comes to her children. I want very much to be a strong, forbearing woman like her"

Bolaji and Toni quickly ran through five more questions about me then Effiong said, "if you could change anything about the past what would you change?"

I caught my breath and my eyes clouded, I could feel my throat constricting; I would change my father's story – he wouldn't have cancer nor die from it, he would be alive and well. I would have him around to moan about like all my friends moan about their dads and how annoying they are. I wouldn't be this dysfunctional, my mother wouldn't have to do so many things alone, she wouldn't have to stand up to dad's family alone, she wouldn't have to teach and run a sweet shop, she would be a doctor's wife, and we would be his happy children.

"Adunni?" Jay cut into my thoughts.

"Let me think about that one, can we take a break now?"

"One more question and we are done – what is the most daring thing you have ever done?"

"Bungee jumping off the Bloukrans Bridge in South Africa" I replied with reckless abandon, the feelings brought on by memories of my father strong and goading me.

"Bungee jumping you say?" Bolaji asked disbelief clear in his voice.

"Yes"

"It's not a good idea to make up fascinating answers, the judges might decide to dig deeper and catch you out, won't look good"

"I did go bungee jumping in South Africa" I replied.

"Off the Bloukrans bridge which is just like one of the most popular bungee jumping sites?" Bolaji pressed.

"Bolaji? How do you even know which bungee jumping site is popular?" Toni asked.

"I have a subscription to a sports magazine that did a feature on the Bloukrans Bridge and other extreme hobbies last month and it just stuck with me"

"Okay, practice questions over, let's go get some food" I said cutting in and they all got up pushing back chairs and tables.

"So tell me about this bungee jumping thing" Effiong said quietly linking his fingers into mine as we walked out of the admin room.

"I was in South Africa to visit a friend and he told me about bungee jumping off Bloukrans Bridge, he's a total adrenaline junkie and had already done it a few times" I stopped and smiled at the memory of Aidan, "so he encouraged me to try it, he wouldn't stop talking about the feelings of excitement and pride you get when you bungee jump and how safe and exciting it is, so I agreed"

"And what was it like?" Effiong asked.

"I can tell you now that it was one of the best and most rewarding moments of my life. The adrenalin rush is crazy and I felt totally accomplished afterwards. It was an excellent way to confront my fears and I even found it therapeutic"

"Well done you, although I think it's a horribly dangerous thing to do. I mean jumping off bridges with I presume a deep body of water below?" Effiong said shaking his head.

"Yes but it's actually safe, the company that's been running it have been doing it for over twenty years without incidence and their staff were very friendly and helpful although you do sign a form indemnifying them of any injuries to you"

"I'm not sure I could do it"

"You will be surprised what you can do under the right circumstances" I replied.

I shouldn't have talked about bungee jumping, or anything that reminds me of him, but I am a fool for pain. I tell myself I want to stop thinking about him, the good, the bad and everything in between but here I am having conversations that remind me of him, letting him prey on my mind, live in my head. No single day goes by without me thinking of Aidan; sometimes the thoughts of him pretend to go away, they pack their bags and leave my head like they have gone forever and I focus on other things, on camp life. I turn my whole mind to doing mundane things like marching excellently on the parade ground, listening to conversations intently and taking part. I told myself if I was busy the thoughts would not come back; how naïve and stupid of me. The thoughts were merely teasing me, as my mum would say "they were doing the mess about" all that packing up and heading out, head hung low in shame and remorse is a ruse. Once the lights were out and the energetic girls I share the hostel with have finally given up their fight with sleep and collapsed on their beds in a tired heap, the thoughts come running, without a pause they flood my mind in vivid technicolour. I see him, hear his laugh, his growling voice, I see his even white teeth, his square nails, and the glasses perched on his nose as he reads a medical magazine by the light of the ugly owl-shaped bedside lamp he loves so much. He is there, talking, smiling, loving me, deceiving me, and killing me.

At the Mammy market, we found our way into one of the more popular canteens, it was half full and we quickly crowded on the one bench that was unoccupied.

"Twenty plates of rice and forty bottles of beer, we are starving" Bolaji shouted.

"Ahhahhh don't mind him oh madam, there are only five of us" Jay said, laughing.

"What do you want to eat?" the madam said smiling as she stood in front of Toni, one hand on her wide hips.

"Rice, plantain, beef, and goat meat, everything two hundred naira" Toni replied.

We all requested variations of Toni's meal and settled down to wait.

"I had one bad scare last year" Bolaji said abruptly into the waiting silence, "It was bad"

"What kind of scare?" Effiong asked.

"HIV scare oh"

"Are you serious?" Toni said, not actually asking a question.

"Man I'm telling you, I had these boils – one on my arm and the other somewhere crazy, and malaria which I treated for a month, after that I began to cough"

"That's crazy" Toni nodded.

"Was I scared or what? I ran off to the clinic to get tested for HIV/AIDS oh"

"But why would you suspect you had HIV off the top of your head?" Effiong asked.

"I don't even know, but you know HIV was all we heard about in school, there was such a heavy campaign to bring awareness that it only brought fear with it"

"But voluntary testing?" Toni said "how can I go for voluntary testing? I can't oh" he said shaking his head adamantly.

"But it's good to know, so you can do something about it" Jay replied.

"Do what about it? What can be done? In that kind of case what you don't know won't kill you. I know I can do nothing, so the knowledge will only kill me"

"You have a point there, but at the same time, knowing means you can take care of yourself better. Nobody is saying you should know so you can get cured, but it's so you can manage yourself and all that" Effiong said.

I was silent, fiddling with my phone.

"So what did you do when you got the result of the test? Toni asked turning back to Bolaji once more.

"Ah, what of the waiting? The time between taking the test and getting the result? It was a time of reflection. I sat in the clinic lounge and prayed like I had never prayed in my life. I promised God everything. I tried to think back to who could have given me the infection and one Port-Harcourt girl I shagged for a week kept coming to my mind and I almost wept at my own folly; but when the result came out, it was negative. You should have seen me. I ran all the way back to my room screaming and singing praise and worship songs. I even vowed to stay celibate till marriage or something like that"

"And have you?" Jay asked giggling at Bolaji.

"You know how these things are" Bolaji said laughing softly "I survived for about two months, and then this Calabar girl came into my life" he said with mock gravity.

"And you went back to a life of unprotected sex" Toni said his eyes twinkling.

"No. No. God forbid...I went back to sex not to unprotected sex, there is a difference my friend. Now I'm smart, no more nonsense messing around, no condom is equal to no sex... finish" Bolaji said frowning slightly.

Good for you Bolaji, good for you on dodging the bullet, there will be other bullets in your life and I pray you dodge them as beautifully and obliviously as you have dodged this one. I don't know how many bullets I have dodged in my life but the bullet that ends my story already caught me, I couldn't dodge that one; maybe it is Karma, fate I don't know. I have thought about me for many days and nights, I have raged in my mind and willed time to turn back. What would I have done differently, if I hadn't been in that place on that day maybe I would have dodged the bullet? Or maybe Karma or fate would have found another way to bring me the bullet; maybe some things are bound to happen no matter what and we are just pawns in the hand of Karma. Interestingly, there was a time when I was a fan of Karma, I was convinced it was the ultimate payback queen, leave everything to Karma she is a fair judge with a penchant for dark humour, she will sort everything out in her own good time but now I don't think so anymore; now for me Karma is just a bitch, a cold bitch with a dark sense of humour who has it in for some people and lets the rest slide through her fingers. Malevolent, cruel bitchy Karma, she has me by my non-existent balls and I can't for the life of me understand why she is squeezing so hard.

"That thing is easier said than done" David said continuing the conversation.

"My guy, don't say that again, I believe it strongly too, no condom no sex" Toni said reiterating Bolaji.

The conversation continued around me and went on till the canteen madam and her service girl started to pack up their utensils signalling to us that it was time to leave.

Day 18 NYSC Camp

BECKY

Dariye the camp handy man, my Dariye the sewer king has been declared missing today and expectedly Adesuwa came to impact this bit of news to me very importantly.

"Why do they think he's dead?" I asked.

"I didn't say he's dead, I said he's missing" she replied. Stupid girl, if only you knew, I thought.

"I bet he's not even missing, he has just decided he is tired of this crappy place and left" I replied

"But he couldn't have, he didn't take anything at all and his phone was found in that his little workshop where he bangs things together" Adesuwa answered, still in her important tone of voice; "that's what Malik said anyway" she finished.

A chill ran down my spine, they say people who commit a crime always make a mistake or two; although I wouldn't personally categorise Dariye's death as a crime, his existence was the crime but I've just found my first mistake – I should have searched for his phone and thrown it into the sewer with him. I wonder what other stupid mistake I made; I can't imagine that anyone would think of searching for Dariye in the sewer behind his shed; why would they? UK and US this is not, CSI and NCIS we do not have; you could kill a thousand people for all the investigative skills the Police force in this country have.

There was excitement in the air as Adesuwa and I left the hostel and it was because all Platoons had been mandated to cook lunch for the day. Each Platoon was allocated the ingredients and utensils needed to cook lunch and was solely responsible for feeding its members – just for the day.

The excitement was understandable, the general consensus was that we could cook better meals than the fat tired women who had been grudgingly cooking and serving our meals for the last two weeks.

I however was not excited. I was in a quiet rage over that god-forsaken-son-of-a-no-good-whore called Mahmud and had been spending considerable time thinking of creative ways to punish him; the bastard needs a lesson like no other.

After morning devotion and exercise, Sergeant Ahmed Platoon Commandant appointed me as the lunch coordinator for my Platoon and asked me to build a team. It was gratifying to have Sergeant Ahmed acknowledge my leadership and organisational skills and I proudly set about choosing a cooking team. I quickly chose Chinyere and Jumoke as I had heard both of them at different times boasting about cooking for large parties, time to live up to their boast. I also picked four boys and four girls to support the cooking, wisely choosing the heavily built ones. Every Platoon got an unlucky goat and I promptly handed our Platoon goat over to the four men on our cooking team to kill, clean and cut up in readiness for the ladies to cook.

Most of the Platoons including mine opted to cook Jollof rice which is the only meal I know that is universally loved by all Nigerians.

Chinyere and Jumoke started the cooking by washing the rice in a large metal basin while the other ladies pealed onions, washed tomatoes and fetched endless buckets of wa-

ter from the water tank to our assigned kitchen corner - a
wooden shed opposite the dining hall.

An hour into our cooking enterprise, the boys returned
with the goat cut up in large pieces in a rotund aluminium
pot, and the pieces looked five times bigger than what would
normally be served with lunch.

"The pieces are so big, will there be enough for the whole
Platoon?" Jumoke asked turning to Ade and Hafeez who had
brought the pot of meat.

"Definitely" Hafeez nodded "Pappy and I counted the
pieces and there are more than enough pieces for all of us including our Platoon Commandant and some"

"Really? I'm starting to think they need to let us do our
own cooking everyday" Chinyere added.

Ade and Hafeez chuckled as they left, their part of the
cooking effectively completed.

"Guys please come back" Chinyere called after them "We
need more firewood and coal for cooking, where are the other guys? We still need you guys to help around here"

"That's Pappy over there, I'll get him, but I have no idea
where Constantus has disappeared to, don't worry Pappy and
I will stay and do whatever else is needed. Ade can you stay
and help the ladies here too?" Hafeez said.

"Yes sure" Ade said smiling.

"Okay we will be back with more coal and firewood
then" and they both left again.

While Jumoke sliced onions and sprinkled spices into
the pot of goat meat, Chinyere and I cautiously tipped the
washed rice into two big pots of boiling tomato stew in
roughly equal amounts. The stew spat and boiled and we hur-

riedly added some water, just enough to cover the rice, we planned to add the stock from the goat meat once the meat was cooked.

Now the rice was cooking and the meat was boiling, we all settled on wooden chairs and Chinyere started telling us a story about a big party she once cooked for; two of the ladies who had been washing up utensils and fetching water joined us while the other two left.

"The stewed spinach we made for the party had everything, smoked fish, dry fish, periwinkle, cow hide, tripe, beef, chicken, mushrooms, name it, it was in there" Chinyere said telling her story with animation.

The mention of mushrooms reminded me of the pretty little mushrooms I had wrapped away in the corner of my bag and a thought started to formulate in my mind, wonderful thoughts about what I could make with those powerful little beauties.

***

The lunch we cooked was delicious and there was plenty of it; it did a lot to improve my mood.

Jumoke and I were in charge of dishing out the hot fragrant Jollof rice while Chinyere plopped juicy goat meat on it with a metal fork. The three of us became hugely popular in no time as we heaped huge amounts of rice on the plates of every corper in our Platoon – there was more than enough to go around.

"You girls are saints. Beautiful angels from heaven who cook like superstars" Effanga a painfully thin guy in our Platoon declared coming back for his third plate of Jollof rice. This time Chinyere did not give him any meat to go with it and he did not seem to mind.

"Do you know that the camp commandant provided us with just a tenth of the ingredients and materials they normally provide the camp cooks daily?" he asked loudly, not addressing anyone in particular, " and yet you guys have managed to turn out delicious food in such huge amounts, God bless you richly"

"Amen" Jumoke answered him.

"Those haggard looking witches who cook food in this camp daily, they are thieves and marauders, we should chase them out of camp" Effanga added talking through a mouthful of rice as he walked away, plate in hand.

"He is lying though" Chinyere whispered to me smiling, today's cooking was sponsored by that popular noodles brand" she paused trying to remember their name and then giving up said, "what are they called again?"

"Indomie" Jumoke offered.

"Yes those ones, so we got way more ingredients and materials than the cooks"

"Each Platoon got one goat each, I can't imagine the cooks get ten goats to cook everyday" Jumoke added.

"No they don't" Chinyere replied.

When the trickle of corpers queuing for food slowed down, I dished a large amount of food into a big plate and covered it with another plastic plate, "I'll be back in a bit, I promised one of the camp officials a plate of food and you know how these people can be" I said turning to Jumoke and Chinyere.

"No problem, don't take too long so you can eat lunch too, you deserve it" Chinyere said smiling at me as I left.

"And thanks for today" Jumoke called after me.

At the hostel, I dug out the little bits of mushroom hidden in a side pocket of my bag, they were now dry and shrivelled, even better. I wore nylon bags over my hand as gloves and then placed a tiny bit of shrivelled mushroom in my palm and rubbed my palms together till the mushroom was powdery, then sprinkled it over the Jollof rice and mixed it in.

Now to find that dirty old man who was so nasty to me on the first day of camp – his nemesis is in a plate of delicious orange coloured Jollof rice.

Day 20 NYSC Camp

ADUNNI

It was the bon-fire night and a lot of wood was piled up in what looked like an Indian pyre. I was also getting ready for the Miss NYSC beauty contest. Mr Adelakun, the Camp Director who offered to help me win in exchange for torrid favours had since informed me that he would do all in his power to make sure I came last in the competition. His threats merely added fuel to my determination to take part in the contest.

A big box of clothes arrived from Lagos for me earlier in the morning courtesy of my fashion mad sister Abeke. She had raided my wardrobe and hers for clothes, mummy's wardrobe for jewellery and even had two new outfits made, one from Toju Foyeh and the other from APK, both very popular frock designers in Lagos.

The smell of food wafted into the admin room where I was getting ready and my stomach rumbled. Jay looked up at me, "are you hungry?"

"Not really, but the smell of food is very distracting, is that food from the food competition?"

"Yes, tonight's events will be starting with the judging of the cooking competition, so all sorts of dishes are being prepared just over there. You should eat a little food though if you are hungry"

"I don't want to ruin the lines of my outfits and I'm probably too excited to swallow anything"

"I'll get you something little, something to keep your mind off all that cooking going on around here" Julia, one of my Platoon members smiled kindly before heading out of the room. Jay and three other girls were helping me get ready; one of them worked as a makeup artist to supplement her student allowance during university and was my makeup artist for the event. She was already laying out endless tubes of concealers, liquid foundation, lipsticks and eye shadow. She had a huge bag of makeup which she assured me was just a small part of her whole collection.

Julia returned a half hour later with a steaming bowl of spicy noodles and a bottle of Sprite.

"Wow Julia how did you know what I needed exactly? This has become my favourite food in the last two weeks"

"Dr Effiong is outside, he heard our conversation and suggested I get you this, I'm glad you like it"

"Thanks a lot"

After much debate my outfit for each segment of the pageant and the right accessories to go with it was agreed and set aside.

I was still getting ready when the judging of the cooking competition started and we were informed by Effiong and Toni who were sitting outside the room that someone from Platoon 2 who had cooked edikaikong - a Calabar dish had won.

"If edikaikong wins another food competition, honestly I will scream" Jay said, "these days, all anybody had to do is cook edikaikong and they win every food competition"

"If it makes you feel better, the second place went to someone who made Amala and abula" Toni said smiling.

"That's more like it"

"But have you ever eaten Edikaikong?" Toni asked her from his doorway chair.

"Once, and I don't see what the noise is about"

"Then you haven't eaten a good one, edikaikong is everything, it is life.

"What is Abula?" Effiong asked.

"It's a Yoruba soup that is in truth a mix of two soups, ewedu and gbegiri"

"Never heard of that combo"

"You have never eaten ewedu?" Toni asked him.

"No I haven't, but I have heard of it"

"Okay, and gbegiri?

"Never eaten it never even heard of it"

"It's made from blended beans, you combine those two soups together with a little stew and you have abula"

"I see"

"Yes and abula is to Yoruba people what Edikaikong is to Calabar people"

"There are other Calabar soups that I personally prefer to Edikaikong because I think they taste better" Effiong answered.

"You would know, but Edikaikong is the one we know and love, my ex-girlfriend is Calabar and I sold my soul to that girl for Edikaikong soup and a few other things" Bolaji said seeming to materialise from nowhere to join the conversation.

"Me thinks you still like that Calabar girl sef" Toni said, "we hear about her a lot"

"True that Toni but she is married now" Bolaji sighed; "to an old white man and has moved to Russia or Germany or something with him; I swear if she comes back today I go forgive and forget everything"

"Hehehehe Bolaji oh" Toni laughed.

After the cooking competition there was a sack race and then the crackly voice of the programme MC announced that the beauty pageant was about to start.

I was ready to go out in my first outfit as a Calabar bride in a rich gold lace blouse and skirt with a sparkly red underlay. Heavy gold pieces were pinned into my hair in a star shape jutting up above my head like an imperious crown and trailing down to the middle of my back; a heavy necklace in a similar design rested coolly on my collar bone and covered my neckline.

My lips were stained red with MAC Rubywoo and my eyes emphasised with sparkly gold eye shadow with a smoky black tint in the outside creases of my eyes. Evelyn accentuated my nose and cheekbones with her contouring magic and shaped my brows into a perfect arc. Julia painstakingly painted my nails a sparking red colour to match my lips and the underlay of my lace outfit. I clutched a gold purse to match my gold Jimmy Choo five inch heels and Julia handed me a gold plated sceptre decorated with gold and red silk to complete my look.

I could only look in rapture at my own transformation. "I look and feel like a princess and I'll be damned if I don't walk out there feeling and acting like one when my Platoon number is called" I said to my helpers, "thank you so much guys, you are the best"

"You are beautiful beyond words" Effiong said staring at me as I left the room to join the queue of contestants waiting to be called out.

"Go get them tiger" Toni shouted.

The beauty pageant progressed very quickly with not nearly enough time between segments to change outfits and Evelyn insisting on retouching my makeup each time.

It was a mad dash out of one outfit into the next but I enjoyed every bit of it strutting down the stage like a professional fashion model at the London Fashion Week.

I changed outfits four times in all, starting as a Calabar bride for the cultural segment, then on to the APK cocktail dress for the party segment where we were each asked to dance to one indigenous music track; then on to sportswear, I whipped out my swimming trunk and showed my long pin straight legs. My trunk was a one-piece suit in pink and blue with a low back and the sides cut out. The final outfit was a formal dinner wear; the Toju Foyeh dress in white chiffon overlaid with hand cut lace fit every curve of my body and showed off my shoulders which Evelyn had decided to dust with shiny highlighting powder; the dress spread out from my hips and trailed the floor.

All the contestants stood like statues on the stage for a few minutes in each segment while the watching crowd cheered and screamed. I could hear the rapid breathing of the Platoon four girl beside me; her foundation was running slightly under the heat of the lights and made me wonder if mine was running too.

There was a dance, a choreography, and a song between each of the segments and in the formal wear segment which was also the last segment, the judges asked each of us one question. I got one of the questions I had rehearsed with Bolaji earlier, the one about if I won ten million naira. I sailed through my practiced answer to a loud applause.

Then it was time to announce the winner of the beauty contest- the next Miss NYSC Jos Nigeria Batch A. The hall fell silent and you could hear an ant's fart. We were all waiting with baited breaths; audience and contestants, the judges smiling smugly, with satisfaction.

After a short speech about unity and cohesion and the admirable game spirit of the contestants, Mrs Amoo lifted the microphone to her pink tinted lips and announced the second runner up - Olaide Martins from Platoon 9. The Platoon 9 corpers went mad with joy screaming and shouting and running amok. Mrs Amoo waited a brief minute for order to be restored, then she announced the first runner up as Hassana Garba from Platoon 2; there was more screaming and shouting and Hassana burst into tears.

Then I heard my name as if from inside a distant fog – Adunni Momora, Winner of the Miss NYSC Competition NYSC batch A, Jos Nigeria.

I smiled fixedly, the surprise rooting me to the spot as the Camp Commandant came to shake my hand and the only lady judge put a sparkly crown on my head. In as much as I wanted to win, I didn't think I would actually win; I was partly doing this to show that camp official that I didn't care to be threatened.

The Camp commandant was saying something but I couldn't hear through the fog in my head, Jay and Toni were hugging me and I was soon surrounded by my Platoon members. Effiong hugged me and planted a kiss on my cheek, Evelyn and Julia were crying happily, Jay too.

We went back to our changing room and I changed out of my outfit into a pair of jeans, a beautiful cream jewelled blouse with tiny straps and fringes at the hem and red stiletto shoes, ready for the after party.

The after party went on till midnight and I was delighted to be surrounded by my friends Jay, Toni, Bolaji and Effiong. It was incredible, I felt loved by people, life, by the universe. It was my first time winning any competition.

I danced vigorously and took endless pictures with camp officials, corpers and the numerous event sponsors, there must have been ten different sponsoring companies all bearing gifts for the winner.

I saw Mr Adelakun from the corner of my eyes watching me, he saw that I had seen him and started to walk over, I turned away from him resolutely and ignored him for the rest of the night.

At twelve midnight, tired and falling asleep on my feet, I called it a night. Effiong walked with me to the lodging quarters for camp official where a room had been reserved for me. At the door he stopped and held my elbow, "I love you Adunni, with all my heart and I'm glad you won today"

"I'm glad too"

"Good, I will see you tomorrow, I'm not going to let go, I'm going to stay till you fall in love with me, till you love me like I love you, I'm staying"

I didn't say anything, I could only smile sadly, "Goodnight Effiong"

"Goodnight"

I wish I could say I know what to do; actually I do; I should nip this in the bud now, stop listening to his solemn promises of love. I'm not ready for another relationship, not one complicated by my situation and I don't believe Effiong is. My situation requires that I be alone, that I deal with things alone. Today's victory and happiness doesn't change that, Effiong's affection and ardent declarations of love don't change that, nothing changes that and giving any consideration to Effiong would just be futile senseless dreaming. I've had my chance and I blew it and that's that.

In the online community which I finally convinced myself to join just before I came to camp, 'Surviving_0210', one of the major commenters and admin was always talking about how surrounding yourself with loved ones who understand and care helps and how finding love again has contributed hugely to his improvement and well-being; but candidly I don't see it. I don't see how I could tell my loved ones, or help them understand; how can I burden them with this? They already lived through daddy's cancer and I know what that did to us all; I can't ask them to understand or live through this again.

And finding love is something I can no longer imagine after Aidan, after everything with Aidan, how can I find love? Effiong doesn't love me, he just thinks he does, he is merely suffering from the effect of being far away from the normal world, everything is skewered around here and even if he won't admit this, I know it.

Members of my new online family usually choose names that tell you something about their journey to this place, the 0210 in 'Surviving_0210's' online name is the date he found out he was positive. I'm HBroken_1113 because Aidan left me heartbroken, lost and bewildered when I found out in the cruellest way possible that he had HIV/AIDS and I possibly had it too.

I had gone to Jo'burg for another long weekend with my lover. I was feeling particularly tired after the flight and the many hours spent at the airport waiting for the delayed flight so I was having a nap in the coolness of his wood panelled bedroom.

I woke to hear Aidan and his cousin Katleho having a heated conversation, the sound of their voices was probably what woke me up.

"You have to tell her Aidan, It's not fair, in fact it's a crime" Katleho had shouted.

Tell who what? I wondered, coming wide awake.

"She doesn't need to know; I take precautions so she's not going to catch anything"

"You take precautions? Are you being funny? Is this a joke? Taking precautions doesn't make it right, she needs to be in this with her eyes wide open"

"Keep your voice down man. She's sleeping in there" I could imagine him jerking his head in the direction of his bedroom.

"You think she will stay with me if I told her?" Aidan asked.

"That's for her to decide, she has a right to know, this is so wrong, you can't do this"

"Have you seen her? She is the most beautiful, exciting woman I have ever been with, I love her"

"I don't know what your definition of love is, but what you are doing to Adunni is not love, that girl loves and adores you"

"If she knows I have HIV she will leave me and I can't live with that, I just can't"

"Yes you can Aidan, yes you can, you are already living with HIV, I'm sure you can live with a little heartbreak and if you truly love Adunni, you will tell her you have HIV" Kathelo replied, "that girl does not deserve what you are doing to her, nobody deserves this kind of subterfuge"

That was when my world crumbled around me, I did not wait around to hear the rest of the conversation; I had heard enough. I ran off to the nearest haematology clinic and got tested.

Even though I prayed and hoped that the precautions Aidan talked about had worked; I also remembered the many times we had made love, unprotected because I was on the pill and we both believed we were exclusive. My test results were positive. I was; I am HIV positive.

Day 21 – Last day of NYSC Camp

BECKY

"Becky, Malik wants to meet you" Adesuwa said smiling.

"Why?"

"Well because you are my best friend and I'm always talking about you and today is technically the last day of camp, everybody leaves tomorrow morning with posting letters"

"Yes tomorrow it all ends"

"Please join us for lunch, I want my two best people to meet each other, you will like him"

I was not sure I wanted to meet this Malik, with his small smiles and confident nods.

"We can do lunch at that popular Mammy market canteen, I hear the stew is mad and their Jollof rice is the best in the world and Malik is paying anyway"

The thought of free food swayed me, I could endure the two of them for an hour in exchange for that.

"Okay when?"

"One pm? I could send him a text now to let him know" she replied grinning.

"Okay that's fine"

We met Malik in front of Mama Basira's canteen and after quick introductions we all went in.

He talked quietly and easily, his voice belying the strength of his mind, but I could sense a rapier sharp mind behind his words. Adesuwa had one hand on his thigh and smiled at everything he said.

He ordered Jollof rice for all of us and cold Coca-Cola without asking me what I wanted. I felt irritated by this peremptory attitude but I swallowed my irritation and waited for the famous Jollof rice which appeared almost immediately, hot and steaming with two large pieces of fried beef taking pride of place on top of the heap. I dug in immediately while Adesuwa continued to talk non-stop, sharing her fantastic experience of camp.

"Camp would have been perfect for me too" Malik said, "except for the death of that elderly admin staff Baba Ahmed, it sort of mired things"

"Someone will clear out that mountain of trash in his room, all those smelly bags and boxes, bit of a trash collector that one" I said, unthinking, my mind taken over by the delicious food in my mouth.

"Don't speak ill of the dead, he died a horrible death" Adesuwa replied.

"I'm not surprised, I bet he died of poisoning, the mean old git" I answered back.

"Why do you think he was poisoned? Malik asked.

I felt a sudden chill, I knew I had made a fatal error and quickly tried to recover "Adesuwa just said so"

"No she didn't" Malik said.

"Yes she did" I insisted, the cold feeling spreading through my limbs, I forced myself to concentrate.

"No I didn't" Adesuwa suddenly burst out, "I said he died a horrible death"

Bitch, thoughtless big-mouthed bitch; I am going to kill you, I wish I already have.

"Do you think he was poisoned because you poisoned him?" Malik asked, still smiling but the smile not reaching his eyes. I suddenly recognised a worthy adversary and kicked myself.

"Oh come on, don't be ridiculous, you have watched too many movies, why would I poison that dirty old man, I don't even know him"

"Why you poisoned him is something we will find out, but yes I think you killed him. I'm also pretty sure you killed him by poisoning him"

"I did not"

"Yes you did, you poisoned Baba Ahmed with funnel oyster mushrooms, you told Adesuwa about them remember? How they almost killed you and what the symptoms are when a person has been poisoned with them"

"I don't know what you are talking about"

"Baba Ahmed showed all the symptoms of poisoning with funnel oyster mushroom; bleeding through the nose, vomiting blood and sweating profusely. We couldn't save him and he died shouting that there were knives in his stomach, all the symptoms you described to Adesuwa and a few more"

"You brought him that plate of Jollof rice in his room didn't you?"

"I didn't bring him anything, I have never had any interaction with that stinky old man and I'm not going to sit here listening to this bad reality show crap you are spewing" I got up with all the bravado I could muster.

"Sit down Becky" he ordered, his voice cold and authoritative, "let me ask you two more questions"

I stared at him levelly and sat down.

"If you did not take him that plate of Jollof rice, if you have never had any interaction with him, how did you know he had a mountain of trash in his room?"

"Anybody can see that old man is a dirty old man, you don't have to visit his smelly room to know that"

"But you did visit his smelly room didn't you? That is how you know about all those smelly bags and boxes in his room. For reasons best known to you, you visited him with a plate of Jollof rice that you had poisoned with funnel oyster mushrooms to kill him. You visited Baba Ahmed to kill him"

"I did not. You are crazy"

"You know after you told Adesuwa that incredible story about the funnel oyster mushroom, I wondered if they grew around here and coincidentally they do. There is a profusion of them behind the female hostel and on the pathway to the camp fellowship house, those and a few other varieties of poisonous mushrooms; you are not the only one who foraged as a child you know" Malik replied.

I glanced at Adesuwa who was staring at me with repulsion, her mouth wide open. I felt an incredible urge to slap the teeth out of her tattling, snitching mouth; instead I got up again and pushed the bench away, ready to walk out of the food shed on shaky jelly like legs, cold air kissing the sweat beads on my forehead and arms.

"Becky where is Dariye?"

This question stopped me cold in my track and I could feel the blood leaving my head and pooling in my feet. I grabbed the bench for support.

"Who?"

"You know who"

"Dariye the handyman" Adesuwa hissed.

"Why are you asking me? He is missing, did I steal him?"

He smiled, "Becky when Adesuwa told you he was missing, do you remember what you said?"

"No I don't keep track of every conversation I have with this garrulous idiot" I said pointing at Adesuwa who was still glaring at me.

"You asked why we think he's dead, why did you think he was dead when Adesuwa had merely said he was missing?"

"I didn't say that"

"Yes you did, Adesuwa found your question so strange she once again narrated the whole conversation to me"

"She is crazy"

"No Becky, you are the one who is crazy and an amateur who thought herself above the long arm of the law. You are under arrest for the murders of Dariye Aduwo, Baba Ahmed Langtan" he paused, "and also Daniel Okereke of Brethren of God Assembly"

I made a dash for the door and Malik grabbed me; we were immediately surrounded by four burly men who I now realised had been sitting in the wooden shed with us all the while.

"Rebecca Oni you are now surrounded by the esteemed men of the Criminal Investigation Department of Lagos State, please do not resist as you will be removed from this camp with all necessary force. Once again I would like to repeat that you are under arrest for the murders of Dariye Aduwo, Baba Ahmed Langtan both employees of the National Youth Service Corps and Daniel Okereke of Brethren of God Assembly"

I looked around, the sweat streaming into my face, I felt cold and dead.

"Take her out of here" Malik ordered the four burly men.

In the cramped bus taking me back to Lagos and retribution, I found out that Malik was a senior officer of the Criminal Investigation Department. He had come to camp to question me about Daniel Okereke's disappearance from the Brethren camp. When he met Adesuwa, he decided to watch me through her.

He had seen me going to Dariye's shed the first two times, but had missed my third visit so when Adesuwa told him what I had said about Dariye being dead he realised I had killed him.

When I asked him what linked me to the missing Daniel Okereke, he said – my blood stained dress which I had thrown into one of the camp bins had been found and identified. Daniel had also mentioned to one Brother Caleb that he was going to talk to me, so I was the last person believed to have seen him; more fool me.

"Where is Dariye?" Malik had asked me in return.

I shrugged. I was never telling him that, ever.

JAY

At 9am, the public service system which had somehow survived the three weeks of camp announced that Jumoke Morales was here to see Jadesola Savage – my mum had come to see me. I walked out of the hostel determined to keep a rein on my emotions, to repair bridges for the sake of my baby who was now in my every waking thought.

She hadn't changed much; she was as slim and spry as she looked in the one grainy picture of her I had. Her hair was in long dark tresses flowing around her shoulder, fanning her face and bare shoulders. She was wearing huge round glasses that looked more like a fashion statement than anything an ophthalmologist would prescribe. Her dress was wispy, a smart bodice with a thin green belt emphasising her small waist, the skirt of the dress danced around her leg; it was clearly a very expensive dress, simple but perfectly cut.

She looked like she was doing everything to keep the hands of time away, to stay young. She smiled at me uncertainly, "Mojadesola?"

"Yes... Mummy?"

"That's me, baby"

I couldn't help running into her arms, I couldn't help the tears. I started bawling like a child whose mother was leaving, mine was not leaving she was returning, but I was still terribly upset. It was as if all the emotions I had kept bottled up inside me since she left were now being released.

"There, there, don't cry honey, we are making a scene now" she said patting my head gently and walking determinedly away from the press building and the scene we were making in front of other waiting visitors.

"Why did you leave?" I asked the moment I caught my breath and we were alone again, "Why did you leave me behind? Why didn't you take me with you?"

"One question at a time honey, first of all we sit down no? Where can one sit in this godforsaken place?"

I suddenly remembered that she used to swear a lot and daddy would tell her off for swearing in front of the kids; she would reply with "block your ears my puppets, don't learn from mummy"

The tears welled in my eyes again as I led the way to one of the admin rooms, hoping it would be empty. Sunday mornings were usually the laziest day in camp so the admin room I turned into was expectedly empty as were the ones on both sides of it.

"We can sit down here"

She wrinkled her nose daintily, "I've forgotten how everything in this country always has a layer of dust" she brought out some wet wipes from her bag and wiped futilely at the wooden bench before sitting down gingerly on the edge of the bench.

I sat down without wiping the bench, careless of the cut-off jeans and t-shirt I was wearing. On Sundays we wear our own clothes and not the khakis that were the compulsory uniform the rest of the week. My camp issued whites were already a suspicious shade of beige and I hoped to never wear them again after camp.

"So how are you? You look well" she said.

"I am well mummy, I am well now; not so much before but now I am well" I felt treacherous saying this to someone who was literarily a stranger but I said it anyway.

"Hmm, and your father?"

"He is fine"

"As dashing as ever? As stubborn as ever"

"Yes"

"Those monumental rages?"

"Not often, Fola has them instead"

"Ah, Fola... his father's son"

"Why did you leave mummy?" calling her mummy came to me as easily as if she had never left, helped by the fact that my father never remarried; so I have never called anyone else mummy. She was never replaced in my heart.

"And you, your father's daughter, gentle in spirit yet direct in speech"

I wouldn't describe my father as gentle in spirit or direct in speech, his friends call him the old war horse and he was a diplomat for over thirty years, direct in speech he was not, but I let that slide, I did not want to be distracted from the questions I wanted answers to.

"You left" I pressed.

"I had to" she answered, she spoke softly and her smile was wry.

"Why?"

"Your father was a difficult man to live with, his mood swings were legendary and he worked extremely long hours; going from long office days to long diplomatic dinners in the evening, some of which the wives could attend and others we could not. To be fair to him his job was high pressured, the Military regime took power August of '85 and even though your father managed to keep his job, there was a lot of reshuffling of diplomatic posts. Diplomats lost and gained jobs every day and they were constantly under the shadow of an unpredictable and despotic ruler.

I spent a lot of time alone at home with your brothers, we had only Dele and Dayo"

"Richard" I replied automatically, "he doesn't like being called Dayo"

"I was lonely and bored and your father would come home and go straight to bed, no conversation nothing, most days I was lucky if I got a perfunctory hello kiss" she continued like I hadn't interrupted her.

"You are blaming my father for your affair and absconding with your lover?" I asked with incredulity. "He was working to put food on the table; how can you even not appreciate that? What kind of wife were you?"

"Be patient with me love, I'm not finished" she said holding up her perfectly manicured hand, her nails were a black matte finish and sharply curved and I was momentarily distracted by their exquisiteness. I will never be as beautiful and glamorous as this woman, this selfish self-centred woman, I thought.

"I continued to endure and support your father; I wasn't working, there wasn't much point to that, he could be posted out of the country anytime, we had just returned from a Switzerland posting. So I stayed at home and loved my babies, and did homework and drank wine. I was devastated to find out at an embassy event no less that your father was having an affair with one of his assistants – Aina Maxwell, she went on to marry Akin Balogun, heir of Premium Bank, did well for herself that one"

Yomi's mum?" I gasped.

"Who's Yomi" she asked.

"My ex-boyfriend, the one who contacted you and asked you here"

"Oh right, is he Akin Balogun's son? His father is Premium Bank?"

"Yes he is"

"And you have broken up with him? Why?"

"I don't want to talk about that now"

"Okay, that's sad though, he sounded like a lovely chap, although knowing that Aina is his mother now, I don't care much for him"

"Can we not talk about that now? You are saying dad had an affair?"

"Yes he did, with Aina Maxwell, it wasn't his first and it wasn't his last. He would beg and apologise and be contrite for a few months, then he would do it again with someone new. It was a relief when we got a posting back to Switzerland, but he had already done the unforgiveable before we left; his current girlfriend at the time was pregnant with his child. He came to Nigeria at every opportunity he got; which wasn't hard, there was always need for someone to come for some event, some meeting or the other, but he was visiting the mother of his child. The treachery of that hurt for so many years afterwards"

"What happened to the child?"

"Oh the child was fine, your father's lover unfortunately died when the child was about 9 months old and her family didn't want the child anyway. They were ashamed that she had a child without a husband so they were happy to give the child to my husband when he came looking for them. Your father took the child and gave it to his mother till we returned from the Switzerland posting six months later.

"You keep saying 'the child', was that me? I am my father's illegitimate child?" I asked, everything suddenly made sense to me, of course she would leave me, I am not her daughter;

my real mother is dead. I am the living proof of all her husband's infidelities.

"No you are not, you must learn to be patient. Your father's illegitimate child is Fola; not you, Fola"

"Oh God, I don't believe you"

"You have to" she shrugged, "it's the truth, why would I deny my own son? Fola is not my son, he is his father's son and his father insisted on bringing him to live with us. He wasn't satisfied with having this child, he was hell-bent on bringing him home and raising him with his half-brothers. He genuinely couldn't see what I was so upset about, after all the boy's mother was dead, what else did I want? I honestly wished his mother wasn't dead, I have never wished someone alive as much as I wished that woman alive; but she was dead and I was raising her son. I tried to live with it, my parents were very supportive especially my mother, she would explain repeatedly that I would be fine with time and at least the boy's mother was not here to be a rival with me in my husband's house. Nobody understood that she was a bigger rival in death than alive. Your father quickly grew to love Fola with so much intensity it was frightening to see. Fola was his orphan son, his motherless baby. He forbade anyone from telling Fola his true story until the boy was much older although since I haven't stayed around, I'm sure he has not bothered to tell Fola anything.

"I don't think he has" I agreed.

"Anyway, I met Toye" she stopped and smiled, her face filling with happiness from whatever memory was filling her mind.

"Toye was everything and a little more, he brought sunshine and joy. He came and took me out of the darkness I was in and gave me reason to live. Toye is the doctor I was referred to when it was obvious I was starting to suffer from some form of depression. Toye and I fell in love"

"So you decided to have an affair with your doctor to cure your depression?"

"You are rather the judgemental goody two shoes aren't you? I took love and affection where I could find it, you shouldn't be so quick to judge"

"I'm sorry mummy, I'm not judging you"

"I got pregnant"

"Oh lawd. Was there no contraception at that time?"

"You are a smart mouth too; after I had Dayo, sorry Richard, I had been told by my Gynaecologist that there wouldn't be any more babies for me, faulty uterus and so on, so there wasn't any reason for contraception or so I thought; but you wanted to come, and here you are"

"What do you mean I wanted to come? Me? I was the product of your affair with your doctor?"

"You are my love child; you are the product of the best year of my life with a man who showed me what true love was but we couldn't be together"

"Of course you were still married" I was struggling to keep the sarcasm and tears out of my voice.

"Yes I was still married and so was Toye, his wife just had a baby girl too so I couldn't exactly ask him to leave her for me. I simply went ahead and had you and your father didn't know any better. He was over the moon anyway to get a surprise baby when we already thought there wouldn't be any more babies. I stopped seeing Toye shortly before you were born, I didn't want any suspicions over who your father was. Toye and I parted ways amicably and agreed to go and do better in our respective marriages"

"And then?"

"It didn't work out, there was a sort of truculent peace for a year after you were born then everything degenerated again. We were fighting every day, your father was seeing other women again, working late and travelling alone. We were both miserable beyond belief and you kids were growing up in a very sad and tense environment; then I met Gonzales"

"Your Spanish doctor lover?"

"Yes"

"It's true then, you do have a thing for doctors"

"Says who?"

"Never mind, doesn't matter now"

"Anyway your father found out and in his utter selfishness wouldn't forgive it; suddenly he hated me more than anyone else in the world"

"So you left him and your kids"

"He wouldn't let me take your brothers or you, your father can be extremely menacing when he wants to be and I'm sure you know this. He has some dark connections and is owed favours by a few unsavoury people. I didn't want to wake up in an empty warehouse or dead in a ditch"

"My father wouldn't have hurt you, he is not that kind of person"

"I'm sorry but you don't know your father and he hated me passionately and completely"

"But after you left, you never wrote nor called"

"Oh I did, I wrote to your brothers in their schools and called, your father intercepted calls and ordered school authorities to withhold letters. I don't know what he told them about me but they withheld my letters. I visited the boys in their Swiss school once and they wouldn't let me see them, it was so devastating that I cried for days afterwards. It almost ruined what I had with Gonzales. I had to put it all behind me, put you all in a corner of my mind to survive, it was that or lose my mind. I didn't want to lose my mind, I knew that one day you would all grow up and I would find you. I decided to wait till then and here we are"

"You could have kept trying, you didn't try hard enough" I insisted.

"I did, I had to stop trying because it was killing me; destroying me inside out"

I was speechless and for a minute I sat there shell shocked.

"So Fola is not my brother?"

"Biologically no, of everything I've said that's the one that sticks with you?"

"He is not even my half-brother?"

"No he is not, he is Dele and Richard's half-brother as they are yours"

"Thank you mum"

"Why? What have I done? Apart from leaving you? I'm sorry I left you, I'm sorry I didn't come back earlier; I'm sincerely sorry"

"I forgive you mum and thank you again for telling me the truth"

"You are kind Jay"

"Mum?"

"Yes?"

"I'm pregnant"

"Oh dear, perhaps you shouldn't have broken up with Yomi then, I'm sure you both can patch things up and work something out, he sounds like he loves you"

"It might not be Yomi's baby"

"Oh; who then?" she hesitated and stared at me, "who else might it be" she asked in her gentle voice.

"Fola" I whispered, "I think it's Fola's baby"

"Fola? Oh my God. How long have you and Fola?..." she left the rest unsaid.

"Since I was about 14, we tried to stop but we couldn't, Fola couldn't"

"That son of a bitch, that worthless son of a bitch"

"It's not his fault alone, it was both of us"

"You were 14" she insisted.

"And he was 19, not much older"

"Old enough to know"

"I don't want to argue mummy"

We both sat there silently for a few minutes, collecting our thoughts.

"He is not your brother" she suddenly said, her voice tinged with desperation.

"What?"

"He is not your brother" she repeated, "you were raised together but he is not your brother, you are not related"

"What is wrong with you Mum? Is that supposed to make me feel better? I might be having a baby with my brother who is actually not my brother and that is what you say?

Don't you get how horrible and bizarre this is? Before you came along with your dramatic stories it was incest. I don't even know how you can suggest what I think you are suggesting" I screamed.

"Don't scream at me young lady" her voice is authoritative, "Do you love him?"

I nodded shamefacedly.

"There you go, there are 90 something other countries apart from Nigeria where you can live together as a married couple without the people who know you as siblings to peer over your shoulder; that's if you want him that much. Personally I don't see why you would want that badly behaved young man, I can't count the number of times he has banged the phone down around my ears when I called to speak with you, it was like your father had poisoned him against me completely"

"He didn't need to poison us, we all saw you leave, storming out and driving off without a backward glance"

"You remember?"

"Do I remember my mother leaving me amidst a lot of screaming and crying and then never seeing her again? Yes, I do remember mum, surprisingly, some things are hard to forget even for a four year old"

"Oh, I'm sorry Jadesola, I'm truly sorry"

"I know you are trying to make me feel better but I could never live with Fola as a husband. He will always be my brother and as much as I love him, what we did was terrible. Nothing you say can change that"

"Then go and make up with Yomi, he loves you and wants both you and the baby, you could build a life with Yomi"

"That would be deceit, I have thought of that but I don't think I could live with myself. I'm keeping and raising the baby anyway"

"Alone?" she asked.

"Yes"

"It's very tough to raise a child alone" she replied.

"How would you know? You didn't bother to try raising yours at all"

"Fair enough"

"Does my father the doctor ever ask about me?" I asked, even though I knew this was a dangerous road to tread.

"He can't, he's dead"

"Everybody keeps dying conveniently for you"

"Toye Momora died of cancer, I didn't kill him or anybody else you may be referring to"

"Did you say Toye Momora, it would just be my luck if the daughter his wife had was called Adunni"

She screwed up her face for a few seconds and slowly said, "Actually she was named Adunni after his mother"

"Perfect, just perfect, my whole existence is a joke"

"Please don't tell me you are dating Adunni too" she replied, a silly attempt at humour which fell completely short.

"I'm not, thank God, I'm not; Adunni is my friend and thanks for coming by" I got up from the bench tiredly. I felt like I was suddenly carrying the weight of the world on my shoulders and the world was damn heavy.

"Can I call you sometime, just to check how you are doing?" She asked me.

"Yes, I guess so"

"Thank you love" she reeled out her phone number, "how are you getting home tomorrow?" she asked.

"Daddy" I paused, suddenly wondering if I could still call him that, "daddy is sending the car down"

"Okay good, take care of yourself and the baby"

"I will"

"I love you and I'm a phone call away if you need me"

"Thanks, that's good to know"

Epilogue - Post NYSC Camp

ADUNNI

A few months after camp, I worked up the courage to tell Effiong I was HIV positive. He smiled and kissed me hard and shocked me by saying he knew. He had seen the drugs in my medicine cabinet and was waiting for me to tell him in my own time. I am glad I did. He is optimistic that with diligent management and the right diet I might never progress to AIDS. I am optimistic too because he is. We are still together and I'm taking it one day at a time. Together we also found faith and a God who makes all things beautiful in His time. Jay and I are closer than ever, her daughter Esme is so beautiful, I feel like the more time I spend with her, the more Esme looks like me; wishful thinking I know. Kathleo sent me an email last week, Aidan died; I did not reply. Writing about pivotal moments is the therapy assignment this week in my HIV support group hence why you are reading my story.

BECKY

I am writing my story from the Women's section of Kirikiri prison Lagos. The visiting Psychiatrist insists that writing my story is the next step in my journey to recovery; recovery from what, I do not know but she is nice and I am bored so I am humouring her, by writing about the three weeks when it all came to an abrupt end.

I expect to be here for another 40 years or till I die. Rachel and Caleb are my only visitors, Abraham has refused to visit me, my parents have disowned me, the thought of that still has me howling in laughter till I'm peeing myself. My only regret is that I didn't kill them when I had the chance. I should have killed that philandering Mahmud too or castrated him. I bet he's still out there somewhere, breaking hearts. Adesuwa the brainless snitch, married Malik; according to the Prison warden they have two daughters. Malik and his interrogation team took most of my teeth and the sight in my left eye just to know where I buried Dariye; the bastards.

JAY

I gave birth to my beautiful perfect daughter Esme Boluwatife in London on a clear September morning, six months after camp. I am raising her alone. I don't care who her father is, I am not telling anyone anyway because it doesn't matter. Fola died in a plane crash last year, Esme was 11 months old. I am just coming out of those dark days and seeing the sunshine. Yomi keeps trying to be a part of our lives and I continue to resist him. I know it will soon stop, he is getting married next month to the heir to a manufacturing conglomerate – a perfect match.

I have decided to write about those three weeks at NYSC camp because it was a pivotal time of my life, it was when I met my sister who still doesn't know we are sisters and met my mother again. It was where I decided to live with my choices without lies or regret; where I realised that Esme's life is worth living, that she has a right to life just like everyone else.

THE END